P9-CNI-027

BEVERLY JENKINS

Rebel

—❧ WOMEN WHO DARE ❧—

AVONBOOKS

An Imprint of HarperCollinsPublishers

This is a work of fiction. Names, characters, places, and incidents are products of the author's imagination or are used fictitiously and are not to be construed as real. Any resemblance to actual events, locales, organizations, or persons, living or dead, is entirely coincidental.

First Avon Books mass market printing: June 2019

Print Edition ISBN: 978-0-06-286168-9
Digital Edition ISBN: 978-0-06-286169-6

Cover design by Patricia Barrow
Cover illustration by Anna Kmet; font © iralu/Shutterstock (letter R)

Avon, Avon & logo, and Avon Books & logo are registered trademarks of HarperCollins Publishers in the United States of America and other countries.

HarperCollins is a registered trademark of HarperCollins Publishers in the United States of America and other countries.

FIRST EDITION

19 20 21 22 23   QGM   10 9 8 7 6 5 4 3 2 1

Dedicated to the real Valinda for her support of education, history, and the romance genre

Rebel

Chapter One

April 1867

Twenty-eight-year-old Valinda Lacy greeted her fifteen students with a smile as they filed into her classroom. Due to New Orleans's postwar chaos, she was teaching out of an old barn a few miles from the docks and warehouses on the Mississippi River.

Offering smiles and words of greeting in return, some of the students took seats on the rough-hewn bench at the back of the room, while the rest made themselves comfortable on the clean-swept dirt floor. Her pupils varied in both age and gender but had one thing in common. They were former slaves, freed by the South's surrender. Now they wanted to learn to read and write in hopes of bettering their futures.

"Did you get a chance to practice writing your names?" Val asked from behind the small listing table that served as her desk at the front of the room.

Many nodded affirmatively. Since the school opened a month ago, most had learned to recognize and pronounce the letters of the alphabet and write their names. She was now guiding them in the basics of reading simple one-syllable words like *cat*, *hand*, and *fish*. The excitement they expressed upon mastering the tasks put tears of pride in their eyes and joy in her heart.

However, like most of the schools dedicated to the recently freed, there weren't enough books, slates, or other supplies necessary for a well-stocked classroom, but Val made do with what she had.

She was passing out her five precious copies of the McGuffey primer when two White men appeared in the doorway. Everyone in the classroom froze. Val dragged her attention away from the long guns they were carrying, drew in a deep breath to tamp down her uneasiness, and met their hard eyes. Many schools serving the freedmen were being burned to the ground by supremacists, their teachers murdered. She didn't want to be next.

"May I help you?"

"You the teacher?" one asked contemptuously. Both were of medium height, unshaven and dressed in clothes that hadn't been new in quite some time.

"I am. Welcome to our classroom. We usually begin our day here at nine, so please try and be prompt. If you'll leave your guns outside, we'll kindly make room for you to sit and join us. Can you read?"

A flush rose up their necks.

"There's no need to be embarrassed. We're all here to learn. I teach children two days a week also, so if you have little ones, they are more than welcome to join us, too."

One of the men opened his mouth to speak, but she didn't let him. "I'll need your names so I can add you to the rolls. The Sisters of the Holy Family sponsor this school. Did you hear about us through them?" She waited, saw bewilderment pass between them, and added, "Never mind. How you heard about the school doesn't really matter. But I do need your names."

She walked back to her desk and picked up a pencil and a piece of paper. "I'm always pleased to welcome new learners. Being able to read and write proficiently can impact your future in many positive ways, but I'm sure you know that. Otherwise you wouldn't have come."

They stared as if she were a talking horse.

"Please, have a seat." She gestured, smiling falsely. "We don't have enough books but we're accustomed to sharing here."

The men glanced around at the angrily set faces of the men and women in the room and stammered. "Uhm. We need to go."

And they left in haste.

In the silence that followed, Val dropped into her chair and let the fear and tension drain away. When she looked up, her students were smiling, and she smiled, too. Forty-two-year-old Eb Slayton called out, "Miss, you had them so confused they didn't know General Sherman from their mamas."

And everyone burst into laughter. Val laughed, too, but inside knew they'd been lucky the two had been so easily baffled. She hoped that luck continued.

Two hours later, Val dismissed her class. Many of the students drifted away to return to jobs and families, but others like seventeen-year-old Dina Watson lingered.

"What's it like living up North, ma'am?"

Val placed the five McGuffey readers into the small strongbox for safekeeping and glanced to the young woman. "The weather's certainly cooler," she replied. For a Northern-born woman, being in the New Orleans heat was akin to walking into a foundry furnace: She was right now roasting in her attire of proper long-sleeved, high-necked blouse, flowing skirt, and hose.

"You'll get used to it," the smiling Dina promised. "Are our people there free?"

Val nodded. "In New York where I'm from, since 1827. Almost fifty years." Seeing Dina's surprise, she added, "But it isn't true freedom. We're still unable to vote or own property in many places. Social mixing is frowned upon, so we have our own schools, churches, and businesses. Some communities even have their own newspapers."

"Your parents free, too?"

"Yes. My grandmother Rose ran when she was about fourteen."

"From where?"

"Virginia. She first went to Philadelphia, then to New York and opened a seamstress shop. My father's parents escaped from Charleston when he was an infant." And unlike Rose, her father was embarrassed by his slave birth and spent his life claiming he'd been born free.

"You got somebody you sweet on back home?"

Val thought about her intended with a deeply

felt fondness. "Yes, his name is Coleman Bennett. We've known each other since we were children."

"Is he in New Orleans with you?"

"No, he and his business partner are in France seeking financial support for their newspaper." They'd be back in the States soon. She missed him and could've used his support in her battle with her father over her desire to travel to New Orleans to teach. In the end, she was allowed to go until Cole's return. Her time in the city would undoubtedly be shorter than she wanted, but in dealing with her father, she'd learned to take victory where she could.

"The French built New Orleans."

Pleased with Dina's knowledge of that fact, she said, "Yes, they did." In addition to the Spanish, and an influx of Haitians who'd fled the island after the revolution there.

Eb Slayton stuck his head in the door. "You ready to go, ma'am? I don't want to be late for work." He often gave Val a ride back to the Quarter after class ended.

"Yes. Dina, be careful going home. I'll see you on Thursday."

"I will."

School was held on Mondays and Thursdays. Val devoted the other days of the week to teaching freedmen children at the convent of the Sisters of the Holy Family, one of the few orders in the nation run by nuns of color. Val picked up her worn brown leather satchel and took one last look around at the neatly swept, makeshift classroom. She was proud to have such a space and even prouder of her eager and focused students. Closing the door, she secured it with the padlock and joined Eb on the seat of his rickety wagon.

Even though it would take his old mule, Willie, some time to get them to the Quarter, she preferred that to being at the mercy of the city's segregated streetcar system. Men and women of the race could only ride cars bearing black stars on the side. Whether intentional or not, there were never enough vehicles to be had, they didn't keep a consistent schedule, and because Whites could ride them, too, gangs of toughs often filled them to purposely make them overcrowded and to harass Black women going back and forth to work.

"I liked the way you handled the Cranston brothers," Eb said to her as they got underway.

"Those men with the guns? You know them?"

He nodded. "Pete and Wesley Cranston. Before Freedom, their daddy was the overseer on a big sugar plantation west of here. Mean as a snake. He died during the war, and now his boys go around causing trouble trying to be like him."

"Are they truly dangerous?"

"They can be, but mostly pick on women and old people. Heard they roughed up some of the teachers and missionaries to the point a few went back North. I'm pretty sure seeing the men in the classroom made them think twice about whatever they'd planned to do. I know they didn't expect you to stand up to them the way you did."

"My grandmother always told me that no matter how scared you are, never show it."

"You did her proud. Watching you run circles around them made my day."

She appreciated the praise. "Do you think they'll return?"

He shrugged. "There's no telling. After you dismissed the class, some of the men and I talked about it outside. We'll be bringing our guns with us from now on. Freedom says we can protect ourselves and we mean to."

She didn't care for violence but if it meant she and her students stayed safe, protesting the men's plan made little sense.

With the issue settled for now, she asked, "Has the Freedmen's Bureau found your daughter a position?"

He shook his head. "They keep telling her she has nothing official that says she knows how to teach."

Val sighed. The Freedmen's Bureau had been established to assist the three and a half million formerly enslaved men, women, and children freed by the South's surrender. Created over the objections of many in Congress and hampered by sometimes conflicting rules and regulations that varied from state to state, it was a bureaucratic nightmare that ofttimes hindered freedom as much as it assisted. Eb's daughter, Melinda, had been enslaved by the family of a wealthy college president whose three daughters secretly taught her to read. Having met Melinda last week, Val found her personable and intelligent, and thought her skills would be a blessing in a classroom. "Let her know if she hasn't found a position soon, she's welcome to help me here."

His face brightened. "I sure will."

Still trying to get the Bureau to pay her the stipend she was owed, Val had no idea how she'd compensate his daughter, but would cross that bridge when she came to it.

Eb then asked, "Do you think you can help my brother put a plea in the newspapers? He's trying to find his wife."

"Of course. Have him stop by the school when he can, and we'll talk it over."

"Thank you. Since Freedom, he's been walking plantations in the area looking for her, but so far nobody knows where she is."

"Does he have children?"

He nodded. "But they were sold years ago to a man in Texas. My brother doesn't think he'll ever see them again."

She couldn't imagine what Eb's brother and the thousands of others searching for sold-away family must be going through, but offering her assistance in any way possible was the reason she'd come south. She credited her grandmother Rose for instilling that desire. Rose had been helping to uplift the race in their New York City community for as long as Val had been alive. Whether it was aiding the elderly and poor with food and clothing, attending abolition rallies and marches, or staying after church to read articles from the newspapers published by Mr. Garrison, Mr. Douglass, and Mr. Martin Delany to those who couldn't, Rose and the women of her circle were who Val aspired to be.

As the slow ride continued, she thought about her own efforts. She'd been in New Orleans for a month now. The city was so different from the strict, staunch confines of New York, it was like being in another country. Music seemed to be everywhere. The women of the race wore head-wraps called *tignons* that could be plain and un-assuming, or colorful and decorated with items like beads and cowrie shells. Back home the pri-mary foreign language was Dutch. In New Orleans people spoke French, Spanish, Italian, and all manner of variations in between. New York had its street vendors, but the ones here sold fruits and vegetables she'd never seen or eaten be-fore like okra and sugar cane. She'd come to love the little baked balls of rice called *calas* that were dusted with sugar and sold in the mornings by women of color. On Sundays, people of the race gathered in a spot called Congo Square, some-thing they'd been doing since slavery. There was music, dancing, and more vendors. She'd never seen anything like it before. Also new to her was the selling of charms and potions that supposedly cast and counteracted spells. The food in New Orleans was rich with cream, sea-food, and yeast, and the streets were thick with armed Union soldiers, poor Whites, and crowds of freedmen searching for work. There was also a volatile undercurrent of fury from the former masters who'd lost their way of life. Some of the local newspapers were filled with vitriolic edi-torials directed at the soldiers and the Radical

Republicans. Most alarming were reports of the increasing incidents of violence visited upon the freedmen and their families from terrorizing Lost Cause groups.

Eb halted his wagon in front of the house in the Treme section of the city where Valinda rented a room. She waved goodbye and he and Willie drove off towards the St. Louis Hotel where he worked as a pastry chef. Ironically, at age nine, he'd been sold at a slave auction in the same hotel. She found it hard to reconcile the city's most famous hotel hosting fancy balls and celebratory dinners while slaves were also being sold under its roof.

Another thing Val found hard to reconcile was her Creole landlady, Georgine Dumas, who shared the home with her older sister, Madeline. Both were elderly but had personalities as different as night and day. Where Madeline was kind and considerate, Georgine was haughty and intolerant. Georgine complained about everything from the weather to Madeline's cooking, but saved her most acerbic vitriol for the Union soldiers and the newly freed.

"They should ship them all back to Africa," she declared angrily during dinner the day Val arrived. "They're as ignorant and useless as the bluecoats."

Later, Madeline explained that her sister's anger was rooted in how the surrender changed their lives. Their plantation was gone, as were their slaves, leaving them to do the mundane yet necessary chores tied to living like cooking, cleaning, and the rest. Luckily Madeline knew how to cook. But many of the South's mistresses hadn't touched a stove for generations, and now, not knowing turnip from tripe, couldn't feed their families.

Entering the small flat, Val found Madeline in the kitchen. The fragrant spicy aroma of gumbo cooking filled the space. Val had known nothing about the flavorful stew before coming south but now loved the dish as much as she did the morning *calas*.

"And how was school today, Valinda?" Madeline asked, putting a lid on the gumbo on the stove and taking a seat at the small table where they shared their meals.

"Good. Two new students showed up, so I now have fifteen. I'll need to find more spellers somehow. Having the students share makes teaching a challenge."

"Do you think your grandmother's church can help?"

"I'll write her tonight and ask." Her grandmother's church back home in New York was her sponsor. In response to a plea for help from the American Missionary Association and the Sisters of the Holy Family, Val and other teachers had traveled south.

They spent a few more minutes talking, and Madeline rose to check on the gumbo. Determining it ready, she called out to her sister. Georgine entered and, upon seeing Val, glowered and took her seat.

Madeline said, "You could at least speak to her, Georgie."

The response was an impatient huff, before Georgine asked Val, "Have the blue bastards paid you yet?"

She replied simply, "No, ma'am."

"Food and a place to sleep is not free."

"I understand."

Madeline spooned the gumbo into bowls, and said tightly, "She's paying us what she can, Georgie. You know that."

"I know nothing of the kind. Who's to say she isn't giving the money that should be coming to us to those wastrel freedmen?"

Val didn't reply. The Freedmen's Bureau was supposed to pay teachers a stipend. Since her arrival a month ago, she'd spent her free time standing in long lines for hours on end only to be told she needed a different requisition form, was at the wrong office, or the person she needed to speak with was unavailable. It was maddening. Having to endure Georgine's caustic tongue was worse. "I'll be writing my grandmother to ask if she can send me extra funds so that I may meet my obligations to you and your sister."

"Otherwise you'll be asked to leave."

"Georgie!"

"We can't afford to keep her here for free, Maddy. She isn't a pet spaniel."

"But we promised the Sisters we'd let her stay with us."

"In exchange for funds. We have no money, Madeline, and no prospect of receiving more. She either pays or she goes."

Madeline's voice tightened. "We have money in the bank, Georgie, and you know it. It may not be as much as it was before the surrender, but we won't starve. You're just being nasty."

"You have one week, Miss Lacy."

Val met the cold black eyes. "Yes, ma'am."

The meal was eaten in silence. Madeline shot her sister angry glares which Georgine ignored. When they were done, Georgine left the kitchen. Val helped Madeline with the dishes, then sat at the table to begin her letter.

Before exiting Madeline said, "Don't worry, I won't allow her to put you on the street."

"Thank you."

It had been a week since Val had written to her family, and like the last time, a bout of homesickness came over her as she began. She missed her mother, her older sister, Caroline, and her grandmother Rose, with whom Val and her parents lived. It would be uncharitable to admit to not missing her father, Harrison, but being alone and so far away from home, she even missed him and his overbearing ways a bit as well.

She wrote first to her mother and sister, and lastly to her grandmother about how she was faring, the challenges she faced, and the progress of her students. She also asked for help in acquiring more books, supplies, and an increase in her personal funds so she could pay what she owed the Dumas sisters. When she finished the letters, night had fallen. She prepared her letters for the post, then went to her hot windowless room and changed into her night things. In the morning, she'd go back to the Freedmen's Bureau office. She didn't relish another day of standing in a mile-long line, but the pay issue had to be resolved, so Georgine wouldn't toss her out on her ear. After saying her prayers and dousing her lamp, she stretched out on the thin uncomfortable mattress and hoped the oppressive heat would eventually let her sleep.

Chapter Two

*S*eated at his desk in the city's smallest Freedmen's Bureau office, Drake LeVeq, former captain with the Louisiana Native Guard, inwardly debated what to do with his anger tied to knowing the freedmen still in line would not be helped today. Mothers searching for stolen children would endure another night of fear and worry; men needing approved work contracts faced being snatched off the street by unscrupulous planters and forced to work for free, or worse, arrested for not being employed. And Drake would go home frustrated because he hadn't been able to do more to assist them.

The reason they wouldn't be helped was the man now approaching Drake's desk, the office's new supervisor, a snippy, thin-faced lieutenant from Boston named Josiah Merritt. "We're not going to get to the rest of them today," he told Drake. "I have a meeting to attend, so send them away."

Under previous commanders, the office usually stayed open until dusk. Since Merritt's arrival three months ago, the formerly four-person staff had been pared down to just Drake, and the doors often closed early, sometimes, like today, before three in the afternoon.

"You're in charge. You send them away," Drake countered.

Merritt drew back, his whiskered face reddening. "May I remind you that I'm in command."

"And I'll remind you that I'm a volunteer not under your command."

Drake knew that many Bureau offices were supervised by good men like the two officers he'd previously worked under, while others may as well be supremacists for their lack of commitment to the freedmen's plight. Merritt was among the latter. Drake longed to walk away from the inept commander but refused to leave the freedmen without a true advocate unless it became absolutely necessary.

Merritt, not getting the outcome he wanted, stormed off. His announcement that the office was closing was met with protests. Many of the men and women had been in line since dawn.

Drake's lips thinned but there was nothing he could do.

Once the office was empty, Merritt, on his way out, said, "Make sure the door is locked, LeVeq."

Angrily eyeing his departure, Drake sighed, then spent a few moments straightening the small mountain of files on his desk holding reports on work contracts, schools, emergency requests for food, and everything else the Bureau handled on behalf of the newly freed and the thousands of poor Whites displaced by the war.

Lincoln began the operation in 1865 as the Bureau of Refugees, Freedmen, and Abandoned Lands. Because a disgruntled Congress refused to appropriate a budget for the Bureau, the funds came from the War Department, which was also charged with implementation. Led by Union General Oliver O. Howard, the Bureau was initially set up for one year, but its mandate had been grudgingly extended. Rules, regulations, and enforcement varied by state, sometimes by offices, resulting in chaos, ineptitude, and graft.

Southerners were clamoring for dissolution of the offices, so Drake wasn't sure how much longer the service would survive, or what the freedmen would do once it was gone. At its inception, there had been wrongheaded regulations demanding Blacks have passes from former masters in order to travel. In Virginia and elsewhere, some offices had forbidden rural Blacks from entering the cities to look for employment, then sent troops to round them up and force them to return to their masters. That the Army was more supportive of the old system than the new had been quite apparent. But, in spite of the shortcomings, the freedmen continued to support the Bureau, because it was all they had.

After locking up, he left. His sister-in-law, Sable, would be returning from Biloxi shortly, and he'd volunteered to meet her boat at the docks. Her husband, his oldest brother, Raimond, was in an all-day meeting with the local Republicans to hash out solutions to combat the violence being spread by White supremacist groups like the Knights of the White Camellia, the Seymour Knights, and the Crescent City Democratic Club. A big family dinner to welcome Sable home was being held at the Christophe, the hotel managed by their brother Archer.

The day was hot as always, and the traffic in the street thick as the air with all manner of vehicles pulled by everything from horses to mules to slow-moving dairy cows. With another sigh, Drake joined the masses of freedmen, soldiers, Northern carpetbaggers, and city natives on the crowded walks going about their day.

AFTER RECEIVING PERMISSION from the nuns to forgo teaching the children for the day, Valinda spent all morning and into the afternoon standing in line at the city's largest Freedmen's Bureau office and finally received a scrip for payment. Relieved, she walked down the street to wait for the appropriate streetcar to take her to the docks. Yesterday, one of her students employed there told her of a small unclaimed crate of slates and chalk being held at the shipping office. The clerk in charge, having given up on finding the owner, kindly offered them to the student for his classroom, so she was going to claim them.

But first she had to get there.

Withering in the late afternoon heat while streetcars with empty seats passed by her and others due to their race left her and everyone else waiting fuming. It took over an hour for a black-star car to finally arrive and it was so overcrowded there was barely room to squeeze inside. At the end of the line, she got off, temper still high over the insulting treatment, and walked to the docks.

True to his word, the clerk gave her the slates with no fuss. Pleased with his generosity and her anger soothed, she made the short hike back to the barn she'd claimed as a classroom to leave the crate there. The six slates and sacks of chalk were as valuable as gold. Admittedly, a small pang of guilt plagued her, seeing as how they rightfully belonged to someone else, but the clerk said they'd been there over a month and were destined for the burn barrel.

Approaching the barn, she was brought up short. The padlock was gone, and the warped wooden door stood wide open. Glancing around but seeing no one about she entered cautiously. Inside, the once cleanly swept floor was now lined with thin, dirty pallets, and littered with empty spirits bottles, candle stubs, and discarded rubbers. There was even a pair of faded blue Union army trousers someone had left behind. Her jaw dropped. Yesterday, this had been her classroom. Now, it was apparently being used for nefarious carousing. As she tried to imagine who might be responsible, the smell of smoke reached her nose. Alarmed, she looked around. Once confident nothing was burning inside, she set the crate on the floor and hurried back outside to find a small fire burning under the nearby trees. In it were the five readers she'd been using with her students, and her heart jumped into her throat.

"No!" She began stomping the flames with her worn brogans. She kicked dirt and ashes, hoping to smother it. Seeing a long thick branch on the ground nearby, she grabbed it up and tried to move the readers out of the flames. The books were all she had, and if she didn't save them, she didn't know what she'd do. But the pages were old and brittle, and even in the humid New Orleans air, the flames licked greedily. Heartbroken, she stopped fighting and watched helplessly as the wind caught the charred, red-edged pages and carried them away.

"Problems, little lady?"

Still holding the charred, red-tipped branch, she turned to see three men dressed in dirty Union blue uniforms approaching. Two were men of color, the other White with blond hair. As they came abreast of her, the mocking gleam in their eyes set off an inner warning, but her anger over the destruction took precedence. "Someone burned my schoolbooks!"

The tallest man, who was thin and brown-skinned, showed two missing front teeth when he replied, "Now, who would do such a despicable thing?"

His grinning companions offered exaggerated shrugs.

"Guess this means school is dismissed," offered the shorter, heavier, gray-eyed man of color at his side.

The tall one with the missing teeth slowly looked her up and down. "Where you from, girl? You don't sound like you're from round here."

They were behind the barn in a cove of tall trees. Valinda knew she needed to get back into the open where she could be better seen from the road. "Excuse me. I need to go." She moved to walk past them, but the skinny blond man latched onto her arm.

"He asked you a question."

She eyed his dirty hand, then his smirking gaze. "Let go!" she snapped, jerking her arm, but he held on.

The tall one drawled, "Y'all ever know a teacher that didn't answer questions?"

"Not a one," replied gray eyes.

"I think we should take her inside and teach her some manners."

She was one woman against three men, and if they wanted to hurt her, the odds were in their favor. The only thing she had close to a weapon was the thick branch in her hand, so she jammed the smoking end into the blond's throat. As he screamed and dropped to his knees, she ran.

Heart pounding, every breath filled with fear,

she was fast enough to clear the trees and head to the road. His companions, initially caught flat-footed, immediately gave chase. Halfway to the road, she was tackled from behind. She hit the ground so hard, pain exploded in her ribs, and her head spun, but she screamed and fought.

A gunshot rang out. The world froze.

"Move away from her. Now!"

Valinda was so filled with relief, a sob escaped. Approaching was a tall bearded man of color wearing Union blue. Behind his raised rifle, fury ruled his dark-skinned face.

"Ma'am, come stand behind me, please."

Struggling to her feet, she didn't hesitate.

The toothless one snarled, "Boy, you're meddling in something that's none of your business."

A bullet blasted the ground by his feet and he jumped with a scream.

"This is my business," the soldier snarled ominously. "Who's your commanding officer?"

The two assailants shared a look, hesitating as if weighing whether to answer the big man or not.

He walked closer, rifle still raised. "Do you really want to die today?"

Their eyes widened.

Another shot sounded. Val spun and saw a golden-skinned woman wearing a blue dress and a matching blue *tignon* standing in a wagon that had a magnificent ebony stallion tied to the back. She, too, had a raised rifle, and it was pointed at their blond companion who'd just stepped out of the trees. The woman called out a warning. "Stay where you are!"

He didn't move.

Still shaken, Val wondered who her saviors were. The woman seemed as fierce as the man.

"Going to ask one more time. Who's your commanding officer?"

Though visibly shaking, they held their tongues.

He eased the trigger back.

Gray eyes shouted, "Lieutenant Crane Jacobs!"

His tall companion snapped at the soldier, "You got no authority here. She's my wife. Caught her bouncing on another man. Teaching her to respect her vows."

The bearded soldier turned to Valinda. "Do you know him?"

She shook her head.

He asked, feather soft, "You wouldn't lie to me, would you, *cheri*?"

Flooded by a reaction that temporarily swamped her fear, she managed to reply, "No."

"Good. Hold this, please."

When he handed her the rifle, her eyes widened. Before she could ask why, he turned back and planted an explosive fist in the face of the man claiming to be her husband. The blow shattered his nose. Blood erupted, and he slowly fell to his knees, then keeled over, out cold.

Her eyes shot wider.

The angry soldier asked the now slack-jawed man with the gray eyes, "Do you want to teach the young lady some respect, too?"

Terrified, he hastily shook his head. "No."

"No, what?"

"No, sir!"

The soldier responded with a deadly smile. "Smart man." He then asked him, "That your friend over there?" He was referring to the blond man still standing motionless under the watchful eye and raised rifle of the woman in the wagon.

He nodded.

"What's his name?"

"Appleton."

"What's yours? And don't even think about lying to me."

Gray eyes swallowed. "Billy Baxter."

"And this one?" he asked of the man on the ground.

"Walter Creighton."

He glanced across the field and called out, "Appleton! Over here. Now!"

Appleton appeared torn. His friend was lying unmoving in the dirt. Valinda guessed he wanted no part of what was going on. But when a blast from the woman's gun tore through the air only a few inches above his head, the matter was settled. He quickly crossed the open field.

When he arrived, the soldier took in the angry bleeding gash on his throat. "What happened there?"

Giving Valinda a death stare, Appleton wheezed out angrily, "Bitch tried to shove a burning branch through my windpipe."

The surprised soldier swung her way. He assessed her silently for a moment, before saying, "Good for you."

Once again, something unnamed washed over her.

Returning his attention to Appleton and Baxter, the soldier warned, "If either of you ever encounter this lady again, I want you to run away like your drawers are on fire." He leaned down from his impressive height to add, "Because if I hear that you were anywhere near her, I will find you. You understand me?"

"Yes, sir!"

"Now pick him up and get out of my sight."

The directive didn't need repeating. Dragging the still-unconscious Creighton between them, they left.

"Are you hurt?" her rescuer asked.

She handed him the rifle. "Once I stop shaking I'll know." The fear was still raw. Her ribs and chest hurt from hitting the ground, but it was her inner self that hurt most of all. What if he and the woman hadn't come along? Trying not to let the thought of what might have happened take hold, she forced herself to draw in a few calming breaths.

He withdrew a handkerchief from the inside pocket of his coat and held it out. "Your chin and cheek are scraped and bleeding."

She glanced down at the linen.

"Here. Let me help."

He pressed the square to her cheek and chin, applied a bit of pressure, and gently stroked it over the now stinging skin. He handed her the handkerchief, and she took it with unsteady hands, wondering how such a titan-sized man could have such a light touch.

In a tremulous voice, she said, "Thank you for the rescue."

"You're welcome. That's my sister-in-law, Sable, in the wagon." The woman was now heading towards them, rifle in hand. "I'm Captain Drake LeVeq. And you are?"

"Valinda Lacy."

"Miss? Missus?"

"Miss."

"Pleased to meet you, Miss Lacy. Can you tell me what happened?"

Gathering herself, she explained about the school, what she found inside, and the burned books. "Two days ago, it was my classroom. Now it's a den for fornicators."

His gaze softened with amusement.

"Something funny, Captain?"

"My apologies. That's just not a word one expects to hear from a schoolteacher."

"Sometimes the unexpected is necessary."

"Like stabbing Appleton in the throat?"

She nodded. "Will you report them to their commanding officer?"

"I will."

The woman reached them and said to Valinda, "I'm Sable LeVeq. Are you okay?"

Valinda looked into her brilliant green eyes. "I will be, thanks to you and the captain."

"I'm glad we came along when we did."

"So am I."

That she might have been assaulted in the worst way reared its head again. She relived the terror of running, being tackled, and how powerless she felt trying to fight them off. The memory made her stomach roil. "Excuse me, I think . . ." She took a few steps away and her stomach emptied itself.

Moments later, LeVeq handed her a canteen so she could rinse her mouth. That done, she handed it back, took a seat in the grass, and waited for her world to right itself. The captain and his sister-in-law sat with her. Worry and concern were on their faces, but they remained silent, letting her collect herself as best she could.

"Where do you live, Miss Lacy?" he asked quietly.

"I'm renting a room in the Treme with Madeline and Georgine Dumas."

"How are you going to get back? Do you have a mount, a wagon?"

"No. I came as far as the streetcar would take me and walked the rest of the way."

"You're not walking back alone," Sable replied firmly. "Drake and I will spend all evening worrying whether you made it back there safely. We're on our way to the Quarter. We can drop you off on the way."

"Thank you."

Sable added, "Drake may have put the fear of

God in those men for now, but who's to say they aren't stupid enough to target you again if they find you alone?"

Valinda shivered at the thought of another encounter.

He stood and put his hand out to help her rise.

Valinda looked up into the concern he exuded and accepted. His scarred hand over hers was calloused, large, and warm.

He said, "I'd like to take a look in the barn before we go, if you don't mind."

"I don't. I've no idea what to do about it now that I have squatters. Someone cut the padlock, which means there's no way to keep them out until I can obtain a new one."

Sable said, "They'll probably just cut it off again."

Val agreed, and she wasn't happy knowing she no longer had a viable classroom.

LeVeq asked, "Does the school have a sponsor?"

"Yes, the Sisters of the Holy Family. This property once belonged to one of the convent's benefactors."

Together they walked back to the barn. He looked around the fouled interior, and said, "If it were in my power, I'd station a few guards here so you could continue to use it and be safe, but with so many other pressing issues in the city, I doubt the Army will see that as an efficient use of personnel."

"I know," she replied, and the reality of that saddened her. She'd had such high hopes. Now she'd have to find a new classroom and start over. "I'll talk to the Sisters and see if they can find another place."

"I'm sorry," he said, sounding sincere.

She nodded.

Sable said, "We should go. Is there anything in here that you need to take with you?"

"Just this." Val picked up the crate with the slates and chalk and took one last look around.

"Come," he said, eyes now soft. "Let's get you home."

Chapter Three

Drake did his best to dampen his lingering fury as he drove Miss Lacy home. He wanted to draw and quarter her attackers until they screamed for a mercy he'd not give. There was no need to imagine what would've happened had he and Sable not come along. He knew. Glancing over at the teacher as she sat silent on the seat between them, he wished for the power to turn back time and erase the terror he'd seen in her brown eyes when he'd approached. The incident wouldn't be something she'd easily forget, and he wanted to punish the men for that as well. Yet, she hadn't gone like a lamb to the slaughter. She'd fought back and that impressed him. The throat wound she'd given Appleton appeared serious enough to warrant medical attention. If Drake had his way, it would fester, rot, and never heal. A gruesome thought for a man raised in the Catholic faith but genuine for one descended from pirates.

By the time they reached the Treme, the Creole enclave on the edge of the Quarter, it was nearly dusk. In a short while, the New Orleans night would belong to those without shelter, drunken revelers, and the shadowy forces that preyed on both.

After receiving directions from her, he stopped the wagon in front of the Dumas's small home.

"Thank you both again," she said in a sincere voice and met Drake's eyes.

Though Drake knew nothing about her, he realized he very much wanted to. Her accent wasn't Southern, so where was home? Was she in the city alone? How long had she been there? Detaining her to satisfy his curiosity made no sense though. After the attack, she was probably of no mind to entertain frivolous conversation.

Sable's voice broke into his thoughts.

"Miss Lacy, if you need anything, let us know. The nuns are very familiar with the LeVeq family. In fact, my daughters are enrolled in their school."

Drake added, "And I'm a volunteer at one of the Freedmen's offices. If I can help you find another site, I will."

"Thank you," she replied. "I've had an awful time collecting my stipend. I wish we'd met earlier. But under better circumstances."

"So do I," he said quietly, taking her in. *Who are you, lovely Valinda? Will you have dinner with me?* Instead of him asking the questions aloud, they discussed finding another place to teach. Although funding and building schools was part of the Bureau's many tasks, places were being burned down as fast as they were established by those intent upon reinstating slavery. "Free space is at a premium."

"I know."

Because she impressed him as someone who'd want to know the truth, he added, "Now that you have no classroom, you may not qualify for another stipend until you find another."

"Then that will present a problem."

"Meaning?"

She explained her problem with Georgine Dumas.

"No one is going to allow you to end up on the street," he told her. Reaching into his coat pocket, he withdrew the small tablet of paper he used for his field notes and a pencil. "If you need assistance at any time, these are the addresses of my Freedmen's office and my brother Archer's hotel, where we're headed." He handed the paper to her. He'd wanted to write down his home address, too, but knew that would be improper.

She gave him a small smile. "Thank you again. I feel as though I've said that a hundred times, but I can't say it enough."

"I'm just glad Sable and I were nearby."

Sable climbed down from her seat to the street to allow the teacher to do the same.

Holding his gaze one last time, Miss Lacy said, "Goodbye."

He nodded and watched her walk to the door. Once she was safely inside, his curiosity remained. Would he see her again? Now that he knew where she lived, could he call on her? His mother, the Lovely Julianna, was a patron of the Sisters. Might she know anything about her?

Sable waved a hand in front of his face. "Drake. We need to go. Rai and my children are waiting. You can think about seeing her again later."

Embarrassed, he smiled and set the team in motion.

They arrived at Archer's hotel a short while later. Upon entering, they walked through the small dining area and made their way to the back room. The LeVeq family was a large one and the noise of the gathering could be heard as they approached.

Applause and cheers rang out when Sable made her entrance. Drake chose an empty chair at the end of the elegantly set long table to allow the honoree her moment in the sun. Her husband, Raimond, grabbed her up, and swung her around into a deep, welcoming kiss. The moment he put her down she was swamped by their children: the fifteen-year-old twins, Cullen and Hazel; their younger sister, Blythe; and two-year-old Desiré, who scrambled off her grand-mère's lap and ran to Sable shrieking, "Mama!" Sable scooped her up and hugged and kissed them all. Famous in the city for her work with orphans, she'd made the trip to Biloxi to escort three of her charges to a new, loving home. Drake, like the rest of the family, was glad she'd returned safely.

Drake was the third oldest son. Ahead of him were Archer and the eldest, Raimond. Their brother Gerrold, born between Raimond and Archer, lost his life during the war, and his high-spirited presence was sorely missed. Behind Drake in the line of LeVeq sons was Beau, then Phillipe, the youngest.

"So," said Phillipe. "Have you figured out a way to kill Lieutenant Merritt, and not be blamed?"

Drake picked up one of the wine bottles

placed atop the white-clothed table and poured a portion into his glass. "No. But I am working on it."

They all knew of Drake's frustration with the man. Their brother Raimond also had ties to the Bureau, but he'd left recently to devote more time to politics, and to the group of Black war veterans known as the Council.

Beau asked, "What happened to your hand? Did you use it on Merritt, I hope?"

Drake glanced down at the bruised skin over his knuckles and flexed the slightly swollen fingers. "No." He then told them what happened.

Both were outraged.

Beau said, "Your restraint is admirable, brother. I'd still be kicking their arses. Is the lady okay?"

"As well as could be expected, I suppose." His mind floated back to the scratches and scrapes on her smooth brown cheeks and his anger rose again. "I told her I'd report the men to their superior officer, but I know him to be as useless as Merritt, so there's no sense in it. He won't reprimand them."

"Maybe we'll be lucky enough to come across them again. At night. In an alley."

Drake chuckled and excused himself from his bloodthirsty siblings to go and say hello to their mother, Julianna.

* * *

AT THE DUMAS residence, Val stared at Georgine in disbelief. "Madeline passed away this morning?"

"Yes. An hour or so after you left for the Freedmen's Bureau. The doctor said her heart gave out. She's with the undertaker."

Val thought back on Madeline's kindness to her and wished her soul peace.

"Which means I can now rid my house of you."

Val stared. After the terrible day she'd had, this was the last thing she wanted to hear. "I received my stipend, so I have the money you're owed."

"Your things are there by the door."

She saw her green embroidered carpetbag and brown leather valise. She was hot, tired, and still reeling from her attack. "Miss Georgine, please," she begged. "I was attacked less than an hour ago. May I at least stay the night?"

"Go. I need to grieve."

Fighting tears and the urge to shake the old crone until her false teeth rattled, Val picked up her things, left the crate with the chalk and slates behind, and walked back out into the night.

The convent was a short distance away. Gathering herself, she set out. She'd been warned against being out alone after dark. The streets weren't safe, and as she now knew, they weren't safe during daylight hours either, so she set a quick pace. Seeing the dark shape of the convent's house ahead bolstered her flagging spirits. Reaching the gate, she pulled. It didn't move. A second pull offered the same result. It was locked.

"No!" she cried softly.

Standing under the street lamp, she searched the elaborate ironwork for a bell pull or some other way to alert the nuns that she needed entry but there was nothing. *Now what?* She toyed with the idea of climbing the fence. She was once the best tree-climbing child in her neighborhood, but unlike trees, the gate had sharp arrowhead finials and she'd undoubtedly puncture her hands using them for balance to drop down to the lawn inside.

Discouraged and deflated, tears stung her eyes, but she wiped them away and started walking again. She'd only met a few people in the short time she'd been in the city, mainly friends and acquaintances of the Dumas sisters, but she didn't know any of them well enough to ask for a place for the night, even if she knew where they lived. She thought about her rescuers, the LeVeqs. She didn't know them either, but they'd been kind. She hated the idea of having to lean on them twice in one day, but what else could she do? She reached into the pocket of her skirt and withdrew the small piece of paper she'd received from the captain. He said he and Sable were going to his brother's hotel. The lack of light made deciphering the address another test. Taking a wild guess, she set out, praying she'd find it and that he and his sister-in-law were still there.

The street was as crowded as if it were noon. Vendors selling spirits plied their goods beneath the light of the street lamps, while girls of the night sold themselves on corners and in the dark doorways of brothels. She stepped around people sleeping on the walks. Saloons blared the music of horns and drums to the delight of the drunks dancing and swaying near the entrances.

"Hey there, lovely lady!" a man called to her. "Do you want to keep me warm tonight?" Laughter followed from his companions.

She kept her eyes straight ahead and ignored them as she pressed on. Her shoulders ached from the strain of carrying the heavy carpetbag and valise. Her ribs were sore from the attack. She was tired and felt terribly alone. She wanted to stop someone and ask if they knew of the hotel owned by the captain's brother, but the attack was still fresh in her mind, and she was too wary. Off in the distance she heard gunshots, more gay music, and the laughter of New Orleans revelers. She kept walking.

Her hope failing, she came upon an old woman of color seated behind a table. Her position beneath a street lamp allowed Val to see her thin, aging, nut-brown face, and the colorful red *tignon* covering her hair.

"Want your fortune told, miss?" the woman asked.

"No, ma'am, but can you tell me if I'm near this address?" Val handed her the paper.

The woman took the paper, eyed it, and handed it back. As Val reached out to take it, the woman gently took her hand, picked up a small lamp beside her, and studied Val's open palm under the flickering light. "You will lose a love, reject a love, find a love."

Val didn't put much stock in the predictions of fortune-tellers. "Thank you. But the address?"

The fortune-teller smiled. "It's there," she said, and she pointed. "Right across the street."

Relief filled her. "Thank you."

"Dare to love him, miss."

"Who?"

"Him," came the reply, as if it were a silly question.

Skeptical, Val offered a respectful, "Thank you again," and crossed the street. Behind her, she heard the old woman laughing softly.

Grateful to find the hotel's door unlocked, Val stepped inside. There were a few white-clothed tables spread out across the small dining room. The people seated at them glanced up from their meals at her entrance, and the way they stared made her conscious of her wrinkled, disheveled appearance.

A man in a crisp black suit stepped to her and said, "I'm sorry, miss. We're about to close the kitchen, so I can't seat you."

"I'm here to speak to Captain LeVeq, if I may."

The man took in her shoddy appearance and the bags she carried. Disapproval lined his dark face. "I'm sorry. The captain is attending a private family gathering, and they've asked not to be disturbed."

"I just left him and his sister-in-law, Sable. They told me if I needed assistance, to come here."

He forced a smile. "I'm sure they did, but they're unavailable."

She fished the paper from the pocket of her skirt. "He wrote this for me."

He gave the note a cursory glance. "I'm going to ask you to leave before I call the authorities."

"You believe I'm a liar?"

Another forced smile. "Leave, please."

His condescending attitude coupled with her awful day, and the prospect of spending the night on the street, forced her to grit out, "Either take me to him or I will shout this place down!"

He opened his mouth to respond, but she was quicker. "Captain LeVeq!" she called out in a loud voice.

Diners jumped with surprise, and a buzz filled the room.

She yelled again, louder, "Captain LeVeq!"

"Miss!" Black Suit snapped, staring around at the unsettled guests. "Keep your voice down!"

"Captain LeVeq!"

A blink later, LeVeq appeared at the edge of the dining room. Confusion filled his eyes and voice. "Miss Lacy?"

"Hello," she said with relief. "He wouldn't take me to you."

Black Suit said, "I'm sorry, Drake, but—"

LeVeq held up a hand that stopped him in mid-speech. "It's okay, Raoul."

Val had been so focused on the captain and the relief his presence generated, only then did she notice the other concerned-looking people he was surrounded by. Most were men, but she spied Sable holding a little girl. Beside Sable stood three other children. An emotion-filled Val gathered herself and whispered, "I'm so sorry for interrupting you, but Georgine Dumas threw me out, and I've no place to go."

A beautiful, older, ebony-skinned woman stepped out from behind the men. "Drake, do you know this young woman?"

"Yes, I do."

"Then have her join us."

Val shook her head. "No, please. Can you just tell me where I can get a place to sleep for the night? I don't want to disturb your party."

The woman asked Drake, "Is she always this stubborn?"

Appearing amused, he replied, "I don't know, Mama. I only met her today."

His mother smiled her way, and Val saw that Drake had her dark eyes. "Have you had dinner?" the older woman asked.

"No, ma'am."

"Are you hungry?"

Val couldn't lie. "Yes, ma'am."

"Then, come, eat. After that, we'll get you a place to lay your head. I promise."

Val glanced around at all the people awaiting her response. She looked to Drake last.

"She likes stubborn women," he told her.

Amusement cut through her weariness. "Okay. I accept."

The family applauded.

Chapter Four

$\mathcal{D}$rake couldn't believe how happy he was to see Valinda Lacy again, but it was a happiness coupled with concern. She'd had an awful day. First the attack, and then being cruelly served by her landlady—he wanted to take her home and dare anyone to hurt her again. Instead he stood off to the side and let his mother and Sable fuss over her and show her to the buffet. As he sipped from his wineglass, his eldest brother, Raimond, drifted over. "Tell me her story."

Eyes never leaving her, Drake related the details of the attack.

Raimond's face clouded with anger. "Glad you were there. So many women have no champions when facing such violence—especially women of the race."

"I wouldn't call myself a champion."

"What would you call yourself?"

"Just someone who helped."

"Uh huh. Is that why you're looking at her as if she's the only person in the room?"

Drake did his best not to show his embarrassment.

Raimond said, "It's okay. I acted the same way the first time I met Sable. Thought I'd lose my mind when she was taken."

A few years ago, Sable, along with their three adopted children, was stolen away by her former master. Seeing Raimond's pain when they couldn't be found was something Drake would never forget.

"I'm not going to marry her, brother."

"That's what I said about Sable. Now I can't imagine being without her."

LeVeq men had a history of loving their wives fiercely. The love between their ancestors Dominic and his Clare was the stuff of legends. Drake was eight years old when their father, Francois, lost his life at sea. The only thing that kept the Lovely Julianna from walking into the Mississippi to join him in death was her concern and love for the six sons she'd be leaving behind. Last year, she'd married longtime friend Henri Vincent and loved him very much. Drake assumed he'd love his wife just as passionately—once he found her, but presently, he wasn't ready. He was content with his mistress, Josephine.

Raimond said of Valinda, "She's a little thing."

"Yes, but don't let the petite stature fool you." He told Raimond about the stick she turned on the attacker Appleton.

"Nothing like a woman who won't go quietly."

"I'm sure Raoul learned that a few moments ago. He's probably still appalled by her defiant shouting."

Rai chuckled and took a sip of his wine. Drake watched Valinda talking to little Desiré, and was pleased to see the teacher smiling.

Archer joined them. "Your lady has Mama eating out of her hand." Julianna had moved her seat to sit beside the teacher.

"She isn't my lady."

"No? Then you should tell Mama. I think she's eyeing her as a potential daughter-in-law."

Drake sighed. "I just met her earlier today."

"Doesn't matter," Archer replied. "Sable seems taken with her as well."

"I doubt either is planning a wedding, Archer."

He shrugged. "That mysterious sixth sense women seem to have lets them know things we men find out only after the smoke has cleared. How much in love with her are you?"

Drake gave him an exasperated look.

Beau joined them and said to Drake, "Phillipe and I've decided, if you don't stake a claim, we will."

"You don't know anything about her."

Archer said, "Since when has that been a deterrent?"

Drake told Beau firmly, "There will be no claim staking. Let her be."

Beau said, "Fine. You have one week." And he walked away.

Seeing him take a seat near the women then lean in and start up a conversation with Miss Lacy tightened Drake's lips. He asked Raimond, "Can you take him out to sea and drop him over the side?"

"Ten years ago, I asked Mama the same question about all you Brats. She said no."

"Pity, he'd make fine shark bait. You'd think he'd be content with those two mistresses of his."

Archer said, "He's always looking for new candidates for his harem."

"He should look elsewhere before I smother him in his sleep."

Both brothers turned his way.

"Just because I'm not staking a claim doesn't

mean I'm not interested." And admittedly, he was. Very. In spite of his mistress and a few other lovelies he called on from time to time, something about the feistiness inside Valinda's small frame drew him. He didn't know any woman with the temerity to cause the ruckus she'd had out front. Any woman not already named LeVeq, that is. Hearing a woman's voice yelling his name had brought the entire party to a halt, and then to discover who the voice belonged to? He wanted to know more about her.

Sable, holding her sleeping daughter Desiré, walked over and said, "Rai, we should head home and put the children to bed."

He nodded.

She then turned to Drake. "I hate to be the bearer of bad news, but your lady has an intended. He's in Paris presently, but will be back in the States, soon."

Drake felt like he'd been hit in the chest by one of Raimond's ship anchors and that surprised him. By all accounts, her ties to another should've made him shrug and move on, but for unknown reasons, it didn't.

Archer patted him on the back. "Sorry, brother."

Rai said, "Maybe he'll fall overboard on the passage back."

Amused, Drake raised his glass in toast, but it didn't numb the disappointment.

"At least she's safe from Beau's harem."

Archer disagreed. "No woman is safe. I told him the next time he has a duel with an angry husband, I'm staying home. Someone else can be his second."

Drake prided himself on hiding his feelings. It was necessary with so many brothers, but somehow Rai could always see behind the mask. "You'll survive, Drake. You still have Josie and whoever else you're dabbling with."

"That you don't know who they are proves I'm discreet."

Archer rolled his eyes. "I'm going to console Raoul. Safe travels home. Good night."

Julianna beckoned Drake over.

"Yes, Mama?"

"Valinda is going to spend the night with me. Will you drive us home?"

He looked at Valinda sitting next to his mother. He was touched by the weariness in her shoulders and eyes. "Of course, but didn't you come over with Phillipe?"

"I did. He's had a bit too much wine, and I don't want us to end up in a ditch. Valinda's had enough for one day."

He agreed and searched the room for his baby brother. "Where's Phillipe now?"

"He and Beau just departed."

"Did he drive you here in your carriage? I came in a wagon from the livery. It needs to be returned and Havana's on a lead tied to the bed." Havana was his stallion.

She nodded. "Archer will have one of his staff return the wagon in the morning."

"Good." He was a man of many talents but not even he could drive two vehicles and ride a horse at the same time. He glanced between the two women. "Are you ready to leave now?"

His mother nodded but Valinda said, "I just need to get my bag and valise."

"Where are they?" he asked. "I'll get them."

"By the buffet table."

He fetched them and led the ladies out into the night.

By the time they made it to his mother's large house in the Treme district, their guest was asleep.

"Poor thing," Julianna said, glancing at Valinda curled up on the back seat. "I don't want to wake her. Can you carry her up to Sable's old room?"

Drake knew that the close physical contact was sure to ensnare him further, but he couldn't tell his mother no. After assisting Julianna out of the carriage, he reached in and gently eased Valinda into the cradle of his arms.

Inside, he laid Valinda down on the large four-poster bed and stepped away.

Julianna covered her with a light blanket and they closed the door behind them.

He asked, "How long will she be staying with you?"

"I don't know. She and I will discuss that in the morning. Little Reba and I are the only ones here, and there's plenty of room, so she's welcome as long as necessary. Are you staying over so you can take care of that leak in my greenhouse roof?"

Guilt singed him. He'd been promising to see to the roof for weeks. "I'm sorry I haven't gotten over here to fix it."

"My orchids don't like being dripped on."

"I understand." He was building a house on his portion of the LeVeq land and had been concentrating on that. "I'll stay and go home when I'm done. It shouldn't take that long."

She smiled. "Thank you. I'll see you in the morning." She beckoned him down. When he complied, she raised herself on her toes and placed a motherly kiss on his cheek. "Good night, son."

"Night, Mama."

Settling into the bedroom he once shared with Phillipe and Beau, Drake continued to think about Valinda. The feel of her slight weight in his arms and the sight of her peacefulness had indeed tightened the snare. She belonged to another, however, which meant he needed to tamp down any thoughts of pursuit. The idea left him grumpy though. Determined to put her out of his mind, he undressed and climbed into bed.

WHEN VALINDA AWAKENED, she groggily noted that she was fully dressed and had no idea where she was. Shaking away sleep's lingering fog, she sat up and looked around the beautifully appointed room. The dark gold drapes were drawn closed but a line of light at the base gleamed brightly against the polished wood floors. The bed was enormous, and the tufted gold upholstery on the dainty ivory chair by an ivory-colored vanity table matched the drapes. *Where am I?* Her last memory was getting into the carriage with Captain LeVeq and his mother. Had she fallen asleep on the drive? That had to be the explanation as to why she didn't remember. The knowledge left her appalled and more than a bit embarrassed. Granted, she'd had a long terrible day, but she could've at least stayed awake long enough to thank his mother for generously offering a place to sleep for the night. And how had she gotten to the bedroom? Had someone carried her? That it might have been the captain left her cheeks hot.

Surveying her wrinkled, soiled clothing, she wondered where she could wash up and change into something cleaner. She spied her carpetbag near the vanity. Leaving the bed, she noticed three doors. One turned out to be a large closet. The other led into a quiet hallway, and the last one opened into one of the largest and grandest bathing rooms she'd ever seen. There was a water closet and a sink with shiny brass fixtures. The claw-footed tub, big enough for two people, drew her in and she ran a hand over its smooth curved edge. Having had nothing but tepid hip baths at the Dumas house, she longed to immerse herself and take a long hot soak, but she wouldn't be so presumptuous without the permission of her hostess, so after availing herself of the facilities, she dug out the sliver of soap from her carpetbag and washed up as best she could. The injury on her cheek was now bruise blue. Viewing it in the mirror brought back those terrifying moments of her attack, and she closed her eyes, forcing herself to draw in a deep breath until the lingering fear receded. Wondering if she'd ever rid herself of the incident, she set it aside for the moment, donned clean clothes, redid her bun, and left the room. A short walk down the hallway led to a staircase. Descending the steps to the floor below, she found herself facing a grand door she assumed led outside. To her right was a large parlor with many windows, fine furniture, and expensive-looking lamps, but no one was about. Trying to determine where she might find the captain's mother, Val heard, "Valinda? Is that you, my dear?"

"Yes, ma'am."

"I'll be right there."

A few seconds later, the LeVeq matriarch appeared wearing a lovely gray morning dress. "Did you sleep well?"

"I did. What time is it?"

"Almost one."

"In the afternoon?!"

Julianna chuckled. "Yes. Is something wrong? Did you have an appointment of some kind? If you missed it, my apologies for letting you sleep. I thought you needed the rest."

"I did want to see the Sisters this morning. I'm not accustomed to rising so late." And she wasn't. Back home, she was up every morning by six to start the fires and light the stove for breakfast. The Dumas sisters had been early risers as well. Thinking about Madeline's death made her send up another silent prayer for her soul.

"I sent them a note earlier to let them know

you were here. They sent back that the bishop was visiting, so they'll be in prayer and there'll be no school."

Valinda sighed. Even though her visit would only be delayed a day, it felt like another setback.

"We need to get you something to put on your cheek. Hold on."

She left for a moment and returned with a small jar. "This should help with the healing."

Val walked over to the large mirror hanging above the fireplace mantel, and dabbed a bit of the creamy substance on her cheek.

"It has witch hazel in it, so it shouldn't sting."

"It doesn't. Thank you." She handed the jar back. "I'll put more on this evening. I need to wash my hands." Remnants of the salve were on her fingers.

"Let's go to the kitchen. Are you hungry?"

Val heard hammering off in the distance. "I am."

"Come. Little Reba will whip something up for you."

"Just toast will be sufficient."

Julianna stopped. "I've worked hard to provide a good life for myself and my children. We have more to offer you than toast."

The soft scolding made Valinda drop her head and smile. "Yes, ma'am."

Little Reba turned out to be a small well-built woman about Val's age. She had a ready smile and sandy skin dotted with freckles. Her *tignon* was gray and decorated with cowrie shells. While Val dried her hands after washing them in the sink, Reba said, "I'm cooking chops for Drake, along with some yams and collards. He's going to be hungry when he gets done. Would you like some?"

Val went still at the mention of Drake's name. "Um."

"Or if you want something a little lighter, I've bacon, shrimp and grits, and eggs."

Val preferred the second offering but didn't want to make more work for her.

Before she could ask for the chops, Julianna, as if reading her mind, said, "Give her the shrimp grits and eggs. She just awakened. Chops and the rest may be a bit heavy for now."

Little Reba nodded. "Yes, ma'am."

Val tried to protest. "Mrs. LeVeq—"

"It's LeVeq-Vincent, but please call me Julianna. My husband, Henri, is currently in Cuba."

Val wouldn't think to be that familiar with a woman of her age. "But—"

"Julianna," she voiced again, a bit more firmly. "Everyone calls me that. Even my sons at times."

Val sensed she stood little chance of winning this, so she surrendered. "Julianna."

"Good. Now, let's step outside while Little Reba fixes your food. I want to check on Drake's progress. He's repairing the roof on my greenhouse."

Mentally preparing herself to see the captain, she followed Julianna down the gravel path that cut through the well-groomed landscape of shrubs and trees to a large glass-sided greenhouse. Her son was on the wooden roof hammering nails into shingles. At their approach, he stopped, and when his gaze met hers, Val's heart skipped in her chest. With his dark skin, close-cropped beard, and Herculean build he was breathtaking, a description she'd never attached to a man before. The men she knew back home were fine upstanding examples of their gender, but none as riveting as Drake LeVeq.

"Good afternoon, Miss Lacy."

"Captain."

He picked up a towel and wiped the perspiration from his brow, his eyes still on her.

Julianna asked, "Are you done?"

"Almost," he replied, but kept his attention focused on Val. She'd never had a man view her with such intensity before. She wanted to look away but the will to do so seemed beyond her grasp.

"Did you sleep well?" he asked.

"I did. Much longer than I planned."

"Which I take full responsibility for," his mother said lightly. "But she apparently needed the rest."

"Apparently," he echoed.

"Valinda, Drake built this greenhouse for me years ago. Would you like to see the beauties inside?"

"I would." If only to get away from the overwhelming presence that was her son.

Drake protested, "And here I was hoping to have the company of two lovely ladies while I worked."

"Finish my roof, and maybe I'll let you eat."

He chuckled and commenced his hammering.

Inside the greenhouse, the hammering could be heard, but the wealth of beautiful plants immediately grabbed Val's attention.

As Julianna pointed out the colorful array of specimens from faraway places like Borneo, India, and Australia, she explained, "My late husband, Francois, was a merchant sailor and picked up my first orchid on a trip to Brazil. I didn't know anything about the care and tried to grow it in the house. It died, of course, and

I was devastated. He searched high and low for someone I could learn from and found an elderly Dominican named Yves, who tended orchids on a plantation north of here. Yves said I needed a greenhouse, so Francois built the original one for me. Every time he went on a voyage, he'd bring back orchids, and with each one I grew better and better at their care."

"What a lovely gesture."

"He held my heart in so many ways. He died in a storm off the Cape of Good Hope when the Brats, as Raimond calls his younger brothers, were little. I didn't think I could live without him. I never knew losing him and his love would bring such pain."

"My condolences on your loss."

"Thank you."

Val had never heard anyone profess to loving someone so intensely. Her parents had an arranged marriage, as did most of the adults she'd grown up around. Some couples treated their mates kindly, but others, like her parents, barely tolerated each other. More importantly, the women, particularly her mother and Val's older sister, Caroline, seemed so unhappy being wives. To escape that unhappiness and the prospect of her father marrying her off to someone she couldn't abide, Val had agreed to marry her dear friend Coleman Bennett. They cared for and respected each other, but their union wouldn't be based on what people termed *love* because it was more of a business arrangement than anything else, and frankly, Val had never witnessed nor experienced love. *You will lose a love, reject a love, find a love.* The fortune-teller's words rose out of nowhere and the hairs stood up on her neck. She shook them off and turned her attention to the next orchid Julianna was describing.

When the tour was done, they stepped back out in the heat and saw the captain gathering his tools.

"I'm done, Mama. All the old shingles have been replaced. Your beauties should be safe for another few years."

"Thank you."

"I'm going to get washed up and eat."

"Reba is fixing Valinda a plate, too. I have some contracts to finish going over. Would you mind keeping her company while I work? It shouldn't be long. Is that okay with you, Valinda?"

Val's original plans for the day had been to thank Julianna for taking her in last night, then depart and speak with the nuns about a new schoolroom and a place to stay. She also needed to contact her students about the closing of the classroom. Nothing in that included eating with her son. Now, her plans in disarray, she had no legitimate reason to decline the invitation, so she surrendered again. "That will be fine."

"Good. I'll have Little Reba bring your plates out to the gazebo. It's such a fine afternoon. You two can eat there."

LeVeq was watching Val with veiled amusement as if he knew the futility in swimming against the strong tide that was his mother. "I'll only be a few minutes," he told them. Picking up his tool belt and the ladder, he strode off.

As he moved away, she couldn't take her eyes off the way the thin sweat-dampened white shirt clung to his broad shoulders and the slope of his back. He walked as if he'd created the world himself. Each step left her so mesmerized, she didn't hear what Julianna was saying.

"I'm sorry, what did you say?"

The matriarch smiled knowingly. "The gazebo is this way."

Embarrassed at having been caught staring, Val followed her down another gravel pathway that led through large stands of red roses, dark pink hibiscus, and fragrant white gardenias. The combination of scents filled the still air with a lovely sweetness. A gazebo made of wrought iron and wood stood beneath the spreading branches of an ancient live oak dripping with its signature pale moss.

"What a wonderful setting," Val said, taking in the surroundings.

"I'm glad you like it. Drake built this gazebo, too."

Val studied the structure and the intricate ironwork. "Who did the iron?"

"Drake. He's an architect, carpenter, and a smith. I doubt there's anything he can't design or build."

Val nodded, fascinated by the swirls and curls of the gazebo's iron walls, but her immediate needs returned. "Might you know of a place where I can stay while I try and find a new classroom?"

"You're more than welcome to stay here, and I have a smaller carriage you may use to get around while you look. Can you drive?"

"Yes." Her intended, Cole, had taught her after her father had forbidden it.

"All of my sons are close by, and I know they won't mind escorting you on your search if they're needed. In the meantime, if you wish to gain some income, I could employ you as my temporary assistant to handle errands and correspondence. I always have more work than I can handle alone."

"What kind of work do you do?"

"I have interests in real estate, shipping, importing, exporting, and banking."

Val found that surprising. Back home, the few women business owners she knew only catered their services to other women as seamstresses, hairdressers, cooks, and laundresses. She'd never met any who moved in the so-called male circles of industry. "Are there other women here with similar interests?"

"Of course. New Orleans has a long history of females in business. At one point during the early years, free women of color owned a considerable portion of the city's real estate." Julianna eyed her for a moment and asked in a serious tone, "What do you want from life, Valinda?"

She'd never been asked that question before. The constraints of society assumed she'd live the life chosen by her father or husband. "To found a school and chart my own course."

"Does your intended want that for you as well?"

"Yes. He's probably the only man I know who does."

"Then you have made a wise choice."

Val thought she had, too, and it felt good

knowing someone else agreed, because her father hadn't. He'd wanted to marry her off to an older man with wealth and status, just as he'd done her sister, Caroline.

Julianna said, "I'll be in my study. Come see me when you finish eating and we can talk further about your potential duties."

"Yes, ma'am."

Julianna smiled and left Val alone.

Chapter Five

$\mathcal{A}$fter Julianna's departure, Val took a seat on the leather pad covering the gazebo's iron bench and drank in the scents and silence. Julianna was certainly a remarkable woman. Val thought the LeVeq matriarch and her grandmother Rose would get along famously should they ever meet. Rose made her living as a seamstress and hadn't remarried after the death of Val's grandfather. Every man who courted her seemed focused on controlling her money, she'd once told Val, so she'd charted her life alone, seasoning it with feistiness and dogged independence.

And now, here her granddaughter sat awaiting her meal with Drake LeVeq. She'd never dined alone with a man outside of her family's acquaintances. What would they talk about? Would she be able to mask her nervousness?

More importantly, would she be able to remain aloof? Something told her that women came easily to him and she didn't want to be viewed as a potential conquest. Yet and still, the prospect of being alone with him filled her with an odd sense of anticipation. She wanted to know more about him, which could be seen as unbecoming for one with an intended, and as the properly raised, straitlaced young woman her father so wished her to embrace and be. But she'd always been daring. Lying dormant inside herself was the young girl who'd enjoyed climbing trees, playing baseball, and who'd without a whimper accepted the whipping she'd gotten from her father in response to her three-day expulsion from Mrs. Brown's School for Proper Girls of Color, for demanding she be taught science. She sensed being around Julianna was going to make that girl regain her wings and rise. What Drake LeVeq might give rise to, she didn't know.

Moments later, he arrived carrying a tray topped by covered silver dishes. His fresh shirt was pale blue. Two buttons at the neck were open exposing the strong lines of his throat. Realizing she was staring again, she quickly looked away.

"Your food, mademoiselle." His French accent was another weapon in his arsenal of things she found attractive. Declaring herself immune was a lie.

"Thank you."

He set one of the covered plates in front of her, placed the rest on the other side table, and took his seat. Avoiding looking his way for the moment, she concentrated on unwrapping her tableware from inside the linen napkin.

"Do you need anything else?" he asked.

She removed the silver top from her plate and eyed the grits topped with shrimp, scrambled eggs, and toasted baguette slices. "No. I should be fine with what I have."

"Excellent." His plate was piled high with chops, yams, collards, and bread. There was also a large bowl of gumbo and rice. He must've seen the wonder on her face because he said, "Roofing is hard work, and I'm still a growing boy."

Amused, she nodded.

"Shall I say grace? Or would you care to do the honors?"

She was so surprised, all she could say was, "No, go ahead, please."

He nodded, bowed his head, and whispered the words. He finished with, "Amen."

She echoed the word and tried not to show more wonder.

He picked up his cutlery and began in on a chop. "Problem, *cheri*?"

"I—wasn't expecting you to say grace."

"No?" he asked with a hint of humor in his voice and dark eyes.

She shook her head.

"We were raised in the Catholic faith and grace is always recited before a meal. In fact, when we were little, my brothers and I would fight over the opportunity. Saying grace pleased our mother and we lived to please her. We still do."

Val forked up her grits and shrimp. It was a dish she'd never eaten before and it was so flavorful, she hummed with delight.

His eyes shot to her.

She froze in response. "I'm sorry. I didn't mean to do that aloud."

"There isn't a man alive who doesn't enjoy hearing a woman's pleasure."

Heat flared inside her and she realized she had no business being alone with him.

"Tell me about yourself, *cheri*. Where's home?"

Deciding that talking about herself was a far safer subject than her pleasure, she replied, "New York City."

"Siblings?"

"One. An older sister named Caroline."

"Are you close?"

"We were before she married two years ago. She lives in Philadelphia now, so I don't see her as often as I'd like. Her elderly husband doesn't care for traveling."

He searched her face as if seeking the answer to something, and she wondered if he sensed the sorrow she felt watching her sister's vibrant personality slowly dimmed by marriage to a man thirty years her senior. She took a sip of water from her glass as if it might wash away her sadness. "Tell me about you. What was it like growing up with so many brothers?"

"Fun. Bruising at times because we fought constantly, and there were times when I wanted to bury one or more under this gazebo. But I wouldn't trade them for all the pearls in the Orient."

She laughed lightly. "Caro and I had our moments, too. The day she told my parents I'd climbed to the top of the neighbor's big maple tree, I wanted to bury her somewhere, too."

"You climbed trees?"

She nodded. "My father was so furious he made me stay inside for a week."

"He was probably worried you'd fall."

"He was more worried about me being a rebellious hellion, as he called me. Proper, well-raised girls don't climb trees, or kneel in the dirt shooting marbles, or play baseball, or all the other things I liked doing."

He'd stopped with his fork partway to his mouth.

"Yes?" she asked, humor in her voice. "Have I shocked you?"

"I think I'm in love."

"No, you aren't. Eat your food."

"How good are you at marbles?"

"Skilled enough that Cole and the other boys refused to let me play with them after a while."

"Cole?"

"My intended."

"Ah."

Once again, he searched her face as if silently seeking answers. He turned his attention to the bowl of gumbo. "Tell me about him."

"My father works for his, so we've known each other our entire lives. He's a newspaper editor. He and his business partner, Lenny, are in Paris hoping to get financial support to start their own paper."

"Is it a love match?"

Val paused. It was now her turn to study him. She replied truthfully, "No, it isn't. I take it you believe there is such a thing?"

"I do. You?"

"There are no love matches in my family or in the families of my acquaintances, so I err on the side of saying no."

"Raimond and Sable have one, as did my parents, as did our great-grandparents Dominic and Clare." He added softly, "Love is real, *cheri*."

The passion he put into the words coupled with his accent were such a heady combination, if he professed the moon was made of ice cream she'd ask for a bowl and spoon. She eyed his full lips and remembered the gentleness of his fingers on her scraped cheek. Common sense urged her to get up and run from him like her slips were on fire because Drake LeVeq was dangerous in ways an engaged, untouched woman like herself couldn't even imagine, but lord help her, she was drawn to him.

"If you aren't marrying for love, then why are you?"

"To be free to live my life the way I want. Cole will allow me that, and I won't have to be chained to a man I can't abide." Like her sister, she silently noted.

"You don't believe a man who loves you will offer you that same freedom?"

"If marriage gives me the freedom I desire, why do I need love?"

"For the companionship. Adoration. Bed games."

"Bed games?" she echoed doubtfully.

From his amused manner she assumed he was talking about marital relations. The proper, well-raised Val would've shied away from such an improper discussion, but the girl her father called Hellion asked, "Are you speaking of marital relations?"

"I am."

"Bed games are played with mistresses and women of the night, not wives."

He sat back, eyes shining. "Are you sure? A wife can be both mistress and wife."

Val decided she was in over her head with this conversation because his statement made no sense. "Do you have a mistress?"

He nodded and said, "I do."

Why she found that disappointing wasn't something she wanted to explore. After all, they meant nothing to each other. "If a wife can be a mistress, do you plan to marry her?"

"No. She'd be appalled if I asked her to." He paused for a moment before chuckling. "I see I'll need to be on my toes debating you."

"I agree."

"Your confidence is intriguing. Were you not intended for another, I'd court you."

Her breath caught. "You're very bold, Captain."

"I'm descended from pirates. Boldness is in my blood."

The warmth coursing through her veins had nothing to do with the New Orleans heat, and everything to do with the dazzling titan watching her so closely. Her ties to Cole notwithstanding, she wondered what it might be like to be courted by such a man.

"If I set aside my boldness and ask very politely, may I call you Valinda?"

"You may, yes." That he was equal parts pirate and gentleman only added to his captivating allure.

"Thank you. Please call me Drake."

"I will."

For a moment the potent silence between them made words unnecessary. The air seemed thicker, charged. Dragging her attention away from his eyes, Val returned to her meal, and missed the titan's knowing smile.

When they were done eating, he gathered the dishes and piled them on the tray with an efficiency that showed him no stranger to the task. "Besides talking with my mother, are you doing anything else today?"

"I'd like to let my students know about the school closing, somehow."

"Do you have a plan in mind?"

"I'm not sure. I know where a few are employed. If I can speak with them, I'm hoping they can spread the word for me." She didn't want her students to think she'd abandoned them or didn't care enough to offer an explanation as to why classes were discontinued.

"Where do they work?"

"One is a pastry chef at the St. Louis Hotel. His name's Eb Slayton. Dina Watson works for a cigar maker. I have the name of the shop on a paper in my bag."

"I've nothing pressing for the rest of the afternoon. I could drive you if you'd like? Mother's coachman has the day off, so I'm sure she won't mind us borrowing her carriage."

Val weighed the offer. Contacting her students was a priority, and truthfully, she was enjoying his company. "If she's okay with delaying our conversation, I'd be grateful for your assistance."

"Then, let's go speak with her."

After Val explained the situation, Julianna gave her approval. The pleased Val went up to her room to get the name of Dina's cigar shop and joined Drake in the carriage for the drive to the Quarter.

Riding alone with a man who wasn't family was also new for Valinda and as they got underway, she tamped down her nervousness. *Were you not intended for another, I'd court you.* His declaration remained breathtaking, but she was convinced it had been nothing more than idle banter. Men didn't court women like herself. As her father once railed after yet another suitor chose to not call on her again, she was too educated, independent, and opinionated. Her eyes swept over Drake's large scarred hands handling the reins and his barn-broad shoulders. Beside him she felt like a Lilliputian from Swift's *Gulliver's Travels.* She'd given him the name of the cigar shop they were bound for and learned he and his brothers patronized the establishment regularly.

"Thank you for helping me with this."

"You're welcome. How many students do you have?"

"Fifteen. We only meet Mondays and Thursdays because those were the days most could find the time to attend. Tuesdays and Wednesdays I teach children at the convent."

"You enjoy teaching?"

"I do." That she couldn't now left her sad and she sighed.

He must have heard her because he looked over and asked, "What's wrong?"

"Things aren't going the way I'd envisioned.

Cole will be returning to America soon and my stay here will end. I don't feel as if I've accomplished much."

"Can some of your students read that couldn't before?"

"Yes."

"Then you've accomplished a great deal. Being able to read will change their lives for the better."

His words soothed her unhappiness. "That's kind of you to say. Thank you."

"It's the truth, *cheri*. If you've only taught one person to read, that's one more able to pass the skill along to their children and others. In your small way you're lifting their future."

She appreciated that balm as well.

"When you leave New Orleans, will you and Cole go back to New York?"

"More than likely." And she would resume her job at her grandmother's dress shop, while searching for a place to teach.

"Is New York a good place to live?"

"If you have money, but where we are is cramped and crowded. The streets are fouled by sewage and refuse. The city fathers have been trying to clean up the area, but it's been slow going."

"New Orleans was that way, too, until General Butler arrived with the Union troops and cleared out all the offal that made the streets so putrid. It was probably the only thing the people on the losing side of the war didn't hate him for."

She'd read about the general in the New York papers and the infamous chamber pots sold in New Orleans that sported paintings of his face at the bottom of the bowl. "Has your family always lived here?"

"My great-grandparents came to New Orleans after their island home off the coast of Cuba was destroyed by a hurricane."

"Were they free?"

"He was. She was a slave. He stole her from her mistress during a sea voyage."

Val stared.

He glanced over and chuckled at the look on her face. "He was a privateer."

"The fancy word for pirate."

"Yes."

"And they had a love match?"

"Yes. She had two children enslaved in Charleston, and after Dominic stole them away, they moved to the island."

"That's quite a tale."

"All true. They loved each other fiercely."

His tone held so much conviction, she wondered what love consisted of. How did it come about? How did it make a person feel? She had no answers.

"Has your family always lived in New York?"

"Only since my mother's parents came north from Virginia. Both were enslaved. My father and his parents were slaves in South Carolina. He was an infant when they escaped to New York."

"Escaping had to be harrowing."

"For my grandmother it truly was because she was fairly young and ran alone."

"Grandparents still alive?"

"My grandmother Rose is, but my grandfather passed on when I was twelve. She never remarried. She said all the men who came around wanted to take charge of her dressmaking shop and her money."

"And her granddaughter has the same aversion to that type of control?"

She looked him in the eyes and said firmly, "Yes."

He gave her a small smile. "Stick to your guns, *cheri*. We pirates don't do well under someone's thumb, either."

Entering the center of the city, he guided the carriage through the congested streets to the St. Louis Hotel. "This isn't a place that welcomes us through the front door, so let me park and I'll escort you to the back entrance."

Once the horses were tied to the post, he guided her down the trash-strewn alley and to the door designated for deliveries and employees. To her delight, Eb and a few other men and women were on the dock eating lunch. He looked both surprised and confused as she approached. "Miss Lacy? What are you doing here?"

He gave Drake a long searching look that held a hint of suspicion, so she made the introductions, then explained, "I'm staying with Mr. LeVeq's mother temporarily, and he was kind enough to drive me here."

"I see." He eyed Drake again, who met his scrutiny levelly.

"Brigands have taken over our classroom, Mr. Slayton, so I have to find a new location."

"No," he replied, voice sharp with disappointment. "That's terrible news."

"Yes, it is. And since I don't know where most of the other students live, I'm hoping you can help me spread the word that there will be no more classes until further notice."

He shook his head sadly. "Of course. How long do you think it'll be before we can start up again?"

"I'm not sure." And she wished she had a better answer.

"Soon as you are, will you let me know? I'm anxious to continue learning. The others are, too."

"I know you are."

Drake spoke for the first time. "There might be openings at some of the few Bureau schools still operating."

Eb nodded. "Before I found Miss Lacy, nobody else was taking new students, but I'll start looking again."

"Maybe you'll have better luck this time," Val said, hope in her voice. "Not that I want to lose you to another teacher." And she didn't, but he needed to continue his education.

"Who else do you plan to see?" Eb asked.

"Dina Watson, Abner Little, and Remus Blue. They were the only people who gave me information on how to get word to them or their families if I needed to."

"I know where some of the others live and work. I'll let them know on my way home."

A man wearing a white chef's coat leaned around the open door and called, "Eb! Time to get back to work."

"Sure thing." He started to the door. "Good seeing you, Miss Lacy. Take care of her, Mr. LeVeq. She's real special."

"I will."

Val forced herself not to meet Drake's eyes to avoid what she might see, and called to the departing Eb, "I can still help your brother, if he needs it."

"He does." And he disappeared inside.

On the walk back to the busy street, Drake asked, "What kind of help is his brother after?"

"He's trying to find his wife. He wants to put a plea in the newspapers, but he can't read or write."

"Nice of you to offer your assistance."

"Were I in his position, I'd want to find my family, too."

"So would I."

She looked up at him as they turned a corner. "We're lucky having been born free, at least in that regard."

He nodded his agreement.

She continued, "My grandmother had a younger brother and two older sisters. She hasn't seen or heard from any of them since she escaped. She continues to hope she will before she passes on."

"I hope the same for her."

The sincerity in his tone matched the look in his steady gaze and something inside her shifted, making her want to further get to know the depth of the man he was inside. "I do as well."

He said quietly, "The cigar shop is just a few doors down."

The bell over the door tinkled as they entered, and the thick scent of tobacco blanketed the air. A short older man with milk-white skin and receding jet-black hair came out to greet them from behind a curtained-off area she assumed led to the back of the place. His face brightened at the sight of Drake. "Drake LeVeq, how are you?" he asked in a heavy French-accented voice.

"I'm well, Eugene. This is Miss Lacy. Val, this is Eugene Bascom, the owner."

He inclined his head chivalrously. "Mademoiselle Lacy. A pleasure to meet you."

"Thank you. I'm pleased to meet you as well."

"Drake, are you here for your cigars?"

"Yes, and Miss Lacy would like to speak with one of your employees."

He paused. "Who?" he asked Val.

"Dina Watson. She's one of my students."

"You're the lady teaching her to read and write?"

"I am. She's doing very well in the classroom."

His manner cooled. "I see."

Drake apparently noticed the change in him as well. "Is there a problem, Eugene?"

"No. Why do you wish to speak to her?" the owner asked Val.

"I want to give her a message about school."

"Give it to me and I will pass it along to her."

"I'd like to pass it along myself, if that's possible." She wanted to make sure Dina received the news.

His jaw hardened, as did his eyes.

Just then a younger man stepped into view. He was tall but his resemblance to Eugene made Val think he might be his son.

"Mr. LeVeq. Your cigars are ready."

"Thank you, Quentin. This is Miss Lacy. She'd like to speak with Dina."

"Of course. Just a moment."

Eugene glared but Quentin stepped back through the curtain. Dina was with him when he returned.

Her dark eyes widened. "Miss Lacy? How are you?"

"I'm well."

She eyed Drake for a long moment then said to Val, "Quent said you wanted to speak to me?"

Val noted the softness in Quentin's gaze as he watched Dina, and the displeasure on the face of Eugene. Having no idea what it meant, she set it aside and told Dina about the school.

"Oh no. I've been looking forward to learning to read better."

"I know and I'm sorry, but it's out of my hands."

Her disappointment was plain.

Quentin said, "I'll help you."

Eugene snapped, "You don't have time."

"I'll find the time," he replied, eyes still on Dina. "It's important that she learn to read."

His soft voice matched his expression.

Dina gave him a smile. "That's very kind of you, Quent, but I don't want your father upset with you. He believes a woman like me is only good for sweeping floors, and has no business trying to better herself."

Eugene turned beet red.

Dina turned to Val. "Miss Lacy, thanks for coming by. Please let me know if you start another class." She added pointedly, "I have floors to sweep." She disappeared into the back.

Quentin glared at his father before telling Drake, "I'll get your cigars."

Drake nodded.

Quentin followed Dina.

Val, simmering over Dina's take on the situation, said as calmly as she could, "Mr. Bascom, please forgive me for asking what may sound rude, but do you really believe Dina shouldn't learn to read?"

His face hardened. "That's none of your concern."

The response made her want to throw up

her hands. She turned to Drake, who said, "I'm sure that isn't what Eugene believes, Valinda, because if he did, the House of LeVeq and its many associates would have to take their business elsewhere."

Bascom's once-angry eyes widened with alarm.

Drake continued, "He'll allow Quentin to assist Dina until she finds another classroom, won't you, Bascom?"

Eugene Bascom nodded so forcefully, Val swore his hairline receded another inch.

Eyes still pinned to the now-quaking shop owner, Drake gave him a cold smile. "Good. I'll check on Miss Watson's progress the next time I visit. How's that sound, Eugene?"

"That's fine. Very fine."

Quentin returned with the cigars. Drake thanked him, and they departed.

Outside, she said, "Thank you. What an awful man."

"You're welcome."

"I know some people aren't happy with the way things have changed since the war, but it's no longer unlawful for her to learn to read."

"Correct. And I applaud you for challenging Bascom the way you did."

"It helped to have a pirate with me."

"Always at your service, mademoiselle. Where to next?"

"To see Abner Little at Caldwell's Butcher Shop and Remus Blue, the sexton at St. Augustine's Church."

Both men were as disappointed with the news as Dina and Eb had been, and on the ride back to Julianna's home, her own disappointment rose again. It lessened as she reminded herself that she had made a difference in their lives, even if she never found another classroom. She also held on to the hope that the nuns would offer a solution.

She glanced over at Drake. He'd been the champion she'd needed back at the cigar shop. Alone, she doubted Bascom would've been brought to heel. Threatening the man's profits had been an excellent strategy. There wasn't a shop owner on earth who viewed losing a group of valued customers as a sound business practice. Having him by her side had made a difference for her and Dina. She'd be forever grateful.

They found his mother seated at her desk in her study. "Welcome back. Did you locate your students?"

Val answered, "Yes, we did."

"Good. Drake, are you staying for dinner?" It was now late afternoon.

"No. I'm going home. I'll see you in a day or two." To Val, he said, "I enjoyed our time together."

"I did as well."

"Maybe we can do it again, soon."

She didn't say yes, but didn't say no, either.

He said, "I'll bring my marbles next time."

She couldn't suppress her smile. "Only if you don't mind parting with them."

"I love a challenge."

"I sense that."

He bowed. "Until we meet again. Goodbye, *cheri*. Goodbye, Mama."

Val watched him leave, and when she turned back, Julianna was viewing her pensively.

"Ma'am?" Val asked.

Julianna waved off the question. "Nothing. Have a seat and let's discuss what we can do about your immediate future."

Chapter Six

After leaving Julianna's, Drake rode his stallion, Havana, down the dirt road that led to his section of LeVeq land. Each brother owned a portion, but Archer lived at his hotel, and Phillipe and Beau maintained apartments in the Quarter. Raimond and Drake were the only two who'd built homes, even though Drake's was still under construction.

As he rode, his mind circled back to Valinda. He'd enjoyed being with her today. She was intelligent, caring, and more than a bit surprising. He certainly hadn't expected her to confront Bascom the way she had, but he supposed that was the hellion part her father disapproved of so much. That she didn't believe in love gave him pause. He supposed if she'd never seen it or experienced it, she wouldn't.

Were her views shared by her intended? If so, Drake thought the man a loon, to have known her for so many years and not be in love with her. He was admittedly halfway there himself and he'd known her a mere twenty-four hours.

Although she was not to be his, he gave himself permission to imagine how it might be if she were, because fantasy hurt no one. They'd shoot marbles, play checkers and chess, and travel to the Orient on one of Rai's voyages. He'd want to hear her positions on the political machinations of the day, and take her to the racetrack and the opera. He wondered if she knew how to swim or ride, and if she still liked climbing trees? And, yes, there'd be bed games. She wore her hair in a tight bun that showed off the beautiful lines of her small brown face and the tempting expanse of her throat above her high-necked blouse. He imagined brushing his lips against that soft column until she hummed with pleasure. Were she his, he'd build her not just a classroom but a school, and gift it to her for her birthday or Christmas, thereby showing her what it meant to be loved and adored by a man of the House of LeVeq.

When he came within view of his house, he heard a woman's screams, followed by keening filled with so much pain he pushed Havana into a full gallop.

It was his housekeeper, Erma Downs. She was on her knees in the dirt by the porch. Head thrown back, tears running down her face, she was wailing as if her heart was broken. Her daughter-in-law, Allie, was holding her and sobbing bitterly.

Dismounting, he ran to her side. "Miss Erma!"

"They killed my boy!" she screamed.

Ice filled his veins. "Who!"

"They killed my boy!" she raged. "They killed my boy!"

His foreman, Solomon Hawk, and some of the freedmen he'd hired to help with the construction of his home looked on gravely.

Drake asked urgently, "Allie, what happened?"

"Daniel wouldn't sign the contract, so Master Atwater shot him." Liam Atwater was one of the cruelest former slave owners in the area.

"When?"

"This morning."

Drake was speechless, then enraged. He calmed himself. There'd be time to let his anger flow later. "Come. Let's get you and Miss Erma in the house. Where's your son, Bailey?"

Allie pointed at the wagon Drake hadn't noticed until then. He turned to see the seven-year-old Bailey sitting still as stone on the seat.

In a shaking voice, Allie said, "Atwater killed him in front of us."

Bailey's small, stoic face warred with the abject sadness in his tear-filled eyes. Drake fought the emotion clogging his throat. "Bring him in. I'll get Miss Erma."

She went to Bailey. Drake picked up the weeping Erma and carried her inside.

Later, after he left Erma resting in one of the bedrooms, Allie told him the story.

"Daniel didn't think the work contract was fair. It said he was to work six days a week from sunup to sundown, be responsible for the animals and the tools, and not leave the plantation without permission. That was the part Daniel didn't like the most. He told Master Atwater, we were free, and when the work was done, we had a right to come and go as we pleased. When the other men wouldn't sign either, it made Master Atwater plenty mad."

Drake knew that many former masters were using the contracts to lock the freedmen into a new form of slavery. He'd seen work agreements that outlined pages of tasks the workers were responsible for, and the penalties meted out if they weren't fulfilled. Very few made reference to what they'd be paid. Some even banned talking during the workday, and demanded the freedmen be subservient in their actions at all times. "Did he allow you to bury him?"

Her tears flowed again and she shook her head. "Master Atwater said anybody defying him would be thrown into the swamp, so they put Danny's body in a wagon and drove him away."

She broke down and Drake eased her against him. His eyes closed as she sobbed out her despair. He said, "I'll file a report in the morning and see if we can't have Atwater arrested." He knew he had a better chance of harnessing a rainbow. The Army would do nothing, and neither would the authorities, but he would take the matter as far as he could. In the meantime, he'd try to retrieve Daniel's body.

Drake rode to the Atwater place accompanied by Solomon. Skirting the house because he knew Atwater wouldn't allow them on his land, they rode another mile before veering into an area that led to the swamp. The realist in him knew the search would be futile. Between the waters darkened by rotting vegetation and the gators, he'd be lucky to find anything. But for Erma, Allie, and her son, Bailey, he at least had to try. He and Solomon slowly guided their mounts through the thick expanse of soaring oaks and muddy ground hoping to find the tracks of the wagon the body had been transported in. If they could, they might be able to determine where he'd been placed in the water. After an hour of searching through the swamp's gloom, they found what appeared to be fresh evidence of wheels. They were visually searching the surroundings when two men on horseback appeared from behind the trees. Both were armed. The older man was Boyd Meachem, Liam Atwater's overseer. The younger, Boyd's son, Ennis.

From behind the raised rifle, Boyd—whose thin face resembled a skull—grinned, showing off tobacco-stained teeth. "Well, lookee here, Ennis. We caught ourselves some uppity trespassers. What're you doing here, LeVeq?"

"Came to retrieve Daniel Downs's body."

Still smiling, Boyd asked, "Who?"

Ennis said, "He's gator food by now."

His father hissed, "Shut up!" before saying to Drake, "Don't recall anybody by that name."

Drake asked through his inner rage, "So, Atwater didn't shoot him dead while his wife and child looked on?"

Something crossed Boyd's face that might have been regret, guilt, or shame but it disappeared as quickly as it appeared. "He didn't kill nobody. And even if he did, what business is it of yours?"

"Daniel's mother works for me."

Again, a fleeting something played over the skeleton-like face.

Ennis spoke into the breach. "Sticking your nose where it don't belong may make you gator bait, too."

Drake knew Ennis was part of a ragtag supremacist group called Protectors of the South made up of illiterate poor White men like himself determined to turn back the clock. Drake looked him in the eyes. "But then Atwater would have the noses of my brothers and the Army in his business. You think Atwater would enjoy that, Boyd?"

Ennis received a sharp look from his father before Boyd settled his attention back on Drake. "Go home, LeVeq. Nothing to be found here and don't let me catch you on Atwater land again."

Drake was well aware that if Meachem were of a mind to kill him and Solomon he could, and their bodies, like Daniel's, would never be found. Rather than be the source of Julianna's grief, Drake offered the overseer an almost-imperceptible nod. Reining his horse around and hoping they wouldn't be shot in the back, he and Solomon rode away.

Dusk was falling. Solomon headed home. Julianna and Erma Downs were acquainted through St. Augustine's Church, so Drake stopped by her house to tell her about the murder.

Upon hearing the news, Julianna wiped the tears from her eyes. Beside her sat a solemn Valinda.

Julianna said, "Erma and I met right after she received her free papers. She saved every spare penny for ten years, hoping to buy his freedom, only to have him drafted during the war, and now this. She has to be heartbroken. Have the authorities been contacted?"

"I'll do that in the morning. Sol and I went to the swamp to try and retrieve his body but Meachem ran us off."

"Will these hatemongers ever leave the race alone so we can live?" Julianna shook her head with disgust. "Is there anything I can do for Erma or her daughter-in-law?"

"I'll ask and let you know."

"Okay," she replied softly. "Tell her I send my condolences. I'll light a candle for Daniel's soul."

"I will."

"And please be careful tomorrow. Some people aren't going to like you bringing the matter to the authorities."

"I know but I owe it to Erma and her family to try and get him some justice."

"I agree, but again, be careful."

He nodded. "I'll let you know what happens."

"Thank you."

He gave the women his goodbyes and departed.

THURSDAY MORNING, DRAKE approached Merritt in his office before the doors opened for the day. The lieutenant was shaving with the aid of a small mirror he'd tacked to the wall.

"I need to speak with you," Drake said.

Merritt paused and turned. "About?"

"A freedman was murdered yesterday for refusing to sign a work contract he found unfair."

Merritt eyed him as if trying to determine how soon this conversation might be swept away. He resumed skimming the razor over and around his beard and sideburns. "As you know, we encourage signing whether they believe it's fair or not. They must work."

"Not under conditions that are a substitute for slavery."

"We don't control the wording."

"But we should stand for a man murdered in front of his wife and seven-year-old son."

Merritt exhaled with what sounded like temper and frustration. He removed the last of the soap from his face with the water in the basin, then dried himself with a small towel. "All right, I'm listening. What happened?"

Drake relayed what he knew, adding, "This is the same Liam Atwater who ran workers off his plantation after the harvest last year to keep from paying them what they'd earned in wages."

"And he was warned not to do it again."

"But not warned against murder."

"What is it you want me to do, LeVeq?"

"Have him arrested."

"Were there witnesses?"

"His wife and son."

"I mean White witnesses?"

Drake's jaw hardened. "I'm sure his overseer was there."

"But you don't know that for a fact."

"No."

"Where's the body?"

"Taken to the swamp and left there."

"So, you have no credible witnesses and no body. The police are going to want at least one part of that answer, if not both."

"Are you saying you won't advocate he be charged with murder?"

"I'm saying, based on what you told me, there's nothing the Army can do. Now, there's a line of living freedmen at the door waiting to be served, so you should go to your desk."

Drake didn't know why he'd bothered. He knew Merritt wouldn't care. Swallowing his rage, he said, "I'm taking this up the chain of command."

"Good luck with that, but don't expect to have a desk when you return. Volunteer or not, I just gave you a direct order. Ignore it, and your services are no longer welcome. And I'll take that up the chain of command."

Drake offered a bitter chuckle. A two-word phrase came to mind, but instead of voicing it, he turned and walked out of Merritt's office. Pausing at his desk, he picked up his valise, and left the Freedmen's Bureau for the last time.

His quest to find someone willing to stand for justice continued at the office of the Bureau's regional commander.

"He's ill, and not taking appointments at this time," Drake was told by his aide.

"When is he expected to return?"

The aide shrugged.

"Then who may I speak to instead?"

"Your local commanding officer."

"He refuses to support charges being brought."

"Then I don't know what to tell you. I'm sorry."

Frustration rising with each breath, he went to the local authorities, only to be told, "A niggress can't testify against a man like Atwater, so until you get someone who can, nothing we can do."

Last year, the city police, aided by men of the fire department, marched on and assaulted the attendees at a Republican convention. When the violence ended, thirty-four Black men lay dead. He knew they weren't going to help Erma and her son, but he wanted to exhaust all possibilities.

In the meantime, to keep from riding to Atwater's place and shooting him on sight, Drake went home and fired up his forge. Once the flames reached the proper temperature, he donned his protective mask, apron, and gloves, and pounded his anger into scrap pieces of iron until it became too dark to see.

As HE LAY in bed the following morning, his mood was as grim as it had been the night before. Seeking justice for Allie's murdered husband had not only been fruitless but had cost him his position with the Freedmen's Bureau. In a way, he was angry at himself for leaving the freedmen's fate in the hands of men like Merritt. On the other hand, slinking back to his desk like a whipped dog and capitulating to Merritt's order meant Daniel's death hadn't mattered, and he'd have had to live with that unfair truth for the rest of his life, just like Allie and her son. Drake's great-grandfather Dominic had saved an island's entire population from being re-enslaved. The least a current LeVeq could do was stand up for the life of one man. He could only imagine what Dominic would do to someone like Atwater, but Drake and his brothers had Dom's blood in their veins, and that pirate blood ran true.

His partially built house had no working kitchen yet, so most meals were cooked out of doors on a grill made of iron and bricks. When he left his bed, he found Erma standing over the grill that held a coffeepot and a few skillets. He knew she was still grieving, so he hadn't expected her to be tending to her duties.

"Morning, Miss Erma."

"Morning, Mr. Drake. Did you find any help for my Daniel?"

He shook his head. "Not so far."

"You probably won't ever."

He knew she was right, and it fanned the embers of his anger. Pulling in a deep breath to keep it from having its head, he asked, "How're Allie and Bailey?" He'd yet to see them this morning.

"Sad. She wants to go home to Texas and be with her family. I'd like them to stay here with me, but she's determined to leave, so I'm giving her my blessing. Nothing's going to bring Daniel back to us, but maybe she can find peace for her hurt with her folks."

"How's she getting there?"

"She has two brothers living nearby. They're going to drive her home. They'll be leaving in a little while."

That he hadn't been able to bring Allie the peace she deserved weighed heavily on his heart. He hoped leaving Louisiana would help salve her grief so she could begin adjusting to life without her husband.

Erma pointed to the skillets. "Get you something to eat. I heard you hammering last night."

"Sorry if I disturbed you."

"You didn't. I couldn't sleep anyway. You pounding on that iron sort of made me wish I knew how to do it. Might have helped me let go of some of this pain."

He thought about helping her find some

peace of her own. "Do you want to go visit your sister for a while?" Her sister, Lena, resided in one of the neighboring parishes.

"I thought I might. Will you be all right if I go?"

"Of course. I can always cook for myself or eat at Julianna's until you return. Stay as long as you need to."

Eyes now wet with tears, she whispered, "Thank you."

They'd gotten to know each other fairly well in the three months she'd worked for him. She was a hard worker, had a pleasant personality, and could cook up an outstanding pot of gumbo. "When do you want to leave?"

"Would today be too soon?"

"No. Do you need me to drive you there?"

"Would you?"

He nodded. Making sure she arrived safely would let him feel as if he'd done something to make her grief more manageable.

"Are you sure you don't mind?"

"I'm sure. If all goes well, I'll be back here by nightfall, so it's no trouble. You go and pack what you want to take, and we'll leave after I've eaten."

Tears filled her eyes again. "You're a good man, Mr. Drake. Thank you."

"You're welcome."

She left him to the silence of the morning. He poured himself a cup of chicory-flavored coffee, put some of the bacon and eggs from the skillets on his plate, and sat down on a crate to eat.

Dusk was just falling when he returned home. He and Miss Erma hadn't encountered any trouble, but he'd worn his uniform and armed himself with a rifle and pistols just in case. There were increasing incidences of supremacists on the roads intent upon showing the former slaves they were no freer after the surrender than they'd been before. There'd been beatings and draggings, lynching and murders. It was his hope that Allie and her brothers would arrive home safely. He didn't worry much though. Both men were war veterans and heavily armed. Any supremacists looking for easy prey would not be met with smiles.

DRAKE MADE BREAKFAST for himself the next day and decided he'd pay his mother a visit. He wanted to see how she and Valinda were faring and if the Sisters had assigned Valinda to another school. Truthfully, he just wanted to see the schoolteacher and her smile. After yesterday, he needed some beauty in his life. That she was pledged to another continued to be a disappointment, but he'd live with that.

First though he had an appointment with Fred Kirk, an elderly landowner who lived nearby. Drake and his men had converted an old stable into a two-stall carriage barn for him, and payment was due today. Kirk wasn't the most honest individual. He had a reputation for offering partial payment and sometimes no payment at all to the tradespeople he hired. He'd promised Drake he would honor his bill, but in case he didn't, Drake went to his shed to get an item that might come in handy and placed it in the bed of his wagon.

Drake drove onto Kirk's property and proudly surveyed the newly constructed barn. It was made of brick and had a flat wooden roof, and small windows had been added to two of the outer walls so the interior would have light. He thought he and his men had done a good job. After parking his wagon, he walked up to the front door and knocked.

Kirk, who resembled an old turtle, answered the summons. "Morning, LeVeq. You here for your money?"

"Yes, sir."

Drake took the bills and counted them. He paused, eyed the old man, and counted the amount again. "You're short."

Kirk raised his chin, showing off his scrawny neck. "It's what I think the work is worth."

Drake held on to his temper. "You gave me your word. The men who helped me build that barn expect to be paid in full."

"You're a wealthy man. You can foot the rest."

Drake had been warned by some of the other builders in the area not to take on the job, but Drake had a soft heart. Kirk swore he'd pay and blamed not being able to hire anyone else on their holding grudges over past misunderstandings. "I need you to pay me what I'm owed, Mr. Kirk."

"That's all you're getting, LeVeq, so be on your way." With that, he gave Drake a smirk and closed the door in his face.

Outdone, Drake stood there for a moment, then growled softly, "Oh, I'll be on my way all right."

Walking to his wagon, he reached into the bed and lifted out a sledgehammer. After rolling the carriage inside a short distance away for safety, he returned, hefted the big sledgehammer, and took a mighty swing. He broke the windows out first. The sound of shattering glass was a symphony to his ears, and he smiled. His next target was the brick wall on the left. It was well-built, and didn't succumb easily, but Drake didn't care. He kept swinging.

Moments later, Fred Kirk came running up

as fast as his ancient legs would carry him and yelled, "What are you doing!"

Drake stopped. "What's it look like I'm doing?" And resumed the destruction.

"You can't do this!"

Drake ignored him. The rhythmic thunder of the sledgehammer filled the air with mortar dust and shards of red brick. And did wonders for his still-angry soul. "You might want to step back out of the way."

"Stop this!" he screamed.

Drake didn't. His campaign soon destroyed the bricks supporting the wood framed roof, and it slumped down like a jilted lover.

"I'll pay!"

"Too late." Drake started in on the right wall.

It took him almost an hour to leave the barn in shambles, and when he was done, he eyed the piles of shattered bricks, glass, and wood, and mentally gave himself a pat on the back. Kirk, whose misery had mounted with each loud crack of the hammer, didn't appear pleased at all.

Drake stretched his sore arms, then handed him back the money. He'd pay the men out of his personal funds. *"Au revoir*, Mr. Kirk."

He walked to his wagon, tossed the sledgehammer in the bed, and drove away.

Chapter Seven

*J*ulianna's driver, Sam Doolittle, guided the carriage through the slow-moving traffic down Canal Street, and Valinda, seated next to Julianna, wondered if they'd ever reach the convent. There were wagons, teamsters, people on horses, people riding cows—something she'd never seen back home—and crowds of people of all colors, shapes, and ages in the street and on the walks. The Sisters of the Holy Family sent a message last evening asking Valinda to stop in. She just hoped she could get there before nightfall.

"After we drop you off, I have some business to attend to," Julianna said. "When you're done at the convent, meet me at the Christophe for lunch. Sable will be joining us as well."

Valinda hadn't seen Sable since the evening

of her welcome-home celebration. Thinking back on that day made the faces of her attackers rise in her memory, so she quickly focused her mind back on the present.

"Do you remember how to get to the Christophe?" Julianna asked.

"I do."

Traffic came to a halt.

Mr. Doolittle said, "Ladies, looks like somebody lost a load of wood up ahead. We may be here a while."

Valinda sighed. They were only a short walk away from the convent and she didn't want to be late. "Julianna, I think it might be faster if I walk."

"Are you sure?"

Valinda nodded. "I'll meet you at the Christophe."

Leaving the carriage behind, she set out and became a small fish in the sea of people moving through the Quarter. Her passage was filled with the singsong calls of vendors, and music from the saloons that never slept. She edged by women carrying piled-high laundry on their *tignon*-covered heads, and soldiers in Union blue. Freedmen in homespun clothing walked beside well-dressed Creoles in expensive suits, while the cacophony of conversations in multiple languages created a music all its own. The longer she stayed in New Orleans, the more she loved its vitality and energy. As she rounded a corner, she came face-to-face with her attacker, Walter Creighton. Alarmed, she jumped.

"Well," he sneered. "Look who we have here." His nose was distended, his eyes bruised and almost swollen shut. "You owe me, you little bitch."

"I owe you nothing. Now, move out of my way." They were on a crowded walk. Not even he was stupid enough to harm her in full view of so many people.

"Next time I see you, ain't going to be no pretty French boy around to keep me from spreading your legs."

Fighting her revulsion, she tossed back, "I'll let him know you send your regards."

He flinched. She pushed by him. Heart racing, her legs shaking, she resumed her journey.

She finally reached the convent, but the meeting didn't last long. Due to pressures from the Creole community, the convent would no longer be enrolling freedmen or their children in their schools. As a result, her services were no longer needed.

As she stood to leave, she thanked the nuns

for taking the time to speak with her and did her best to hide her disappointment.

"God be with you, Valinda," she was told as she departed.

"Thank you."

Outside, she took to the crowded walks again to meet Julianna and Sable at the Christophe and gave her disappointment its head. According to the Sisters, the wealthy Creoles didn't want their children taught in schools that also opened their doors to former slaves and were threatening to withdraw their patronage. Since these families were the Order's main source of financial support, the Sisters had no choice but to comply. They assured her that a workable solution might still be found, but for now, class and wealth overrode the needs of the newly freed.

Valinda wasn't happy. It was yet another blow to her quest to teach and she wondered if it was a sign that it wasn't meant to be. She also learned that due to a lack of funds, the state of Louisiana was closing many of the schools established by the Freedmen's Bureau. In Val's mind, that made little sense because the freedmen and their families needed education for a successful future. Yes, there were those who believed working in the fields was all the formerly enslaved could be expected to achieve, but she didn't agree. During her month-long tenure in her now-abandoned classroom, her students had been eager, focused, and grateful to be learning.

Thinking about them, she wondered if they'd all been contacted by the ones she'd spoken with already. But her own fate was of equal concern. Without a place to teach, the Bureau wouldn't pay her, and without a stipend, she couldn't afford to stay in New Orleans. She was thankful to Julianna for offering her a temporary job helping in her office and running errands, but it wasn't a permanent position. All Val wanted to do was make a difference in people's lives and teach. Even if her time in New Orleans would be ending when Cole returned to the States.

Approaching the Christophe, she saw the corner where she'd met the fortune-teller, but the old lady wasn't there. *You will lose a love, reject a love, find a love.* Val shrugged off the prophecy. She had more pressing things to think about.

When she entered the hotel, she was met by Raoul, and he didn't appear pleased to see her again. "Madam Julianna has been waiting for you," he said in a haughty tone that seemed to suggest she was late. "This way."

Val ignored the dig and followed him to the table where Julianna and Sable were sitting.

"Thank you," Val said to him, but he'd already turned and walked away.

"So, how did the meeting go?" Julianna asked once Val was seated.

Val sighed and relayed the details. Both Sable and Julianna appeared disappointed, and Julianna said, "There've been rumors about this. I wondered if they'd bow to the pressure, but I suppose they had no other choice."

Sable said, "I'm sorry, Valinda."

Val asked, "But why would the Creoles make such a demand?"

Julianna responded, "First, it isn't all the Creole families, but there are enough opposed to be taken seriously. Why? Because they value class and their social position above all else. They don't want to be lumped in with the freedmen just because we all share African blood. They cling to the belief that their education and wealth makes them superior. During the war they went to Washington and met with Mr. Lincoln with the hopes of being designated a special class of individuals, but that status was never granted."

"So, they want to punish the Sisters?"

"If that's what it takes to maintain their positions, yes."

Val found that maddening.

"Looking down their noses at former slaves like myself is nothing new," Sable pointed out. "Some still refuse to acknowledge me when our paths cross."

"I didn't know you were once enslaved," Val said.

"Yes. Raimond and I met in one of the contraband camps. He was stationed with the Union troops and I was a runaway."

This was Val's first time hearing any details of Sable's life.

Sable added, "When Rai and I married, Creole mothers all over the city wept."

Julianna chuckled.

"Some even told me to my face that I had no business being in the House of LeVeq."

Julianna added, "Not that any of us cared what they thought. My son loved her, and she loved him. That was all that mattered. But some of the Creoles are coming around. The *Tribune* has been encouraging them to drop their stance because both groups—the free and the freed—need each other. The country isn't making distinctions between the two, and we'd be stronger if we united, especially on the issue of suffrage."

Val agreed.

As the waiter arrived with menus, the conversation was set momentarily aside. While the man waited for their orders, Val chose the fish. Julianna and Sable did as well.

After he departed, Sable said, "The Sisters closing their doors presents a problem for me as well. My children and my orphans are enrolled in their school, and now I'll have to find a new place for them."

"You run an orphanage?"

Sable nodded. "I do. Twelve children. Seven girls and five boys."

Julianna asked, "Would you consider being their teacher, Valinda?"

Excitement rose. "I would. Do you have a place where they can be taught, Sable?"

"Unfortunately, no. Unless it's out of doors. There's barely room to turn around in the house where they live on our property."

Before Valinda could ask, Julianna said, "And I don't own a property to offer, either."

"Then how can we proceed?"

Julianna replied, "We may be able to find a temporary location, but the facility might not be ideal. Carpetbaggers have descended on the city like the plagues of Egypt and are buying up foreclosed and abandoned land as if it were made of gold, because in truth it is. New Orleans was the richest city in the South before the war, and everyone is hoping it can be again."

"I was teaching in a barn, Julianna. If we can find a place that has walls and a roof, I can conduct classes." Hope rose. "When can we begin the search?"

"Immediately would be my preference," Sable replied. "I don't want the children to go too long without schooling. I'll ask Rai if he knows of a suitable place. How long will you be in New Orleans?"

"At the most, another month or two. My intended, Cole, plans to return around then."

Sable said, "Two months of schooling for the children is better than none, and in the meantime I can search for someone permanent."

Valinda was disappointed that she'd not be that person.

Julianna said, "I'll ask my acquaintances about a place to hold classes as well. Someone has to have walls and a roof they'd let us lease."

Val wondered how to bring up the delicate subject of compensation but decided to just state her concern. "I'll need to be paid."

Julianna waved her hand. "Of course. And if you don't mind my company, you're more than welcome to continue living with me and Reba until your intended comes for you. That way you won't have to use your salary for rent. Housing prices are at a premium as well."

She was grateful for the offer.

Their lunch arrived shortly thereafter, and as they ate they discussed Valinda's qualifications. "I had a standard education, but my father refused to allow me to continue studying further. I begged him to let me attend Oberlin, but he thinks education is harmful to women."

Julianna and Sable shook their heads at that.

"So, I continued on my own. My grandmother Rose is dressmaker to some wealthy New Yorkers and one client is married to a professor at the City College of New York. When my grandmother told him how much I loved learning, he invited me to come and see his library. I'd never seen so many books in my life. When he said I could read what I wanted, I thought I'd died and gone to heaven."

"How old were you?" Julianna asked, smiling.

"Fourteen, and since then, I've read everything of his that I could get my hands on: Greek classics, books on science and astronomy. Philosophy. Architecture. I may not be a formally trained teacher, but I'm a knowledgeable one."

"Maybe more than most," Sable said.

Val appreciated that.

They then spent a few minutes discussing the orphans' ages, and how far along they were in their studies.

The talk was interrupted by Archer's arrival at the table. Unlike Drake and Raimond, his skin was lighter, his body leaner. Julianna's sons came in a variety of colors and builds but all were undeniably handsome.

"Ah," he said, smiling, as he stood over them. "Three of the loveliest ladies in New Orleans. Are you enjoying your meals, or should I fire the chefs?"

"I believe their jobs are safe," the amused Sable replied.

He turned to Valinda. "Are you settling in, Miss Lacy?"

"I am. Your mother has been very generous."

"Good. If I can help in any way, please let me know."

"Thank you."

Valinda saw Julianna look past Archer and smile. "Ah. Here's Drake."

Valinda turned. She needed to tell him about her encounter with Creighton but decided to wait until they were alone. He took up a position behind her chair and his nearness enveloped her like warmth from a hearth.

Julianna asked, "What are you doing here?"

"I stopped by the house to see you, and Reba said you were having lunch with Sable and Valinda." His baritone voice flowed into her blood. Glancing up, she found his eyes waiting.

"Have you eaten?" Julianna asked him.

"No."

"Join us, please."

"Thank you. Get me a chair, Innkeeper," he commanded Archer.

"Get it yourself. And we just opened for lunch so don't eat everything in the kitchen. I have other diners to feed."

"Your food's not that good, brother."

"Would you not say that so loud?" Archer snapped, sounding scandalized and looking around at the other diners with concern.

Julianna and Sable chuckled. Valinda did, too. She enjoyed the brothers' banter.

"Drake, get a chair and sit," Julianna said. "Archer, you go and do whatever it is you do here."

Archer cut his sibling a mock dirty look. "Ladies, your meals are on me. The bear pays for his own."

Drake set a chair between his mother and Valinda, and shot back, "You're so kind."

Archer kissed his mother's cheek and departed.

Valinda wondered if *bear* was Drake's nickname. His size certainly rivalled one.

After Drake gave his order to the waiter, his mother asked, "So, how did things go with the authorities?"

"Not well." And he told them of his unsuccessful quest to get justice for Erma's son. "Allie can't testify because of her race." Val knew that although the practice was considered illegal, many areas of the country continued to abide by it, even in the North.

Drake continued, "And I was so furious with Merritt's refusal to bring charges, I've quit the Bureau."

Julianna appeared stricken. "Oh no."

He nodded. "It was either that or not be able to live with myself. I'll volunteer my time elsewhere."

Sable said, "I can always use your help with the food distributions."

"Okay. Let me know what day you need me. The Republicans' offices mirror many of the services the Bureau provides in terms of relief efforts, so I'll help out there as well."

Seeing how frustrated and unhappy he appeared tugged at Val's own feelings.

His mother asked, "How's Erma faring?"

"I drove Erma to her sister's place yesterday. Told her to take as much time away as she needed. I'll be talking to Rai about how to proceed next."

Julianna looked very concerned. For a moment, she searched his face silently before asking, "You'll be careful?"

"Always, Mama. Don't worry."

Valinda had no idea what was being referenced but noted the serious set of Sable's features, too. She sensed she was being left out of something important, but was too polite to stick her nose into a matter where it didn't belong.

Drake's meal arrived and in spite of his brother's warning, he appeared to have ordered everything the kitchen had to offer. There was a large steak, three pieces of fried catfish, collards, plantains, a large bowl of rice, and half of a still-warm and fragrant baguette.

His mother chuckled, and he looked over innocently. "Yes?"

"I'm always amazed at the amount of food you put away, my son."

"I'm still a growing boy, Mama. And I worked up quite an appetite earlier tearing down the barn we built for Old Man Kirk."

"Why'd you tear it down?"

"He didn't want to pay the agreed-upon price, so rather than let him keep the barn, I used a sledgehammer to express my displeasure. Took me over an hour to turn it into rubble, but he'll think twice before trying to cheat anyone else again."

"Good for you," Sable said with a laugh.

Valinda was impressed. Most people would've met the man in court or simply taken the incorrect amount and angrily walked away. He hadn't done either, and the hellion in her applauded him for the novel solution.

"How's the search for a new classroom going?" he asked her.

"Not well." And she relayed the problem the Sisters were facing along with the disappointing decision they'd made.

"Those Creoles need to be horsewhipped. Forcing the Sisters into a corner that way is unfair."

"I agree."

"If you were going to stay in New Orleans, I'd build you a school."

She blinked.

Sable asked, "Do you have a teaching position waiting for you back home?"

Still reeling from Drake's words, she finally responded to Sable. "No. Not yet. I shouldn't have a problem though." There were many schools for students of color in the city of New

York and areas nearby, but she was stuck on Drake's words. Would he really build her a school? The offer was as moving as he was. But she wouldn't be staying. Once Cole arrived, she'd leave vibrant New Orleans behind. The thought was unsettling. She glanced his way and wondered how soon he'd forget her once she was gone. Recognizing the foolishness in that, she returned to her meal.

"Do you mind if I move in with you until Erma returns?" Drake asked his mother. "I can cook for myself at my place, but Little Reba's cooking is better, and I'll probably not want to do anything but boil water after working on the house all day."

"You know I don't mind. Move in whenever you like. Henri will be returning from Cuba tomorrow, and once he's rested up, we'll be going up to Baton Rouge to look at some property he's interested in purchasing. I'll feel better knowing Reba and Valinda won't be at the house alone."

Valinda wasn't sure how she felt about being in the house with Drake, even with Little Reba there. "How long will you be away?" she asked.

"Two days. Three at the most. If you get lonely, Sable is close by."

"In fact," Sable said easily, "if you don't have anything pressing tomorrow, I'll come get you and you can meet the orphans you'll be teaching."

"I'd like that." Even though her time in New Orleans would be ending sooner than she cared to think about, teaching the children would be in line with her goals, and she might even get to know Sable better.

Drake looked confused. "You're going to teach the orphans, Valinda?"

"Yes."

Sable explained how the Sisters' decision to close the school was impacting her orphans.

He looked to Valinda. "That's very kind of you."

The sincerity in his gaze snared her and she was at a loss to explain why he affected her in ways no other man had before.

Julianna's voice broke the spell. "But we need a place we can lease as a classroom. Can you ask the property owners you know if they have a barn or a cottage, or anything she can use?"

"I assume you'd prefer a place close to the orphanage."

Valinda replied, "I would, but if I can borrow a wagon, I can also pick up the children each morning before school if it's necessary."

He nodded. "I'll see what I can do."

"Thank you."

"You're welcome."

The soft tone of his voice slid over her once again, leaving her warm and unbalanced. She knew she shouldn't be reacting to him, but her responses seemed to be choosing their own path. Parts of her wanted to explore whatever he'd awakened, only to be reminded that he had a mistress while her future lay with Cole.

Once everyone finished their meals, it was time to depart.

Julianna announced, "We'll be having dinner tomorrow evening at my house to welcome Henri home, so Drake, make sure your brothers know they are to be there."

"Yes, ma'am."

"And tell them that mistresses, gambling halls, or goings-on at gentlemen's clubs don't qualify as legitimate excuses. Only hospitals or death."

He chuckled. "I will."

She added, "Henri's been gone almost three months and I've missed him dearly. I'd like to celebrate him being home again with the entire family."

Sable said, "We'll be there."

Julianna looked to Valinda. "You're part of the family now, too. Will you dine with us and meet my Henri?"

"I'd be honored."

Her husband's dinner would be the second celebratory gathering of the week, and Valinda couldn't help but envy the joy the LeVeqs took in their familial ties. Her family was quite the opposite. There was no bantering or joy. They celebrated Christmas, and little else.

Drake said, "I'll come by later to bring the things I'll need while staying with you, Mama."

She nodded.

He gave Valinda one last intense look, inclined his head her way, and departed.

ON THE SLOW drive back to Julianna's home, Valinda spent the time thinking about her future. In truth, she realized she didn't want to return to New York. A strong sense told her that her future lay in New Orleans. Having heard nothing from Cole about his search for an investor, she wondered if he could be convinced to try his hand at a newspaper here. It might be difficult to learn the ins and outs of the city's volatile political climate and its effects on the daily lives of the citizenry, at first, but might he be willing to try? It was a question she intended to ask.

When they reached Julianna's home, the heat of the day was upon them. There was a breeze however and it made the high temperature at least tolerable.

"I'm going to get away from this heat and rest in my room," Julianna told her. "Feel free to do the same, if you care to."

"I think I'll work on clearing up your correspondences first, if that's okay with you?"

She nodded. "It is. I'll be back down later." She climbed the stairs to her bedroom and Valinda went to the office. Julianna's filing system apparently consisted of tossing all the receipts and bills into a box and hoping they'd sort themselves. Valinda had spent yesterday separating the business receipts from those tied to the household, and the letters from various individuals. Some of the items showed dates of two years ago and Valinda smiled and shook her head as she sorted through them. As she worked, time passed, but she was pleased when she finally reached the bottom of the box and could begin matching like with like.

"Can I convince you to take a break?"

She looked up to see Drake in the doorway holding a glass of lemonade in each large hand.

She didn't want to admit how happy seeing him again made her feel. "For lemonade you can convince me to walk across the Mississippi."

"I think the gazebo will be far enough. It's much cooler outdoors than in here."

The perspiration on the back of her blouse and the skin above the high neck of her lace-edged collar were a testament to that, so she stood. He handed her a glass, she took a sip, and her hum of pleasure brought his eyes to hers.

"You need to stop doing that, you know."

"I can't voice my pleasure about the lemonade?"

"Only if you want me to wonder what else makes you purr."

As if she weren't already warm enough, heat from his words flashed over every inch of her body. "More pirate talk?" she tossed back more boldly than she felt.

"Yes, and it would be courting pirate talk, if you were free."

She drew in a steadying breath. "Let's go to the gazebo."

Eyes sparkling, he stepped aside. "After you."

With his overpowering presence making her insides resonate like a clanging bell she walked with him through the gardens to the gazebo. Due to her father's control of her life back home that frowned on anything tied to socializing, parties, or fun, she had no idea there were men like Drake in the world. Men able to turn her knees into pudding with just a few words or make her heart race from a knowing glance. Even though she had no experience, she vowed to do her best to hold her own.

They sat in the gazebo as they'd done before, and she sipped, savoring the breeze and being away from the stifling heat inside the house. He sat back, watching her.

"You're at an advantage here."

"How so?"

"You're accustomed to playful banter. I'm not."

"It's not hard to learn."

"And if I don't wish to?"

"Then I've overestimated you."

"Meaning?"

"I think the hellion inside you likes a challenge, otherwise she wouldn't have climbed trees, played baseball, or enjoyed whipping those boys at marbles. But I don't think you've let her out to play in quite some time. She showed herself a bit the last time we were here. I got the impression that she liked the verbal swordplay."

She didn't respond.

"Does your intended prefer the hellion or the meek miss?"

"Why does that matter?"

"Because I see a woman settling for a small piece of cake when she can have it all."

"By being with someone who I don't love?"

He nodded.

"We've had this conversation."

"And I'm still puzzled by your choice."

"Which is none of your business."

"True, but—"

"There are no buts. I've chosen Cole. He's chosen me. We don't need your approval or blessings."

He sipped and smiled.

"Something funny?"

"Just pleased that you picked up your sword, *cheri*."

She rolled her eyes. "You really are insufferable."

He toasted her with his glass. "My apologies for making you angry. That wasn't my intent, and you're right, your choice of a husband is none of my affair."

The sincerity in his tone soothed her ire. "He does care for me."

"Then may you have a happy life."

"Do you mean that?"

"If he is your choice, yes."

Valinda didn't know why she'd asked if he was being truthful. As she stated, she didn't need his approval and yet . . . He'd rescued her during Creighton's attack, stood by her at the cigar shop, even offered to build her a school. There were women who'd probably sell their souls for the attention of such a man. Before coming to New Orleans, she'd never doubted marrying Cole. Becoming man and wife benefited them both. She knew nothing about love or adoration, and still clung to the idea that neither were necessary, but the tempting, bearded mountain of a man sitting across from her had put cracks in the firm rock upon which she stood. She hoped Cole would agree to settling down in New Orleans because she dearly wanted to stay in Julianna's and Sable's spheres and learn all they could teach her about navigating life, but doing so would result in ongoing contact with Drake. She met his eyes.

"Problem?" he asked.

She shook her head and lied, "No. Just wondering if I'd be able to convince Cole to open a newspaper here."

"You want to stay?"

"I do. I know the political situation is less than ideal, and I've had numerous setbacks trying to teach, but the city is growing on me." She loved the food, the sounds, the smell of the Mississippi, the never-ending excitement in the air.

"Will he agree?"

She shrugged. "I don't know." And how would

she handle those occasions where Drake was present? She hazarded another glance his way and saw him watching her as if he'd read her thoughts and found her attempts to deny her feelings amusing.

"I wanted to wait until we were alone to tell you. I saw Creighton today before arriving at the convent."

He went still. "Tell me what happened."

She complied and when she finished, added, "His eyes are still so swollen from your punch, I'm surprised he could see me at all."

"I'm sorry I wasn't there," he said softly.

She found that endearing. "You can't be everywhere, and we were in the middle of the Quarter. He did scare me, but I wasn't worried about him assaulting me with so many people about."

"Still, he had no business approaching you, let alone making threats. He was warned."

For a moment he observed her silently and she wondered what might be going through his mind. "Yes?" she finally asked.

"Creighton aside, just enjoying being with you."

In spite of their small verbal dustup a few minutes ago, she was enjoying his company as well.

"Did my mother show you my tree house?"

"Your tree house?" she echoed warily. "No."

He stood. "Come. Let me show it to you since you enjoy climbing."

"I haven't climbed a tree in decades."

"Maybe this will re-spark the hellion."

Amused and not sure what to do with him, she rose and followed him deeper into the trees.

It was a short distance away. She viewed the ramshackle remains of the broken slats and listing wood high up in the thick moss-covered boughs of a great oak. "That's your tree house?"

"What's left of it, yes. Granted, I built it when I was ten, but it served its purpose in those days."

"Now, it looks like it'll serve as a way to a hospital."

"You wound me, *cheri.*"

The tar paper roof had large holes that matched the holes in what had once been the floor. "Anyone foolish enough to go up there will be wounded, too." She eyed the worn ladder nailed to the trunk. "Is that how you climbed up?"

"Yes. Our feet were smaller then, so the slats were shorter."

Val took in the perch. "It's pretty high up. I imagine you could see the countryside for miles."

"I could. Being up there made me feel like the king of the world."

"I did love being high above everything."

"My brothers and I had many an adventure up there. One day we were pirates sailing the seas, and the next day balloonists floating to Haiti. We imagined being members of the Louisiana Native Guards and saving Andrew Jackson's troops during the War of 1812."

She was surprised by that.

"You don't know about the Louisiana Guard saving Jackson's bacon?"

"No."

"It's a celebrated part of the history of New Orleans. Remind me to tell you about it sometime."

"I will." She surveyed the tree house again. "It doesn't look like you've played up there in quite some time."

He nodded. "Once my brothers and I began growing it became too small to hold us, but we had fun while it lasted." The fond wistfulness in his tone touched her, reminding her again of the strong ties he had to his family. He seemed comfortable expressing the feelings he had for them. She never remembered her father voicing such telling thoughts about those he was related to.

He added, "Julianna even let us sleep up

there sometimes, until the night we were roughhousing and Phillipe fell to the ground, breaking his arm. That was the end. She did allow me to sleep there alone after though, because I'd built it."

Val couldn't imagine her father allowing her to have a tree house but could imagine how much fun it must have been. "Thank you for bring me here."

"You're welcome. I'm drawing up plans for a much larger one on the property near my new house. I have a couple of trees I'm deciding between."

"Really?"

"Every boy needs a tree house."

"But you're an adult now."

He grinned. "True, but I'm never too old for adventures. We could have tea."

She laughed. "Tea?"

"Sure, why not? Maybe, if your intended agrees, I can invite you both when it's finished. Do you think he'd accept?"

"I believe he would. We often climbed the trees together, and he was always the one daring me to go higher. When my sister told on me, that was the end."

"You're always welcome to climb mine whenever you like."

She sensed he was referencing more than an oak and she suddenly found it difficult to breathe. "We should probably get back to the house."

"As you wish."

She asked, "Are you having fun?"

"Fun?"

"At my expense?"

"Never, *cheri*, but I am enjoying imagining all the fun we'd have together were you free."

Admittedly, the idea of having fun as an adult was foreign. Her father would find the idea disgraceful. "I've never associated having fun with anything but children."

"Then we need to change that."

"How?"

"I'd build us a tree house we could have tea in, use to escape the heat of the day in, and sleep together in at night."

Val's eyes closed as the seductive wake of his words washed over her.

"We'd catch frogs and fireflies. Take one of Raimond's boats and sail to Cuba to have dinner with my cousins, and then walk along the beach in the moonlight."

She met his dark eyes.

"Then I'd kiss you until sunrise. . . ."

Trembling, she took in the intensity in his

eyes. The air between them was as charged as an approaching summer storm. If he kissed her now, she'd be lost. "Please, don't kiss me."

"I won't. Not unless you're free to ask me to."

She tried to convince herself that being attracted to him served no purpose, yet the urge to throw caution to the wind and walk that moonlit beach was strong.

"Come, *cheri*. Let's get you back." Placing a brief guiding hand on the small of her back, he gently steered her towards the path, and silently walked her to the house.

Chapter Eight

*J*ulianna was seated in the parlor reading the *Tribune*, and as Drake entered with Valinda, she looked up, scanned them silently for a long second before asking, "Are you staying for dinner, son?"

"No. I'm going to see Hugh to firm up plans to complete my kitchen. I'll be back later tonight."

"Give him my regards."

"I will." After offering his goodbyes and sharing a final look with Valinda, he departed.

As he rode away, he thought about how he'd wanted to stay for dinner and share more of Valinda's company, but he needed to distance himself from her and not be the man who wanted to find a secluded corner and kiss her until she melted. She belonged to another and he was undoubtedly being an ass for constantly

voicing how he felt about her, but he couldn't
seem to help himself. In that moment back at
the tree house, the urge to ease her into his arms
and finally taste her lips almost blew past his
defenses. Her softly worded plea not to made
him grab hold of his faltering control. But going forward, should she offer him even the ti-
niest bit of encouragement, her intended might
as well remain in Europe because Drake would
not give her up.

Due to Henri's welcome-home party, he'd have
to cancel the outing to the theater he'd planned
with his mistress, Josephine. That he had a mistress while wanting Valinda was fueling much
inner debate, but he needed to see her before riding to meet with Hugh.

Josephine DuSable lived in the small cottage
she'd inherited from her mother on the edge of
the Treme. Her family's founding matriarch,
Mala, fled to New Orleans during Toussaint
L'Ouverture's rebellion in Saint-Domingue, and
after a few months, caught the eye of a French-
man. In those days, because of the small number
of European women in places like New Orleans,
Biloxi, and St. Augustine, the men of France and
Spain took up relationships with both enslaved
and free women of color like Mala, in what was
termed *mariage de la main gauche*—a left-handed

marriage. In exchange for the lady's favors, the man paid for her home, fathered and educated their children, mainly in Europe, and in some cases, freed her and their offspring if they were enslaved. When the man died, the woman and children were often provided for in his will.

She and Drake had been together for two years. He was not her first protector, and more than likely not her last. For her, the relationship was not a left-handed marriage but a business transaction, nothing more. For Drake, after dodging Creole mamas and their marriage-focused daughters since the age of sixteen, he found her attitude refreshing. There was no talk of weddings or children. She was smart, funny, invested wisely, and could engage in conversation on everything from politics to opera. He enjoyed her both in and out of bed, but neither had any illusions about love. She valued her independence and knew her worth. When her beauty faded, she and her business acumen would probably end up owning half the city.

He rang the bell to her cottage. It was answered by her longtime housekeeper, Selma. The dark-skinned older woman had roots in Haiti as well. "Good afternoon, Mr. LeVeq."

"Hello, Selma. Is your mistress available?"

"For you? Of course." She stepped aside, and he entered. "She's in the parlor."

To his surprise the parlor was filled with crates of varying sizes. Gowns and hats covered the furniture. Shoes and handbags were lined up by the hearth. The statuesque, golden-skinned Josephine was standing in the middle of the chaos as if thinking.

"Josie?"

She turned, and her smile warmed him as it always did. "Hello, Drake."

"What is all this?" He stepped farther into the room and saw books stacked on the floor, more shoes, bottles of perfume, bath salts, along with bed linens, china, and cooking pots.

"I'm moving to Mexico City."

Somehow managing not to be blown over by the unexpected news, he replied, "Really?"

"Yes. I met a Spanish gentleman willing to make it worth my while."

"You're going to miss New Orleans."

"I know, but with his money, I can afford to."

His smile met hers. "Then by all means, do what's best."

"I'm sorry to spring it on you this way. I planned to tell you tomorrow when we had our theater outing."

"That's why I stopped by. Mother's having a

family dinner tomorrow that demands my attendance. Henri is coming home."

"Ah. Then canceling works well for me. I need to pack."

"When are you leaving?"

"Early next week. I've sold the cottage, but I still have to take care of a few items of business."

"If I can assist in any way, feel free to call on me."

"I will. Shall we have one last evening together?"

Valinda's face floated across his mind's eye and he shook his head. "No. I'll let you get back to your packing."

"No?" she responded with a dubious-sounding chuckle. "Are you ill?"

He smiled. "No."

"Have you found someone new?"

"No." He had, but Valinda wasn't his, no matter how much he wished otherwise.

"I think you're lying to me, Drake LeVeq," she said playfully. "But it doesn't matter. I hope she makes you happy."

He walked to her and planted a soft kiss on her brow. "Godspeed, Josie. Enjoy your new life in Mexico."

"Thank you, Drake. Thank you for all the good times, the gowns, and the rest. I will miss you."

"I'll miss our times together as well." He bowed and made his exit.

As he mounted his stallion, he was caught between amusement and humiliation. He knew having a mistress while being attracted to Valinda wasn't honorable, but it never occurred to him that Josephine would remove herself from the equation and settle the matter so uniquely. He wondered if any of his brothers had ever had the rug pulled out from beneath them this way. Not that he planned to ask. They'd never let him live it down if he did. So, having been dismissed by his mistress while pining for a woman who belonged to another, he rode out of the city to the abandoned plantation his good friend Hugh had purchased, and hoped he had some cognac on hand.

"So, Josie's replaced you."

Drake and Hugh were sitting on the front porch of his ramshackle mansion. It had been torched by the former owners to make it uninhabitable when they lost it to the bank during the war. Hugh's plan was to rebuild it and put it up for sale.

"Yes. To say I'm surprised is an understatement."

"You always said she was a businesswoman."

"True, but I never thought I'd be tossed aside like an old bill of sale."

Hugh sipped his cognac. "The price we pay for underestimating the so-called weaker sex."

"I suppose."

Hugh was big and burly like Drake. He was White though, and his hair and beard were red. "You have a replacement in mind?"

"No. Need to lick my wounds first. Although . . ."

Hugh looked over. "Although what?"

Drake told him about Valinda and her intended, to which Hugh responded, "Thou shalt not covet thy neighbor's woman."

"Good thing he's not my neighbor then."

Hugh snorted.

Drake smiled. The two met in '62, right after the Union invaded New Orleans and closed the ports on the Mississippi River. Hugh came to the city to fight on the side of the Union. He was from an area in East Tennessee staunchly opposed to the Confederacy, where people called themselves Unionists and Heroes of America. Like Drake and his kin, Hugh was a Radical Republican.

Hugh asked, "What is this I hear about Liam Atwater murdering someone?"

"He did. His name was Daniel Downs. The son of my housekeeper."

"He was Miss Erma's son?"

Drake nodded. "Killed him in front of his wife and seven-year-old boy, and dumped his body in the swamp."

"My lord."

"I'll be talking to the Council about it. We can't let him get away with this."

"No help from the locals or the Army?"

"None."

"You have something in mind?"

"I do."

"If you and the Council need help, let me know." After his father and uncles were hunted down and killed by the Confederate army for refusing to enlist during the war, Hugh had no love for Democrats of any stripe. He and the Union soldiers he'd served with were now doing their best to counteract supremacist violence by protecting freedmen property, schools, and churches. They'd also infiltrated some of the Lost Cause groups, and the Council relied on them for intelligence. In the bloody, three-day riot in Memphis last year, two of Hugh's childhood friends had been among the forty-six Black people murdered by supremacist supporters. For him, this post-war battle was personal.

"So, what do you want to do about your kitchen?" Hugh asked.

Hugh was a carpenter, too, and he and Drake spent the next hour talking over the plans, etching drawings in the dirt, and speculating on how many additional men they'd need to finish the project. Once Drake's house was done, they'd focus on rebuilding Hugh's mansion.

Their plans made, Drake brought up Valinda's need for a space. "The teacher I'm coveting needs a place to hold her classes. It can be a barn, an old house, a structure of any kind. If you know of anything available, will you let me know?"

"Will an old railroad car do?"

Drake eyed him. "A railroad car?"

"The Army gave me a contract repairing tracks. Any abandoned cars we find along the way are being burned if they're no longer usable."

"How many do you have?"

"Found three yesterday."

Drake was intrigued. "What kind of condition are they in?"

"Wood is badly warped. Some have no doors, but they could be fixed up and they'd be free."

"What about the tops?"

"A few are partially intact."

Drake thought it over for a moment. "Do you

think we can salvage wood from some of the worst ones and fix up say one or two?"

"I don't see why not. You trying to make points with the lady?"

"Of course not. I'm only interested in aiding my fellow man."

Hugh slid across the porch a few inches. "Moving away in case lightning strikes you for lying."

They laughed, after which Drake asked, "Is there a way you can move them to my land where I can work on them?"

"We have some drays, so yes."

"How soon?"

"You are eager, aren't you?" Hugh asked, smiling. "Give me a day or so to make the arrangements, and the men and I will transport them."

"How much do you want?"

"If you pay the owner of the horses for his time, that's all we'll need."

Drake was deep in thought. "Okay." He liked the idea but wanted to see the cars to determine if restoring them was a possibility. "Can we ride over to see them?"

"Now?"

"Yes. I don't want you going through the trouble of moving them if I can't restore them."

"Trust me. They'll be fine."

"I hope that isn't the cognac talking."

"It isn't. You'll make points with your teacher. Promise."

Drake did want to make Valinda happy.

Hugh asked, "Where are you off to now?"

"To the Quarter to make Archer feed me."

"I have some hens we can cook." He held up the bottle of cognac. "And we have this fancy French liquor that needs finishing."

Drake grinned. "Let's eat."

After eating his fill, Drake left Hugh and rode to Raimond's house to attend the Council meeting. Made up of veterans, freedmen, and a few trusted Black Republican party members, the group formed after the surrender to intervene in work contract negotiations, educate people on their rights, and do their best to influence state and local politicians. People in the city knew about their public face, but the more secretive parts of their operation were conducted in shadow.

Drake entered the barn where they were meeting and nodded at the twelve men already inside, four of whom were his brothers. The agenda opened with reports sent in by similar groups across the South on subjects pertaining to land ownership, Black codes, and the overall state of freedmen rights.

Rai began with the good news of the increasing number of schools and colleges being established across the region, most notably Howard College in Washington, named for General Howard, and two in North Carolina: St. Augustine Normal School and Collegiate Institute and the Freedmen's College of North Carolina.

Drake saw people nodding approvingly.

Rai then turned to more serious matters. "General Sheridan has designated May first as the day Louisiana and other states will begin registering voters both Black and White under the recently passed Reconstruction Acts. The elections will be held to pick delegates to form new Constitutional conventions. Violence is anticipated. Sheridan's promised to keep the process as safe as possible, but we all know there aren't enough troops to meet that promise. I've sent word asking veterans to volunteer as peacekeepers, and that they pass the word to all veterans they may know."

Beau added, "And that they be armed."

Since May first was only two weeks away, Drake asked, "Have you talked to Hugh and his Heroes to request their assistance?"

"No, but if you could, I'd have one less thing to do."

"I'll speak with him."

"Thank you."

They spent a few more minutes discussing the logistics of where the registration sites would be. As Rai pointed out, violence was probably guaranteed because Confederates would be forbidden from adding their names to the ballots as delegates.

Mason Diggs, one of the veterans, asked, "So, does this Reconstruction Act give members of the race the right to vote everywhere?"

"No. Just in the states that rebelled."

"That doesn't make sense."

Rai said, "Tell that to the fools in Congress."

They all knew Black voters would hold a numerical advantage in the five states of Alabama, Florida, Louisiana, Mississippi, and South Carolina. If the elected delegates could indeed rewrite their state constitutions, conditions in the South would change for the better. Being a political pessimist, Drake doubted the Confederates would allow them to hold on to power for long, due to the infighting going on within the Republican party, and the ease with which the supremacists were being allowed back into the political arena via President Johnson's toothless Loyalty Oath.

Rebels who re-pledged their loyalty to the Union were being given back their land and their power. That they'd committed treason and cost the country thousands of lives seemingly meant nothing. Regaining their status meant more Black Codes were being put in place to disenfranchise the newly freed, and splintering the state's Republican Party into three warring factions. There was the powerful Custom House Ring, the Radicals flocking to the leadership of young Henry Clay Warmoth, and in Drake's opinion, the most important block of Republicans—the newly freed—because without the support of the third leg, the Republicans' stool could not stand.

But the opposing forces, made up of the Redeemers and other Lost Cause supporters, were fractioned as well. Louisiana's Bourbon Democrats vehemently opposed anything benefiting the formerly enslaved—from owning property to establishing schools. The more practical-minded, conservative Democrats, aka Reformers, supported limited rights, but joined the Bourbons in saying no to social equality—even as they held the Bourbon's hard-line approach responsible for the federal government's intervention in the state's politics.

As a result, the state was a powder keg. The Lost Cause Democrats, in cahoots with some Southern Republicans, were determined to restore the old order by any means. Last year's riot at the state convention, in which the city's police force and firearms descended on the convention hall and murdered thirty-four Blacks and three White Radicals, stood as a sobering example of how far they were willing to go to achieve their goals.

Raimond continued the meeting by asking, "Does anyone know a man named William Nichols?"

No one did.

Rai explained, "Neither do I, but he's one of the leaders of the groups confronting the streetcar companies and their star cars."

As more and more Blacks and allied Whites pushed back against the discriminatory policies, the situation with the streetcars was reaching a boiling point. Many people were attempting to ride the regular cars in spite of the law. In response, White drivers and passengers were routinely dragging the protestors off the cars and assaulting them afterwards. A Black veteran in uniform boarded a Whites-only car with his mother, only to have her "brutally ejected," according to a newspaper account. In response soldiers had attempted to derail a Whites-only car.

"William Nichols plans to get himself arrested and challenge the legality of the star car system in court. We've been given rights, but no one knows what these rights really entail, so this is one way of testing."

Drake was impressed. "Do you think the court will hear his case?"

"If he gets arrested, I'm not sure the courts will have a choice but to hear it."

"Did he say when he plans to do this?"

"I'm led to believe it will be soon, so keep your ears open. We'll support him however we can. Any thoughts or questions?"

When no one spoke up, Rai added, "Now for some humor. Former slave owner Elwood Reynolds wants me to ride out to his place and talk to the freedmen there because they've moved into his house."

Archer chuckled. "What?"

Rai nodded. "He has Black families living in his kitchen, parlor, den, and yesterday a family of five moved into his bedroom. They told him their labor built his place, so they were partial owners."

Drake said, "They have a point."

"I agree."

"Are you going to go?" Diggs asked.

"No. I told him I have no authority, and since the Army has already said they won't evict them—they said they can't spare the personnel—he'll have to work it out on his own."

All over the South, the former masters were having a hard time adjusting to a way of life that no longer put them on the top rung.

Rai said, "Our most serious concern this evening is Liam Atwater. Drake, would you fill everyone in, please?"

Drake took a few minutes to tell the story and finished with, "His widow and son are owed justice."

Council member and Republican politician, Kennard Guyton, a longtime friend of the LeVeqs, said, "Killing us has always been akin to killing flies to him. The number of people who died on his place yearly easily surpassed every other slave owner in the area."

Atwater owned an enormous sugar plantation, and working sugar was by far the most brutal work a slave could be assigned. Most died by the age of twenty-five from infections caused by the serrated leaves, snakebite from the venomous snakes lurking in the fields, and heat exhaustion from having to stir the cane down to syrup in vats heated underneath by flames—vats often positioned in the hot Louisiana sun.

Rai said, "We've all heard Drake's story. All

in favor of seeking justice for Daniel Downs's widow and child, raise your hand."

Each man complied.

VALINDA OPENED THE French doors and stepped out onto the bedroom's veranda. There was a cooling breeze and the night was alive with the sounds of insects and the faint chorus of calling frogs. She took in a deep breath and felt herself relax.

A messenger from the Sisters arrived after dinner bearing a wire for her from Cole. He and Lenny had docked in Maryland and were making their way to New Orleans by train. He estimated it would take three, maybe four days at the most. She was happy to have him safely back on United States soil and couldn't wait to see him to hear all about Europe and how the business quest had gone. His pending arrival also meant she'd be leaving New Orleans much earlier than planned and she wasn't sure what to do about her conflicted feelings. Could he be convinced to stay?

She slapped at a mosquito feasting on her arm for dessert. She returned to her musings, but was soon distracted when Drake's face shimmered over her mind's eye. The more she vowed not to think about him, the more she did. She thought back to that moment when she asked that he not kiss her, and part of her was disappointed with the stance she'd taken. It didn't care about her commitment to Cole, or any of the other barriers she'd erected against Julianna's bear of a son. It wanted to know what a kiss from him might feel like. Would his lips be hard? Soft? Would the kiss be chaste or have the power to make her melt in the way his words did? She had no answers. The only certainty was that she was sliding down a slippery slope in his direction and couldn't find a handhold to stop her progress.

She slapped at another mosquito buzzing around her neck, and another that bit her through the sleeve of her gray satin wrapper, so she went inside. The doors had screening though, so she left them open to the breeze and night songs while she sat on a chair in the darkness. She enjoyed the large bedroom with its beautiful furniture, especially the big tub. With Julianna's permission she'd treated herself to a bath a short while ago and wanted to take it home if she did return to New York.

It was a silly thought, because she doubted she and Cole would be able to afford a place large enough to hold something so big after they married. People of color were relegated to living in some of the most crowded and least cared-for sections of New York City. None of her acquaintances had a home with room to house such a luxurious tub. And yet, living in the five rooms above her grandmother's seamstress shop made Valinda and her sister, Caroline, believe they were relatively wealthy growing up because there'd always been food on the table and their father was employed as a barber in the shop owned by Cole's father. Not until adolescence when she began attending Mrs. Brown's School for Proper Girls of Color did she encounter girls from families with true wealth—girls whose family employed drivers for the carriages that brought them to school each day; girls who lived in places like Boston and Philadelphia with families rich enough to allow them to board at the school; and girls who arrived with furniture for their rooms, including wardrobes filled with dresses. Val had never owned more than two pairs of shoes at one time—one for every day and the other for church and special occasions. At Mrs. Brown's, she met girls who possessed five and six pairs of shoes, and an equal number of coats and gloves. She wondered how their familial wealth measured up against the LeVeqs'. She knew that when she and Cole married they'd never even come close. Having a tub like the one in the bathing room would be the stuff of dreams.

As she closed the doors and got into bed, she

didn't dream of luxurious tubs. Instead, she dreamt of being chased by a pack of feral dogs.

She was running, heart pounding with fear while trying to keep ahead of the snarling, growling pack at her back. Their long, loping legs quickly closed the distance and she was knocked to the ground. Screaming and twisting to get away, she grabbed the neck of the closest animal to keep its foaming fangs from sinking into her skin. The dog's features shifted into the face of attacker Walter Creighton and it smiled evilly. She somehow broke away and was on her feet running again. They gave chase, baying like maddened bloodhounds. Julianna frantically beckoned to her from where she stood on a porch, but the dogs were between them, so Val kept running. The dogs vanished. A wagon appeared. Her father jumped down from the seat. There was fire in his eyes as he wrapped her wrists together tightly with the rope in his hands and tied a lead from the rope to the back of the wagon. He ran back to the seat. Beside him sat a man. He looked at her. Before she could put a name to the vaguely familiar face, the wagon pulled off and she stumbled and fell to the ground. Being dragged over the rough ground, she yelled that her father stop. He didn't. Crying out, she tried to undo the knots but couldn't. She managed to get to her feet only to lose her balance again, and again. Exhausted, she surrendered and was dragged away like a broken doll.

She woke up, shaking. Putting her hands to her sweat-damp cheeks, she drew in a trembling breath. Little pieces of the nightmare floated back. The man with her father. She was certain she knew him, but his identity remained locked behind the door of her mind. She suddenly remembered her sister being in the dream, too. Caroline had been seated high in the boughs of a live oak, watching with tears in her eyes. Leaving the bed, Val walked into the bathing room, splashed water on her face, and took in another deep breath. She crawled back into bed but lay awake until dawn.

Chapter Nine

*W*hen Val came downstairs to the table for breakfast, her disturbing night must have shown on her face because Julianna asked, "Did you not sleep well?"

Val told the truth. "No."

Drake, who was at the table, too, viewed her with concern.

"I can send Drake for the doctor if you're ill. Do you want to spend the day in bed?"

"No. Sable is coming to get me later. I'm just a bit sleepy. I'll feel better by the time she arrives."

Neither LeVeq appeared convinced, but she ignored that and silently added the breakfast offerings of sausage, eggs, and grits to her plate. As Drake continued to assess her, she said, "I'm fine, Drake."

"You wouldn't lie about being ill, would you, *cheri*?"

The gentle sincerity in his tone knocked down another one of the barriers she had in place against him. "No. I had a bad dream. That's all."

She could tell he had more questions, so she tried to reassure him. "There's no need to worry. Please, eat your breakfast, I'll be fine."

He observed her for a few more seconds, then complied.

To change the subject, she asked Julianna, "What time will your husband be arriving? Does Little Reba need my assistance with any of the preparations?"

Julianna shook her head. "No. It will just be family, so she won't need any additional help with things. He's scheduled to arrive by boat at one. Mr. Doolittle and I will meet him at the docks. So excited to have him home again."

"What time is dinner?" Drake asked.

"Seven at the latest. What are your plans for the day?"

"Working on my house."

"Can you save Sable a trip and drop Valinda off at her place on your way? I'm sure Sable would appreciate not having to drive over. Is that okay with you, Valinda?"

Val swore Julianna was subtly trying to put

them together, but she was too polite to voice the accusation. "As long as it doesn't take Drake out of his way."

"It won't."

"Then, thank you in advance."

"You're welcome."

After breakfast, Drake said to her, "I'll saddle my horse and meet you outside."

Once he'd departed, Julianna asked, "Did your intended say where he would be staying when he and his partner arrived?"

She'd shared the wire with Julianna. "No."

"I suppose his early return means you won't be able to teach Sable's children."

"I'm hoping to convince him to start his newspaper here in New Orleans."

"You don't want to return home?"

She shook her head.

"Do you think he'll agree?"

"I've no way of knowing."

"And if he says no? Then what?"

"That's something I've been asking myself." And she still had no answers. All she knew was she didn't wish to return to New York. By staying in New Orleans, she could continue to aid the freedmen, and although her stay these past few weeks had been challenging, being on her own allowed her to test the waters of independence. The plan to marry Cole would offer her a modicum of freedom from society's expectations as well, but would it be enough? Or would she spend the rest of her life haunted by what she might have accomplished had she chosen to remain unmarried or courted by Drake? a tiny voice whispered.

Julianna's voice was sympathetic. "Life can be trying. If I can help in any way, let me know."

"I will. Thank you."

Outside, she met Drake who stood waiting beside his large mahogany stallion. "Does the stallion have a name?" she asked.

"Havana. Rai purchased him there as a colt for my birthday, a few years ago." He patted the horse affectionately and asked her, "Are you ready?"

She nodded. Before she could blink, he lifted her and set her sideways on the horse's back, then mounted behind her. The heat of his big body made it difficult to breathe.

"Problem, *cheri*?"

"I'd rather walk beside you."

"Rai and Sable live almost two miles down the road. I want to get there before tomorrow."

"I think your pirate blood is taking advantage of the situation."

"No pirate worth his salt would let a beautiful woman ride on a horse's rump. Your bruise is better."

The abrupt subject change threw her. She brought her hand up to the spot on her cheek. "Your mother gave me something to help with the healing."

"Is it still tender?"

"A bit." The thought came to her that no man had the right to be so handsome, observant, or have the ability to charm her so effortlessly. Yet, here he was.

"Lean back, so we can go. I'll be on my best behavior."

Every inch of her longed to experience his nearness, if only for the short two-mile ride, and in the end, the longing won out. She leaned against his strong chest and prayed her clothing didn't catch fire as he urged Havana forward.

"Comfortable?" he asked while keeping the stallion to a walk.

Val looked up. "I thought you wanted to get there in a timely manner?"

"I do, but I also want to enjoy your company."

His overpowering nearness and clean male smell played havoc with her senses, making her vividly aware of him from the top of her head to the tips of her toes. To distract herself, she tried picking out landmarks in case she needed to make the trip to Sable's alone someday, but all she could focus on was the measured pace of the horse and the brick-hard chest of the man sheltering her so protectively. "I received a wire from Cole yesterday. His ship's docked in Maryland. He's back early and should be in New Orleans in a few days."

"I'm assuming that wasn't why you had the bad dream." He looked down, and gave her that smile, and she couldn't respond any other way except in kind.

"It was not."

"Good. I don't need more reasons to run him off."

"Promise me you'll be respectful when you meet him."

"I'm a pirate. We lie."

"Drake?" She punched his arm playfully.

"Ow! Just being truthful. Pirates can be bribed however."

"I'm not letting you kiss me."

"That isn't what I meant, but good to know you have kissing me on your mind."

"I don't."

"Are you part pirate, too?"

Embarrassment heated her cheeks.

"Do you like his kisses?"

"That's none of your business."

"Before he arrives, maybe you'll have a chance to compare."

"You're supposed to be on your best behavior."

"I'll be on my very best behavior, when I kiss you, *cheri*. Promise."

Thinking she may swoon, she wondered how serious her injuries might be if she fell off the horse. "You're outrageous."

"No. I'm a son of the House of LeVeq."

She chuckled. "Tell me about your house. What will you be working on today?"

"The ironwork for my gazebo. It will resemble Mama's, but I may put on an iron roof instead of the wooden one she has on hers."

"Where did you learn your skills?"

"Originally from an African man who'd been sold into slavery here. His master let him hire himself out and he eventually made enough money to buy his freedom. I was his apprentice for two and a half years."

"How old were you when you began the apprenticeship?"

"Twelve. I lived in his shop for the first year, but he didn't let me near the forge for the first six months. Instead, I fetched and carried, swept up, and watched while he worked. In the evenings after the shop closed for the day, he'd lecture me on the things that went into being a smith: the African traditions, different methods of working the iron, how to vary the temperatures of the fire. Once he was convinced I had the necessary reverence and knowledge he began my lessons."

She glanced at his scarred hands and ran a finger over one of the larger scars. "Is that where all this comes from?"

"Some. Some come from carpentry. Others are simply from being a LeVeq with five brothers."

She smiled his way.

He met her gaze and said, "If you do leave New Orleans, I'm keeping your smile so I can pull it out and look at it whenever I think of you."

Val scanned his face, expecting to see teasing amusement. Instead, his solemn eyes met hers for a brief heart-piercing moment before turning to the road.

When they reached the tall iron gate that led onto his brother's property, five smiling children came running to meet them, shouting, "Uncle Drake! Uncle Drake!" Having met Sable's children at the Christophe, Valinda assumed these were some of the orphans. They appeared to be no older than seven years of age and their beaming smiles showed Uncle Drake to be a favorite acquaintance. He greeted them each by name and asked how they were faring. They replied with tales of tadpole catching and who won the footrace yesterday and being allowed to stay up late last night to look at the moon.

"Who's she?" a little boy with missing front teeth asked, while he and the others walked happily beside the big stallion.

"This is Miss Valinda."

"She your lady?" one of the girls asked.

He laughed. "No. She's going to be your new schoolteacher."

Val saw the young faces evaluating her in light of the new information.

"Are you mean?" a boy asked.

"No," Val replied.

"Good. Uncle Rai made a teacher leave because he yelled at us all the time."

"I promise not to yell," she reassured him.

"She's pretty, Uncle Drake," one of the girls pointed out.

"You think so?" he asked her.

She nodded.

"I do, too," he replied.

Flustered by the compliment, she turned her attention to the large two-story home. It was made of wood and painted white. There were graceful staircases on the left and right that led up to a second-floor walk bordered by a wrought-iron grille. She wondered if it and the house were more of Drake's handiwork. Sable stepped out onto the porch with her daughter in her arms. Her hair was hidden beneath a green patterned *tignon*, and she was wearing a simple white blouse and gray skirt. She greeted Valinda's arrival with a smile.

Drake dismounted, and before Valinda could react, his strong hands effortlessly lifted her free and set her gently on her feet. Hoping her face didn't reveal how breathtaking she found him, she walked with him towards the porch. The children followed.

"Good morning, Valinda," Sable called. "How are you?"

"I'm well. How are you?"

"I'm well." She then said to her brother-in-law, "Drake, I could've ridden over to Julianna's to fetch her. In fact, I was just about to leave."

"Mama thought this might be easier since I'm on my way home."

Desiré's chubby little brown arms reached out for Drake and he took her gently from her mother. "Morning, sweet Desi. How are you? Are you keeping Papa in line for me?"

"Yes," the toddler said proudly.

"Good girl. Can I get a kiss?"

She pressed her lips to his cheek.

"Thank you. Don't ever let a boy kiss you, okay?"

"Okay."

He handed her to the amused Sable.

Val continued to be amazed by his antics.

Drake said his goodbyes. "Enjoy your day together ladies. I'll see you at dinner." He looked down at the adoring children and asked, "Who wants to ride the bear back to his horse?"

They all screamed, "I do!"

"Get on then."

And to Valinda's amazement, some scrambled onto his broad back, while others latched onto his big arms and large legs. He growled, and with the laughing children hanging on, he roared again, and slowly made his way to the waiting stallion.

Sable said, "They love him so much. I think they know that in his heart, he's really one of them, only bigger."

Valinda watched as the bear reached his mount. After freeing himself of his young barnacles, he got back in the saddle. He offered a departing wave to Valinda and Sable and headed for the gate while the laughing children ran beside him.

"Come on in," Sable said.

Valinda took a last look at Drake galloping away from the gate before following Sable inside. Sable gave Desiré to the smiling housekeeper and led Val into the parlor. The room was beautifully appointed, with fine furniture and lamps. A large oil painting of Sable in a beautiful emerald gown hung above the fireplace. Valinda took a seat and said, "It appears that I won't be here long enough to teach the children." And she told her about Cole's wire and the debate she'd been having with herself.

"If the decision were entirely yours, would you stay?"

"I would, but I made a promise to Cole."

"Is it a love match?"

Val paused, looked into the waiting green eyes, and shook her head. How many more times would she be asked that question? "No, but we do care about each other a great deal. I'm not convinced love is needed in a marriage."

"If you've never known love, I suppose it isn't, but I'd be lost without Rai in my life. Granted there are times when I want to hang him on a clothesline because we're both opinionated and stubborn. In fact, I'm pretty upset with him even as we speak."

Valinda was surprised by the confession and

wanted the details but knew it would be rude to ask.

At that moment, Raimond LeVeq walked into the parlor. He was wearing a dark suit that seemed to accent his build and handsomeness. "Morning, Valinda."

She nodded, noting the way Sable eyed him with displeasure.

"Still angry I see," he said to his wife.

"You can't go around punching people in the nose, Raimond."

"The little runt deserved it, *ma reine.*"

Val didn't understand the French but by the soft intonation, sensed it was an endearment.

Sable's response was just as soft. "Stop trying to sweet-talk me."

"Is it working?" he asked. The amusement in his eyes was very reminiscent of Drake's.

Valinda cleared her throat. "Um. Maybe I should leave you two alone."

Raimond shook his head. "Not necessary." He then turned to Sable. *"Bijou,* when you have a wife that you absolutely adore, and are constantly challenged by a runt calling himself a poet who keeps declaring his love for the wife you absolutely adore, you can choose not to punch him in the nose. I chose differently. Be glad I only broke his nose."

Sable shook her head in response to his defense.

He asked quietly, "Did you hear the part about how much I absolutely adore you?"

"Aren't you late for a meeting?" she asked, looking partly skeptical and partly amused.

"They'll wait. How about after we come home from Henri's dinner, I get down on my knees and—beg your pardon."

She met his eyes, and said to Valinda, "Be glad you're not marrying into the House of LeVeq. The men are incorrigible."

Rai walked over to where his wife sat. "Would you like that? Me, on my knees?" he asked again.

A blush bloomed over Sable's golden cheeks. "Go to your meeting, Rai."

"You're going to be very pleased when I'm done begging your pardon."

She pointed to the door and a laugh slipped free. "Out, outrageous man."

Grinning malely, he leaned down and kissed her so softly and thoroughly, she melted into the emerald settee. Valinda tried not to stare.

He straightened and, after slowly tracing his thumb over her bottom lip, said, "I'll be back around six."

He headed to the door. "See you this evening, Valinda."

After his departure, Sable said, "As I was saying, a clothesline."

But Valinda knew she didn't mean it. She also knew she'd just witnessed something she'd never seen her parents share; something she and Cole would never share, either. Passion.

Val spent the balance of the morning with the children, which freed Sable to handle some business in her office. They read to her and she read to them. She joined them in a rousing game of tag, searched the edge of the pine forest for colorful rocks and insects, and sat with them at the trestle table to eat lunch. It was fun and made her think back on the conversation she'd had with Drake. It had been years since she'd played and she had to admit all the laughter and being so carefree lightened her spirit and banished her nightmare.

After lunch, it was quiet time. Some of the younger ones napped, while the older ones read, painted pictures, or simply lay on their backs outside in the field and contemplated the clouds—an activity a young Val had loved to do.

Val and Sable took their quiet time on the back porch.

"How long will they rest?" Val asked.

"An hour or two. Thanks so much for your

help today. Your being here allowed me time to write letters for some freedmen to their kin. I'm way behind."

Sable must have seen the confusion on Val's face, so she explained. "I began writing letters for those who couldn't read or write when I was in the contraband camp where Rai and I met. Now I do the same for the freedmen here in New Orleans."

Val understood now. "The brother of one of my students asked me to do something similar. He wants to put a plea in the newspapers in hopes of finding his wife."

"I've helped with those, too, because I know what it's like to have missing family members. I've been searching for my sister, Mavis, and brother, Rhine, since Freedom. Each night I pray they are alive and safe, and that we'll be reunited."

Val thought about her grandmother and her siblings.

"Slavery was an awful thing," Sable said. "As a race we've suffered so much pain and sorrow because of it."

Val agreed. "Both North and South. I was eleven when the 1850 Fugitive Slave Act was implemented, and I can recall how terrified everyone was of being captured by all the slave catchers that came north. The catchers didn't care if you had free papers or not. Some of my classmates lost fathers, mothers. Entire families fled to Canada to hide themselves."

"In the South, news from the North was hard to come by so I know nothing about those times."

"Our parents escorted us back and forth to school. The churches passed out whistles to the women and older children because the catchers sometimes came during the day while the men were at work."

"Why whistles?"

"They served as alarms and alerts. I remember my grandmother and some of the other women blowing their whistles while chasing one off our street. The more they blew, the more women joined in. They'd armed themselves with long-handled spoons and forks. Skillets. Broomsticks. The man couldn't run fast enough and received quite a beating."

Sable chuckled. "That must've been some sight."

"It was." She'd watched the episode from the doorway of her grandmother's dress shop.

"When my grandmother returned she marched in, put her mop away, and said, 'He's not coming back.'"

"I wish you were going to stay, Valinda. We'd probably have fun together. I have the family but very few friends."

Val remembered Sable touching on being shunned by the Creole women during their lunch at the Christophe. "Maybe the women here will come around."

Sable shrugged. "Who knows, but I do wish you weren't leaving."

"There's a chance that I'll stay. Let's wait and see what Cole says."

"I'm keeping my fingers crossed."

Val planned to do the same.

THAT EVENING AS Val dressed for the welcome-home dinner in her bedroom, she thought back on her day with Sable and the passionate moment between Sable and her husband. Val wondered what that bond felt like, and if they were that playful with each other all the time. Raimond's pledge to beg her pardon had caused Sable to blush. Val thought he might've been alluding to something more intimate, but being an innocent in such matters, she didn't know.

The large dining room was filled with LeVeqs. There was conversation, laughter, a gloriously set table for the adults, and a smaller one for the younger members. Standing before the mantel and wearing an elegant indigo-hued gown was Julianna. Beside her stood a tall handsome man wearing spectacles. The two were having an animated conversation with Raimond and Sable. Seeing Val, Julianna beckoned to her.

"Valinda Lacy, my husband, Henri Vincent."

"Pleased to meet you, sir."

"My pleasure as well," he replied in French-accented English. "Julie tells me you may not be with us for much longer."

"I'm hoping my plans will change."

"I do as well."

At that moment, Little Reba announced dinner and everyone moved to the table. Val noted that Drake wasn't in the room. She told herself she wasn't disappointed by his absence, but it was a lie. She chose a seat across from Raimond and Sable. As everyone was settling in, Beau walked over to Val. "May I?" he asked, indicating the empty chair to her left.

"Of course."

He sat. "I hear you may be leaving us."

"Possibly," she replied.

"That's too bad. I was hoping—"

A sharp tap on his shoulder caused him to look up.

Drake.

Like his brothers, Drake was dressed in a

well-tailored black suit that emphasized his frame.

Beau held his brother's gaze. No words were spoken. Beau sighed aloud and rose to his feet. "Enjoy your dinner, Valinda."

"Thank you," she said softly.

Drake sat. "Good evening, *cheri*. How was your day?" he asked easily.

She glanced across the table at Sable who cracked, "Lots of clothesline, Val. Lots."

Val leaned close to Drake and asked softly, "Why'd you make your brother move?"

"I didn't. He decided he wanted to sit elsewhere."

She rolled her eyes.

As the meal progressed and the conversation and laughter flowed, Val noted how happy Julianna appeared. She and her Henri were seated next to each other. They shared whispers, smiles, and their feelings for each other were quite apparent. Henri was left-handed. Julianna used her right. His right hand held her left throughout and Val thought the display both tender and sweet.

"How long have your mother and Henri been married?" she asked Drake quietly.

"A little over two years. They married a few months after Rai and Sable spoke their vows."

"They look happy."

"They are. He was my father's best friend and loved Mama from afar. They should've married years ago, but Henri didn't want to disrespect my father's memory."

Another love match, she realized. In fact, Julianna had two in her lifetime. She glanced at Drake.

"Yes?"

She wanted to understand the feelings that tied Sable to Raimond and Julianna to Henri and how it impacted them as individuals, but she didn't know how to express it and have it make sense. "Nothing."

"Are you certain?"

She nodded and returned to the food on her plate.

Dessert was a sumptuous bread pudding topped with a rich vanilla bean sauce. Once everyone had a piece on their dessert plates, Raimond stood up. The room quieted. He raised his wineglass. "A toast to Henri and our Lovely Julianna. May your love endure."

Cheers filled the air. Henri leaned over and gave his lady a kiss, to the delight of all.

At the end of the evening, goodbyes were shared, everyone left for home, and Julianna and Henri retired upstairs to their suite of rooms. Val and Drake were the only ones left in the now-silent dining room, and after last night's restless sleep, she was tired. "Good night, Drake."

She was on her way out of the room when she heard, "May I share your company for a short while?"

She turned. Viewing him and his intense gaze, she sensed herself on the cusp of something she couldn't name. Everything she knew about him, from his love of tree houses to his strong sense of caring, made her yearn to know more. Rather than debate the reasons why she shouldn't accept his invitation, she replied, "Yes."

"The mosquitoes may run us back inside, but shall we sit in the gazebo?"

She nodded. When he offered his arm, the silent gesture made her swallow nervously, but she let him escort her out into the night.

The moon had risen, and its beams bathed the gravel path with pale light. The breeze was soft and the air fragrant with the scent of Julianna's night-blooming jasmine. Val told herself she wasn't really nervous. After all, she'd sat with him in the gazebo before, but never alone in the dark, an inner voice reminded her sagely.

They took seats opposite each other in the

darkened gazebo. She heard the scratch of a match, and light sprang to life on the wick of a small candle that sat on a piece of tin in the center of the table.

"You came prepared," she said.

"I wanted to be able to see you and hoped it would make you more comfortable."

"I appreciate your caring."

"Always the gentleman."

For a few moments, silence rose between them, bringing with it the unique music of the night. She savored the breeze and watched it ruffle the candle's flame.

"Tell me something about you I don't know, *cheri*."

"No one's ever called me *cheri* before," she replied.

"No?"

"Do you address other women that way? Your mistress, maybe?"

"Is that the hellion asking?"

"Yes." She wanted to know because if he used it commonly, she'd rather be addressed by her name.

"Then tell her no, and that I no longer have a mistress. She's received a better offer."

She searched his face in the wavering light. "Are you saddened by it?"

"My ego is. The rest of me will live. I enjoyed our times together, but it was a business arrangement, nothing more."

Val realized how naïve she was. She never considered a man's arrangement with a mistress might be viewed so dispassionately, but that he no longer had a mistress didn't sadden her, either.

"Tell me something else," he encouraged softly.

The passionate kiss between Raimond and Sable rose in her mind, but she shied away from adding that to the conversation. "I'm terrible at singing, embroidery, and playing the piano."

"All the things society expects a good woman to master."

"Unfortunately, yes. I enjoy science, but my father wouldn't let me add more schooling to my education."

"Why not?"

"He believes too much education damages women and makes them unfit for bearing children. Do you believe a woman wanting to learn is damaging?"

"With the Lovely Julianna as my mother? No."

She smiled. He was easy to talk to. In that way he was much like Cole. She thought of him and wondered about their future.

"Penny for your thoughts?"

"Honestly? I was thinking about Cole."

"Give me my penny back."

She laughed. "I was thinking that the two of you are alike in that you're easy to talk to."

"It doesn't matter. A man convinces a beautiful lady to sit with him in the dark, only to be told she's thinking about another man."

"I've never been kissed," she whispered, then wished she could take it back, then decided she didn't. Then decided Drake LeVeq was making her lose her mind.

He searched her face in the shadows. "Ever?"

"Ever."

"Not even by your intended?"

"No. I mean, he's kissed me on my forehead and cheeks. But—"

"Not your lips?"

She shook her head. The candle's weak light showed his unspoken questions.

"Please don't think less of him."

"I don't."

She wasn't sure she believed him but chose to take him at his word. "Cole is incredibly kind and good."

"You don't have to defend him to me, *cheri*."

"I feel as if I do."

"You don't."

Again taking him at his word, she nodded, adding, "So, here I sit, a fully grown woman who watched your brother give Sable a kiss this morning that seemed to melt her from her spine to her toes, and I know nothing about that. But I feel as if I should, even if society thinks a properly raised girl shouldn't." She looked at him. "I blame you and your pirate kin. I was fine until I met your family with all its love and passion."

He laughed. "Will you come sit beside me?"

She stood and joined him on his side of the table. He draped an arm over her shoulder and eased her close to his side.

"We LeVeqs can be pretty contagious."

"My parents can barely tolerate being in the same room, but I saw the way Henri held Julianna's hand during dinner, and it was so touching. This is all so different for me."

"No two families are alike," he said.

"Cole's parents at least like each other, but they don't hold hands during dinner, nor have I ever seen them act the way Sable and your brother did this morning."

"What do you mean?"

"She was mad at him for punching a poet in the nose."

"Ah, the pesky Gaspar Cadet. Rai's been

itching to toss him in the gutter for years, but she didn't look upset with Rai at dinner tonight."

"He told her that when they got home from dinner tonight, he'd get down on his knees and apologize, and that she'd be very pleased. Sable's face turned beet red."

Drake's laughter was loud enough to startle the moon.

"I assume that has something to do with what you called *bed games*, correct?"

"Yes."

"And it means, what?"

"I can't tell you, *cheri*. That will be between you and Cole."

She fell back against his shoulder. "Why do men want unmarried women to be so ignorant?"

"I don't know, but it's how the world works."

"It's very unfair."

He turned to look at her in the shadows. "I adore you so much."

"But not enough to tell me what Rai meant?"

He laughed. "No, so stop asking me."

She sighed.

"Don't pout, *cheri*."

"One more thing on the list women aren't supposed to do?"

"If you were mine, I'd be on my knees right now, believe me."

Not even the shadows could mask the heat in his eyes. He drew a slow finger over her bottom lip and her eyes closed. "May I kiss you instead?" he asked, whispered.

Val had no barriers left. "Yes . . ."

He brushed his lips over her forehead. "Were you mine, there'd be no secrets . . . only pleasure."

He kissed each of her trembling eyelids, traced a slow blistering path down to the space beneath her ear, and gently teased the tip of his tongue against the edge of her lips. When they parted on her sigh, his claimed hers in a kiss that was moan-inducing, head-spinning, bone-melting. She'd never experienced anything like it, and then he slowly drew away. Floating on the sensations, it took a few seconds for her brain to restart so she could move. Opening her eyes, she saw him above her. She reached out and cupped his bearded cheek. The hellion in her leaned up and boldly kissed him again and thrilled to the sound of his groan. The pressure of his lips increased, his arms around her tightened, and she was eased closer, her softness flush against his hardness. Hot lips sought out the thin strip of skin above her high collar, while his large hand explored her back and spine. His lips covered hers again and the world began spinning. There was a yearning between her thighs. Her blood rushed. He then placed his hands on her waist, tore his lips from hers, and set her down a short distance away.

"You belong to another, *cheri*. You're making me forget that."

Val felt as if she'd just run a race. If this was passion, she wanted more.

"Let's go inside."

"Drake—"

"Come on. Otherwise you'll be out here with your dress raised and me on my knees."

Her eyes went wide.

He smiled and stood.

She stood, too. She'd never felt this with Cole or anyone else. "Thank you for the kiss."

"You're welcome." He blew out the candle and walked her back to the house.

Inside it was as quiet as it had been earlier, but Val was not the same. Drake's pirate kisses had opened a door inside herself that she wanted to fling wide open. She and Cole were to be married, but he didn't leave her breathless or make her want to be kissed until dawn because they had no physical attraction to each other, and thus, no desire.

"Good night, *cheri.*"

"Good night."

At two in the morning, Liam Atwater was awakened by the sounds of someone banging on his door. Thinking he might be dreaming, he ignored it at first, but when it continued, he sat up. His wife, Mildred, asked sleepily, "Is someone at the door?"

"Yeah. Go back to sleep."

She rolled over. Dressed in a faded nightshirt that exposed his pale, bony legs, he stepped into his worn leather slippers and picked up the rifle kept by the bedroom door. The knocking continued. He hollered, "I'm coming, dammit! Keep your drawers on!"

He paused for a moment to look out the parlor window, but seeing nothing in the darkness, shuffled to the door and pulled it open. Strong hands locked on to his arms, scaring him badly. He struggled to free himself. They relieved him of the rifle and he yelled furiously, "Let me go! Who are you?"

He was forced to the edge of the moonlit porch. Out of the darkness came five mounted men slowly riding abreast. The wind whipped at the edge of their black capes. Their faces were hidden beneath black hoods and he shook with fear. He opened his mouth to scream Mildred's name, but the gag was faster, tighter. The hood placed over his head plunged him into total darkness, and the terror made him soil himself. His wrists were bound behind him and he was dragged off the porch and down to the night-damp ground.

He lost a shoe, but his captors didn't care. From within the hood, he cried, screamed, and, yes, begged, but the gag muffled it all. Liam was five-foot-four-inches tall. He weighed one hundred and forty pounds. The men from his nightmare had no trouble throwing him into the bed of a wagon. As it got underway, he heard Mildred screaming, but there was nothing he could do.

How long the drive took, Liam didn't know, but not even the hood could mask the smells of rotting vegetation or the distinct song of the frogs and grunts of gators. They were in the swamp. The wagon slowed and stopped.

He was hauled out and placed on his now bare feet. For the first time, someone addressed him. "Liam Atwater, you're guilty of the murder of Daniel Downs, and justice will be served."

He wailed behind the gag. His arms were latched onto again. He tried to wrest himself free but was lifted and set down in what felt like a dugout.

The voice said, "You gave Daniel no chance, but we're not completely heartless. Somewhere near you is a hunting knife. Find it, and maybe you can save yourself, but be quick. There are holes drilled in the bottom of the canoe. It'll sink fast, and the gators will come running."

Bawling, he felt the boat being pushed into the water. As it began to float, he frantically extended his bound hands in a desperate search for the knife, but felt nothing except the water's slow rise dampening his nightshirt. Scooting around carefully but quickly, he finally felt the sheathed blade, and in his elation tipped the dugout over. Hands tied behind his back, he went into the water. Frantic, he tried to hang on to the boat, only to hear three large splashes. He froze. Gators. Screaming within the wet hood, he didn't have to wait long before being dragged under and death rolled until he drowned.

Chapter Ten

$\mathcal{D}$rake came down to breakfast and found only Valinda at the table. "Good morning, *cheri*."

"Good morning," she said shyly.

He ran his eyes over her mouth and forced his mind away from how sweet she'd tasted last night in his arms. "Where's the Lovely Julianna and Henri?" he asked, taking a seat.

"Little Reba said they're eating in their suite."

"Ah, that's what lovebirds do after being apart. Did you sleep well? No bad dreams?"

"No bad dreams."

"Good."

"How was your sleep?"

"Good." He dreamt of her. Hot, lusty pirate dreams.

Reba came in. "Drake, there are some soldiers outside asking for you."

He stood and left the room. Outside was his nemesis from the Bureau, Lt. Merritt, and a three-man mounted detail. "What can I help you with, Lieutenant?" Drake asked coolly.

Merritt glared down from his mount. "Where were you around two o'clock this morning?"

Drake eyed him. "Here in bed. Why?"

"Do you have witnesses?"

"Either tell me what this is about or leave. My breakfast's getting cold." He knew Merritt disliked being challenged, especially by men of color, but that was his problem, not Drake's.

"Liam Atwater was taken from his house by some riders about that time and hasn't been seen since."

"Again, why are you here?"

"To see if you know anything about it."

"I don't." He crossed his arms. He saw Merritt look behind Drake, so he turned and saw his mother, Henri, and Valinda watching from the door. "Anything else?"

"If I find out you were involved—"

"You won't. Good day, Lieutenant." He walked up the steps. The angry lieutenant wheeled his mount around and he and the detail rode off.

Inside, Henri asked, "What was that about?"

Drake explained to him about Atwater murdering Daniel Downs, before adding, "Apparently early this morning, some men dragged Atwater out of his house, and now's he's missing."

Julianna said, "For good, I hope. How dare he murder a man in front of his wife and child."

Valinda said, "The lieutenant thinks you know something about it because you were trying to have Atwater arrested?"

"I suppose so."

She shook her head. "Had the Army been helpful, maybe the murderer wouldn't be wherever he was taken. Come and eat before your breakfast gets any colder."

He smiled. "Yes, ma'am."

Julianna and Henri went back to their rooms and he rejoined Valinda at the table.

She asked, "You said you went to the police and the Army about the murder. If they think you were involved, might the supremacists think so, too, and retaliate?"

He studied her and reminded himself that she was both brains and beauty. "More than likely, but my brothers and I will be prepared."

"I wonder if the country will ever heal from the war?"

He thought back on the reports Rai shared at the last Council meeting about the uptick in the violence sweeping across the South. "It won't be anytime soon. Maybe not even in our lifetimes."

"It's sad to think that the race may still be demanding justice when little Desiré grows up."

"It is."

"So, were you and your brothers involved?"

He studied her again. "Would you think badly of us if we were?"

"No. Someone has to champion us if the government won't. During the Draft Riots back home, mobs attacked members of the race all over the city. They even burned down a Colored orphanage. Those who hate us have no shame, and if dragging them from their houses teaches them a lesson, I'm all for dragging them out every night until they learn."

He was impressed by her fire. "Do your parents hold those views?"

"My grandmother Rose does, but political discussions aren't encouraged at home. My father says only men understand such complex issues, and since he's the only man in our household, he does his debating at the barbershop where he works."

"Your father sounds like most men I know."

"Unfortunately, he sounds like most of the ones back home, too. That's why I take such joy in being acquainted with your mother. She's like my grandmother who I also admire because they've made their own way and are forces to reckon with."

"And that's what you aspire to? Being a force to reckon with?"

"Yes, and to teach girls to aspire to be the same."

"What's your dream, *cheri*?"

"To head up a school where girls who, like me, have no interest in embroidery or playing the piano, can learn as much about whatever they want: mathematics, botany, the stars. They can study animals or anatomy. And I'd have the money to provide excellent teachers who don't believe learning will damage them."

"That's very lofty."

"It is, but dreams can't come true if you don't have them."

At that moment, Drake wanted to give her her dreams and anything else that quick mind of hers desired. She was smart, witty, sassy, and, as he learned last night, ripe with passion. He thought back on her sighs during those two short kisses and the memory made his groin tighten in response. Although he told her he wouldn't judge her Cole, Drake couldn't imagine being content with passionless kisses on her brow and cheeks. Were she his, he'd make love to her from sunset to sunrise, then pray for more hours in the day, and two extra days in the week. And that still might not be enough.

"What are you thinking?"

"Pirate thoughts."

"What kinds of pirate thoughts?"

"Truthfully?"

She nodded.

"Making love to you from sunset to sunrise. Every day."

Her eyes closed for a moment. In response, he smiled. "You asked, *cheri*."

"I did. Didn't I?"

"Yes."

Truthfully, if he were in his right mind, he'd forget about the feel of her in his arms, about wanting to taste her ripe mouth and treating her to a long sultry session of what it meant for a man to be on his knees. In a few days, her intended would arrive. Although she might be having second thoughts now, he doubted she'd stay. Once she saw Cole, their plans would reassert themselves and she'd be on the train back to New York. He wondered how long she'd remember him. And what in the world was he going to do with the two train cars he'd asked Hugh to deliver?

"Drake?"

He looked over.

"Thank you for the kiss last night. I don't feel so ignorant anymore."

He nodded. "I'm glad." He wanted to take the conversation further, coax her onto his lap, and do all sorts of pirate things to her, but decided to begin weaning himself from her immediately, even as his eyes lingered over her sweet mouth. "So, what are your plans for the day?"

"Sable and I agreed that I'd come and teach the children anyway, at least until Cole arrives. Once he does, I'll let her know what my final decision will be."

"Do you need a ride over?"

"I was going to ask Julianna if Mr. Doolittle could take me, so I won't have to impose on you."

"It isn't an imposition." For a man set upon distancing himself, he was admittedly doing a poor job.

"I have slates and books to take. There'll be no room on Havana."

"Okay. That makes sense. I'm going to the stable. Not sure I'll be here for dinner though."

He saw her disappointment. "You belong to another, *cheri*. I don't want these kisses between us to go any further. Passion could lead to a place you'll regret, so I need to let you be."

She nodded. "You're right of course."

"Enjoy your time at Sable's."

She gave him another tight nod and he left her seated at the table.

His foreman, Solomon Hawk, and the five freedmen he'd hired as laborers were already working when he arrived.

"Morning, Drake."

"Morning, Solly." The decision he'd come to about Valinda had left him more than a bit grumpy. "Where are we today?"

Solly studied him for a moment as if assessing his mood, and replied, "Planning to finish framing the kitchen so we can start putting on the bricks."

"That's fine. I'll be working on the gazebo."

Drake led Havana to the stable, then took a moment to say good morning to the men before heading to the shed. Inside was his forge, anvil, and tools of the trade. He donned his leather apron. Valinda tried to enter his mind, but he pushed her aside, picked up a shovel, and dug out the upper layers of ash in the forge. Adding new charcoal, he lit the mass and waited for the coals to reach the proper temperature.

Once it did, he began working on the iron he'd be using on the planned gazebo. He hammered, thinned, and slowly twisted the strands of metal into the swirls and curlicues needed for outer walls. Frustration tied to Valinda lingered, as did his desire. He was doing the right thing, but he didn't have to like it. Glancing up as he worked, he saw his brother Raimond, arms crossed, leaning against the shed's opening. Drake had no idea how long he'd been waiting, but before investigating, he took another few minutes to finish hammering the piece he was working on, then set it aside to cool. He shucked his mask and removed his gloves. "What?"

Raimond walked in. "My, aren't you the surly one? It's good to see you, too. Thorn in your paw?"

Drake sighed.

Rai said, "Mama and Henri are going to Baton Rouge the day after tomorrow. I just want to make sure someone's at the house with Valinda and Little Reba while they're away."

"I told her I'd stay over but if someone else can take my place I'd appreciate it. Trying to get this house finished." And avoid Valinda.

"I'm on my way to Lafayette, Archer can't leave the hotel, and Beau and Phillipe set sail this morning for Cuba to pick up some shipments I have coming in. They'll be gone for four or five days, so you're it, I'm afraid."

"Okay."

"Why the bad mood?"

"I need to stop pining after the lovely Valinda, and it's not sitting well."

Rai scanned his face. "You know her intended is due any day now?"

"I do."

"I saw the way you made Beau leave her side at dinner last night."

Drake walked over and banked the fire in the forge. "He made his own decision."

"His own decision, my ass. You were two seconds away from tossing him into the street. You can't have a woman who's already promised, Drake."

"I know that. Have known that. She climbed trees when she was young, Rai."

Rai dropped his head and shook it with amusement. "Just the kind of woman every Tree House King needs. How far gone are you?"

"Far enough."

"If she leaves, then what?"

Drake shrugged. "Ride north and steal her back?"

Their grins met.

"Spoken like a true pirate." Rai paused for a moment, taking Drake's measure, then added, "I know you don't need my advice."

"Correct."

Rai chuckled. "Never mind then. Do what's best for her. Not you. But if you need me to ride north, let me know."

Drake loved his brothers, but he loved Rai the most. "I will. Safe travel to Lafayette."

Rai nodded and made his exit.

Drake blew out a long breath and went back to work.

VALINDA STOOD IN the back of the wagon and took in the miles-long line of Black and White faces and tried to keep her heart from breaking. She and Sable were among a group of volunteers distributing food, but she hadn't expected it to be such an emotional undertaking. There were families, single men, single mothers holding infants, and elderly women with toddlers latched onto their homespun skirts. There were old people lying in the beds of listing wagons and others perched on the backs of swayback mules. All were hungry. All waited patiently. What pulled most at her emotions was the resignation in their eyes. Many took the rations of pork, yams, and beans with a nod of thanks; others simply walked away.

She dragged yet another ten-pound bag of yams to the wagon's edge. The muscles in her arms burned in response to the unaccustomed heavy lifting. "My arms are on fire," she told Sable.

"It'll go away in a few days. Take a break and go help Mrs. Bentley at the stipend tables. She needs to be relieved. She's seated at the table beneath that oak over there."

Val took in the two long lines of people stretching from the table and back across the open field. "Why are the lines divided by race?" One held Blacks. The other Whites.

"The older White women don't want to be in the same line as the people who once worked for them."

Val found that sad. Everyone there was seeking assistance of one type or another, yet bigotry continued to take precedence in some minds. Wondering if the nation would ever rid itself of the divisive thinking, she left Sable and set off across the field.

Hundreds of people were milling about. On the surface, the gathering could have passed for a country fair, if it weren't for the lack of gaiety. The majority of the people standing in the sweltering New Orleans heat were there for food, to report beatings, murders, and other incidents of violence to the Bureau agents in Union blue, and to apply for government stipends. The only people smiling were the freedmen in line to be married.

Mrs. Bentley, a thin middle-aged White woman from Ohio, was one of the hundreds of missionaries who'd come south to assist the Bureau. After a quick introduction, she had Val take a seat in the rickety cane chair beside her. "Watch me for a moment and then you'll be on your own. I'm going to go help with the marriages. I need some joy after sitting here all morning."

Val read over the government-issued form she had to fill out for each applicant. There were columns for the applicant's name, age, number of children in the household under fourteen, and the reason the person wanted assistance. Her table handled the White women, and after watching Mrs. Bentley conduct a few of the interviews, she was left alone.

"May I help you?" she asked the older woman next in line. Her brown gown was stained and wrinkled, the hem tattered and dirty. Her thin gray hair was pulled back from her bony tight-lipped face and she ignored Val as if she hadn't spoken. "Excuse me, ma'am. If you'll step closer I can fill out your form."

"I'll wait until the other woman comes back," she said firmly, not meeting Val's eyes.

"She isn't coming back."

Hearing that, she immediately got out of line.

As she walked away, Val stared with surprise. A few others within earshot stared as well. Val sighed.

The next woman stepped up to the table. She was middle-aged, wearing a dirty, once-white blouse and a dark skirt patched on the side with green fabric. She was barefoot and had two small, dirty-faced children with her. She looked tired but nodded a greeting.

Val asked kindly, "Your name please?"

"Mary Castle. I'm 47. I have these two grand-children. They're five and four. They belong to my daughter, but she left here a few weeks ago and hasn't come back."

Val wrote it down and asked, "The reason you can't work?"

"Lost my husband in the war and I got these two children."

Val added that to the report.

"Do you know when I'll get the money? This is the fourth time I've applied."

"No, I don't."

"Okay, thank you."

"You're welcome." Mary departed and the next woman stepped up.

Val filled out forms for the next two hours. A few women refused to be interviewed by her, but most didn't seem to care that she was of a different race. Many were elderly and cited their ages and failing health as why they couldn't work. One woman was blind, others like Mary Castle had small children in the home. The stories were sad. Val had come south thinking only people of the race were destitute and in need of help; she was wrong.

At the end of the day, Sable drove the wagon home, and Val asked, "When will the people who applied for stipends get their funds?"

Sable glanced over. "Never, more than likely."

"Why not?"

"There's no money. The forms will be filed and forgotten. The state has no funds and neither do any of the parishes."

Val was stunned.

"The process is nothing more than an exercise, and it's heartbreaking."

Val thought back on all the people she'd met that day: the elderly, the blind, the children. "Is it the same of our people?"

"Yes."

"Why offer hope where there is none?"

"It's a question everyone has been asking. The men in Congress don't see the need to do more than send pennies and offer platitudes and it's infuriating."

Val agreed. Mary Castle had applied four times already. What would happen to her and the hundreds of others of both races who would receive nothing?

"So now that you've seen the depth of problems we're facing, what do you think?"

"I think I need to help wherever I can."

Sable nodded. "Tomorrow is my weekly visit to the Colored Orphanage. Do you want to come along after my orphans are done with school?"

"I do."

The next day's visit to the city's orphanage also fueled Val's need to help. Most of the children had been abandoned and were under the age of ten. The lack of funding showed in the basic meals of grits and toast; the hand-me-down clothing provided by Sable, other volunteers, and the local churches; and the thin worn cots they slept on. But because they were children, smiles greeted their arrival and she and Sable smiled in response. Val had brought along a few books and sat on the floor and read to them.

When it was time to leave, she knew that if she decided to stay in New Orleans, one of her first acts would be teaching reading at the orphanage.

As she lay in bed that night, she thought about all she'd seen and done over the past two days and she also thought about Drake. He hadn't come back to Julianna's since they decided to step away from each other, and she told herself it was for the best, even as the memory of his kisses remained vivid. She was promised to another man, but it was difficult to erase her first taste of passion and the enjoyment she'd found in the conversations she and Drake shared. He'd introduced her to his family, offered to build her a school, and asked about her dreams. Those things alone were enough to endear him to her forever. Since saving her on the awful day they met, he'd been nothing but kind, and caring. Although she was engaged to Cole, she missed Drake LeVeq.

On the second morning of Drake's absence, Julianna and Henri prepared to leave for their trip to Baton Rouge. Henri had sufficiently recovered from his travels and was eager to investigate the land he might want to purchase. Mr. Doolittle would be taking them to the train station. Doolittle and Julianna's gardener, a young man named Frank Poole, were outside loading the luggage into the carriage under Henri's watchful eye.

In the parlor, Julianna asked Val, "Have you heard from your Cole?"

"Not yet. I'm assuming he'll be arriving any day though."

"If he does, don't you dare leave New Orleans until I return."

Val smiled. "I'd never leave without saying goodbye."

"Good. Drake promised to stay here while we're gone to keep an eye on things, but I haven't seen him. Raimond said he reminded him. I hope he hasn't forgotten. Sometimes he gets so focused on whatever he's building he loses track of time."

"I'm sure Little Reba and I can manage alone."

"I don't doubt that, but I worry about the supremacists and their night rides."

Val understood. The newspapers were filled with more frightening accounts of burnings and deaths. There'd also been editorials demanding the arrests of Liam Atwater's kidnappers. That Drake hadn't denied playing a role in his disappearance continued to cause her worry about retaliation against him and his family.

And suddenly he appeared in the parlor—all glorious, six-foot-plus inches—and her breath caught. His eyes met hers. The way her heart was pounding, she was sure everyone in the room heard it. He gave her a slight nod and she gave him a tremulous one in response. He walked over and placed a kiss on his mother's cheek. "Morning, Mama. Came to say goodbye and find out if there's anything you want done around here while you're away."

"I worried you'd forgotten."

"No."

Henri stepped inside. "Are you ready, Julie?"

She nodded and said to Valinda, "If your intended needs a place to stay have him speak with Archer. I'm sure he'll have a room available."

"I will. Have a good time."

"Take care of her, Henri," Drake added.

Henri escorted his wife out to the carriage, leaving Valinda and Drake alone. The silence between them was awkward, but underneath, as charged as it had been the night in the gazebo.

"Is there school today?" he asked her.

"No. The doctor is visiting."

"Are the children ill?"

"A couple have the sniffles. Sable said they'll all come down with it eventually. She just wants to make sure it isn't something more serious."

"Ah."

Even with Cole's imminent arrival, the man holding her gaze illuminated her feelings like a lighthouse in the darkness.

"How have you been?" he asked.

"I've been well," she replied softly. "I've been

helping Sable with some of her charity work. And you?"

"I'm fine. How and where did you help?"

She told him about the first day and the second with the orphans.

"You're to be commended. I've volunteered there, too, in the past. I'll go back to it—but not under the Bureau—once the house is done."

"How's it coming along?"

"Should be finished soon."

Another awkward silence.

She said finally, "Since there's no school today, I'm going to work on organizing the rest of Julianna's files."

"Where's Little Reba?"

"At the market. She should be back shortly."

"I'll see if the gardener needs help with anything," he said.

She nodded and watched him leave.

DRAKE HELPED GARDENER Frank Poole dig out a stand of old hackberry trees that Julianna wanted to replace with magnolias. She'd hired the thirty-year-old Frank a few months ago through the Freedmen's Bureau. She wanted to help the freedmen get started on their new lives, and a job was a good place to begin. Drake and his brothers were of the same mind. The laborers working for him were formerly enslaved, as were the women working as housekeepers at Archer's hotel. Rai had a small army of freedmen working in his warehouses, and on his ships and docks.

Drake knew nothing about Frank's past but learned a bit as they worked and he talked about his ongoing search for his mother. Over sandwiches Little Reba brought out for lunch, Frank told Drake more. "I was sold away when I was five but have been looking for her since the day after Freedom. Searched all over Mississippi where I believe I was born, but no one had ever heard of her or her master."

"Why do you think you were born there?"

"Old woman on my last place said people there told her that's where I'm from, but I could've been born anywhere, so I'll keep looking."

Judging by the number of advertisements and letters in some of the Black newspapers, there was a flood of people seeking sold-away family members just in the New Orleans area. Multiply that by the estimated three million held in slavery across the South before Freedom, and Drake suspected there were thousands upon thousands wanting to reestablish ties to their kin.

"Are you going to stay in New Orleans?"

"Just until the end of summer. I'm going up to Baton Rouge next. If I don't find her there, I may head to Texas. My wife says she's going to leave me if I make her move again. We've been going from place to place since Freedom, so I understand her complaining, but I have to find my mother. She's expecting me to. Otherwise why'd she crop my ear this way if not so she can recognize me?" He turned his head and Drake saw the shortened lobe of his left ear. He wondered how common the practice had been. Hester Vachon, wife of Rai's best friend, Galen Vachon, was born into slavery. Her mother severed the tip of Hester's little finger at birth in case she was sold away and needed to be found. What other methods had slave parents used in the hopes of finding their children again, was a question he couldn't answer. He did know how fortunate he and his brothers were to have been born free. He couldn't imagine the heartache he'd be suffering had he been sold away from his parents. "If there's anything my family can do to assist you, please let us know."

Frank nodded. They finished their lunch and went back to work.

At the end of the day, Frank left for home and Drake went into the house to wash up. As he cut through the kitchen he was surprised to find

Valinda stirring a pot on the stove. "Where's Reba?"

"She had to leave. A man came by about an hour ago with a note from her brother-in-law. Reba's sister is ill. The brother-in-law has to work tonight and needed Reba to come and sit with her."

"Did he say how serious it was?"

"No, but she said if she has to stay longer, she'd let me know."

He didn't want to be in the house alone with Valinda. Just looking at her made him want to throw all good intentions out the door. Desiring her continued to plague him.

"She left dinner. Are you hungry?"

He was, but it had nothing to do with filling his stomach. "I am. But let me wash up first." And he left her alone.

Val admittedly had a moment of panic when Reba was leaving. Being in the house alone with Drake was only going to magnify what they both were determined to avoid. Due to the circumstances of her marriage to Cole, there'd be no intimate relations. Was it selfish of her to want another taste of passion because she'd have none in her life going forward? How would Drake react if she were to ask him for one night in his arms? How might she start the conversation? What should she say? She wished she knew.

Drake came downstairs clean and refreshed but wanting Valinda continued to bedevil him. In a way, he wished her intended had already arrived, so he'd be occupied with other things, like how to send the man back to New York alone, but for the moment, she ruled his thoughts. She, with her sunny smile, honey-brown skin, sharp wit, and lips made for him alone. He was glad to see her, and now he had to get through the evening without pulling her onto his lap and slowly stripping her bare. The thought made his groin tighten and he sighed at the self-torture.

He found her in the kitchen removing dishes from the oven with a towel-covered hand and he enjoyed the view of her skirt-shrouded backside as she bent into the oven.

"Do you want to eat in the dining room, or upstairs in your room alone?"

"I'd like to eat outside with you, if you don't mind."

She turned, studied him for a lengthy moment before refocusing on her task. She removed another dish and set it on the counter. "I don't mind."

Their gazes held. He lowered his eyes to her mouth, reminding him of its taste and shape, before rising them again to her brown eyes. Desire waited, and it was mesmerizing. "You shouldn't look at me that way, *cheri*."

"No?"

"I'm doing my best to keep my distance. You're not helping."

"What if keeping your distance isn't what I want?"

He settled on the frankness in those same brown eyes. "You're determined to make me lose my mind, aren't you?"

Mischief in her smile, she shook her head, then turned serious. "I enjoyed our time in the gazebo. It's probably going to be the only real passion I'll know for the rest of my life. Is it wrong that I want more to hold on to?"

He didn't know how to respond.

"Cole and I don't desire each other. There is no physical attraction. That isn't why we're marrying. You showed me passion, so truthfully, this is your fault."

"Blaming me, are you?"

"You were the man kissing me in the gazebo."

"So, what is it that you want, Lady Hellion?"

"A night, an evening—with you."

"I'm not taking your innocence, Valinda."

"That isn't what I want. My mother says that part is awful anyway. She told my sister and I that when my father insists, she recites the alphabet until he's done."

His jaw dropped, and he laughed. "The alphabet!"

"Yes. She said it's usually over by the time she reaches the letter P."

Laughter erupted again, and he couldn't stop.

"What's so funny?" she asked, grinning.

Still laughing, Drake felt his knees weakening and his ribs vibrate on the edge of pain. "Oh, lord. I'm going to die right here in Reba's kitchen." He finally pulled himself together and with amused eyes viewed her like the treasure he considered her to be. "No lover worth his salt should have his woman so bored she's silently reciting the alphabet."

"No?"

"No, *cheri*. She shouldn't be thinking anything other than how good a time she's having."

She looked confused, then said, "This is why I need more tutoring."

"You'll not get your completion certificate from me though. No matter how you and Cole feel about each other, that's not my place."

"I understand."

"But do you agree?"

"Is this a contract?" she asked.

"You could think of it that way. I don't want

you angry with me when we're done." He studied her. "Are you sure this is what you want?"

"I am."

"Positive?" he asked softly.

She nodded. "Yes."

"Then let's eat. I'll tutor you when we're done."

The thought of gifting her with the pleasure she'd requested made him want to cancel dinner and carry her up to his room then and there. No man in his right mind would say no to a sensuous evening of play, even with the limits he'd set down. But he wanted to court her, seduce her, give her the full measure of how earth-shattering desire could be, so he set aside the urge of having her immediately. With Reba away, they had all evening.

STANDING OUTSIDE ON the terrace connected to his room, Valinda watched the night roll in. The wind had picked up. A storm was on the way. She could hear him moving quietly around inside. She didn't know what he was doing. Preparing things, maybe. Not that she knew what that might be. Having never been in a man's room before, she was more nervous than she'd ever been in her life. So much so, she toyed with the idea of telling him she'd changed her mind, but truthfully, she hadn't. She wanted whatever was to come. With him. And then, he was behind her. His arms gently encircled her waist and the initial touch and feel of him closed her eyes.

"Storm coming," he voiced quietly.

In more ways than one, she thought. Lightning flashed in the distance, followed by the faint, low rumble of thunder.

His lips brushed over her ear. "You sure this is what you want?"

Slow, lulling sensations made everything go hazy. "Yes." His lips slid over her jawline and he gently nipped her ear. Her soft hum of arousal blended with the rising wind.

He whispered, "I'm going to kiss you. . . ." His big hand cupped her breast. "And touch you. . . ." His thumb moved featherlight over the point until her head dropped back and a gasp of pleasure slipped from her lips. "And do it again." Both hands came into play, touching, gently circling until she swore she'd catch fire.

"I can't wait to taste these."

Her knees dissolved, and her breath caught. She hadn't known this touching played a part when she dared ask him for this night. Lost in how he made her feel, she distantly noted the beginnings of wind-blown rain. She didn't care if she was drenched as long as he didn't stop, but without a word, he picked her up and carried her inside.

The lone lamp barely lit the room, leaving most of the contents, including his big four-poster bed, in shadow. He gently set her on her feet in the middle of the gloom, and as she stood there shaking, he ran a slow finger down her cheek. Her shaking increased but she drew in a deep breath, hoping to calm herself, even as her senses continued to spiral.

"I don't want you to be afraid," he said reassuringly. "I want this to be as special as you hoped it would be. If you need us to stop so you can catch your breath, just say so. And at any time, if you want to end the evening, say that, too. I won't be angry or upset."

She gave him a quick nod but was determined to see this through.

"Come sit with me."

He took her hand and led her to the settee positioned near the window. He sat and guided her down sideways onto his lap. His arms eased her closer and he placed a gentle kiss on her brow. "How would you like to take your lessons? Do you wish to be nude, partially dressed, or remain fully dressed?"

His closeness, faint brushes of his lips against

her ear, made it hard to think, and even more difficult to form speech.

He kissed her then, deeply, thoroughly. The world spun. Her senses soared. After a few more moments he drew his mouth away, and whispered heatedly, "Shall I strip you bare so I can kiss every satin inch of you?"

His voice scalded her, and when he leaned her back against his rock-hard shoulder and took her nipple into his mouth, the temperature shot higher. Her thin cotton blouse and shift were no barrier to his mouth's heat. Crooning, she arched to give him more, and he drew her in deeper, his fingers plucking and circling its gem-hard twin.

"I need an answer, *cheri.*"

No matter how wanton he made her feel, this was her first time with a man. She wasn't bold enough to be nude, even partially, so she somehow managed to reply, "Dressed."

"Okay, we'll save nude for another time." He ran a finger down her buttons. "I'm going to open these though, okay?"

Pulse pounding, she nodded.

"But first, I want more of this gorgeous mouth."

He kissed her for what seemed like endless, soul-firing moments. He tutored. She learned.

His tongue tasted hers. She tasted his. He brushed his softly bearded cheek over hers and she savored the feel. He slid searing kisses over her jawline and the bare skin above the high neck of her blouse, and she gasped softly.

True to his word he worked her buttons free, kissing each small patch of exposed skin along the way. His tongue dallied with the hollow of her throat, and his mouth traced a lazy searing path against the top edge of her shift. He eased the cotton aside and for the first time in her life, a man took her bared breast into his mouth and she tightened with a soft cry.

"Small and perfect, just like you." He bit her with gentled teeth. The sensations crackled like lightning. He lowered the other side and treated the twin to the same gasp-inducing feast. He spent an inordinate amount of time leisurely going back and forth, while she groaned, and arousal pulsed between her thighs. His big hand slid her skirt up and down her leg, mapping its length with his heated palm, while the storm of passion buffeted her like the powerful winds of the storm outside.

"Shall I bring you to pleasure, *cheri*?"

She didn't know what that meant, but she was on the edge of something bright, dizzying, and new.

He recaptured her mouth in another searing kiss, and the hand that had been languidly moving her skirt slipped beneath and moved between her widened thighs. When he circled his fingers over the damp heat there, she shattered and cried out.

Drake wanted to immediately take her to the bed and fill her virgin body with as much of himself as she could take. But he couldn't. She wasn't his. Bringing her to pleasure had him so hard, he'd probably never walk again. As she soared on the wings of her orgasm, he helped bring her back to herself with soft kisses on her mouth, and circling caresses. Hearing her breathing slow to a nearly normal pace, he kissed her again, then drew back. "How was that?"

"Oh my," she replied, breathlessly.

"No desire to recite the alphabet?"

"Not even a letter."

"You're a very passionate woman, Valinda Lacy." Having gotten not nearly enough of her, he languidly teased his tongue over a tempting, still-damp nipple, while his fingers between her thighs continued to slide and stroke. "Made enough memories?"

Her moan hardened him further. She was wet and so soft, the urge to taste her there was strong. He forced himself to recapture her mouth instead. She was not his, so he regretfully chose to leave that initiation to her husband.

But that didn't mean he'd deny her more pleasure. Her hips rose in response to the carnal invitation his touch offered. He boldly eased a finger partially inside and began a rhythmic in-and-out that caused her strangled cry to ruffle the silence.

For the rest of the night, while the storm raged outside, passion made them lose track of time. He sucked, she arched. He nibbled, she gasped. When they were finally sated, he knew he should get her back to her room but glancing down he found her asleep. Appreciative of his own memories, he kissed her brow, made himself comfortable, and closed his eyes with her in his arms.

Chapter Eleven

$\mathcal{G}$ood morning."

Drake opened an eye and saw his brother Archer standing by the door, arms folded, amused curiosity in his eyes. In Drake's lap, Val stirred. Seeing their visitor, she startled and quickly turned her back to redo the buttons on her blouse, while Drake glowered at his sibling for his presence.

"You two look comfortable."

"Go away," Drake growled.

"I will in a minute. Just wanted to let Valinda know her intended and his business partner are downstairs."

Panicked, she scrambled to her feet. "Will you tell them I'll be down shortly?"

He nodded.

Before she could hurry off, Drake caught her

hand and met her eyes. He placed a soft kiss on her fingertips and released her. She rushed out.

Drake's eyes stayed on the open door then settled on Archer's face. "Didn't Mama teach you to knock on a closed door?"

"I did. Knocked on her door, too. No response from either. Imagine my surprise finding her here. What the hell's the matter with you?"

Drake stood. "Stay out of my business."

"Drake—"

"Nosy and deaf," Drake said, cutting him off.

Archer sighed. "Okay. I just hope you know what you're doing."

"I don't, but thanks for the good wishes."

Archer shook his head, turned on the heels of his expensive boots, and left him alone.

Drake ran his hands wearily down his bearded face and headed to the bathing room.

In her room, Val studied herself in the mirror. Her eyes were red from lack of sleep, her hair a mess, her lips kiss-swollen, and she needed a long soak in the tub to make herself right again, but she had no time. When had Cole arrived? And what had Archer thought upon finding her asleep in his brother's lap? She had no answers. All she knew was she needed to hurry and make herself presentable to keep Cole from waiting any longer.

When she entered the parlor, Cole and his business partner, Leonard Carson, both smiled. Lenny stood. Cole, aided by his cane, did the same. He opened his free arm and she stepped into the embrace, hugging him tightly. "So good to see you, Cole."

"You, too, Val."

She shared a hug with Lenny and then gestured for them to retake their seats. She hazarded a glance Archer's way as he stood by the windows, and he gave her a smile which made her feel better. "When did you arrive?"

"Last night at the height of the storm. A hack driver gave us the name of Archer's hotel. Imagine our surprise when we told him why we were in New Orleans and he mentioned you were staying with his mother."

"She's been a blessing."

Cole looked confused. "What happened with the nuns? Weren't you staying with them?"

She gave him a quick summary of her housing woes and how she came to be at Julianna's.

Cole asked, "Is she here, so I can thank her personally for offering you a haven?"

"She and her husband are in Baton Rouge. They'll be back in a day or so."

"So, you're here alone?"

"No, her cook is here, but left yesterday to see

to a sick relative. Archer's brother Drake is here, too."

At that moment, Drake entered the parlor. His eyes and manner were distant as he crossed the room and extended his hand to Cole. "Drake LeVeq."

Cole took his measure as they shook hands. "Coleman Bennett."

Drake and Lenny shook as well before Drake took up a position over by his brother. Arms folded, he glowered at them like an angry sentinel. She caught Cole's small show of surprise and the way he turned to Drake as if re-evaluating him. He and Lenny shared a glance before Cole swung his attention to her. Guilt flared inside. She wanted the scowling pirate to leave. She shot Archer a quick look, saw him sigh and shake his head at his brother's actions. Knowing there was nothing she could do outside of yelling at him to be nice, she pasted on a bright smile, and said, "So, tell me about Paris."

Cole, never one to be intimidated, asked the LeVeqs, "Do you mind if we visit privately? I know this is your mother's home, but—"

Archer replied, "Of course not. Come, brother, let's see what we can find to feed you in the kitchen."

He'd left Drake little choice, so Drake inclined his head. "Enjoy yourselves."

When they exited, Val relaxed but saw Cole's unspoken questions. Rather than field them, she said, "So, Paris. Did you find an investor?"

IN THE KITCHEN, an exasperated Archer said, "You really don't know what you're doing, do you? Am I going to have to tie you up outside until Mama and Henri get back?"

Drake glared and set a skillet on the stove. "I think I'm losing my mind."

Archer said flatly, "She's not yours."

Raimond had pointed that out also. "I already have one Raimond in my life, Archer. I don't need two."

"What you need is to take your lovesick self home and let her figure out her future alone."

"I'm not in love."

"Lust-sick, then."

Ignoring that, Drake cracked eggs into a bowl, pulled the cream from the cold box, and poured some into the eggs. He wondered if Valinda was hungry. She hadn't had breakfast, but because of the way he'd acted out there, she'd probably punch him if he disturbed the reunion to ask, so he left the thought alone. "Have you eaten?"

Archer nodded.

He added a pot of grits to the stove, then pulled out the leftovers from last night and added helpings of that to the growing number of items on the stove.

Archer cracked, "You're never going to get married. There's not a woman alive who'll cook that much every day."

In the breadbox, Drake found the last of the baguettes Little Reba baked yesterday. "Have you noticed that I'm doing all this alone? There are also people you can hire called cooks."

Once everything he planned to eat was ready, Drake filled up his plate, and he and Archer went into the dining room. "Are you taking Bennett and his friend back to the Christophe?" Drake asked as he began in on his meal.

"Unless you'd prefer to."

"If you have work to take care of, Valinda and I can do it. No sense in you wasting away your morning." He and Archer may have been going back and forth, but they were still brothers who looked out for each other.

"I do. Roudanez and some of the other news-papermen are having a dinner this evening. I know the staff can handle things, but I want to be there for the preparations in case I'm needed. However, I'll stay if you plan to drop the man in the swamp."

"I promised Valinda I'd be nice. I just hadn't planned on sharing her this morning." And he hadn't. He'd been looking forward to a nice quiet breakfast with just the two of them. "Go on. I'll take care of her precious intended."

Archer smiled. "Try not to further embarrass your lady."

"She's not my lady, remember?"

Archer gave him a brotherly pat on the back and exited.

IN THE PARLOR, Valinda listened to Cole and Lenny talk about their trip to France, the sights they'd seen, the people they'd met. It sounded like a wonderful experience, but the main question remained. "Did you find an investor?"

Cole and Lenny smiled.

She laughed. "Quit teasing me and tell me."

Cole replied, "We didn't, but we did find someone willing to sell us his newspaper, along with his presses and the shop he runs it out of."

Surprise filled her face and voice. "Oh my goodness. That's wonderful."

"He's elderly and wants to step away from the business. The price he quoted is a bit more than what Lenny and I can scrape together right now, but he's willing to wait for the rest."

Lenny added, "The fact that Cole and I have

actually published a newspaper was in our favor. He's had a few people interested in his operation, but none had ever put out a paper before."

Cole continued, "He said the paper has subscribers all over California, and if that proves true, we should be able to turn a profit soon and to pay off what we still owe him."

Val paused. "California?"

"I know that isn't what we initially planned but we can't pass up this opportunity."

Val looked between them. Their excitement was evident, and she was pleased that they'd found such an excellent prospect. But California? "I was hoping to convince you to start a paper here in New Orleans."

They stilled, and Cole scanned her features. "You like it here, I take it?"

"I do. Very much. The situation for people here is so dire, I'd like to stay and help. I know we agreed to marry, but I'm not sure about California, Cole."

"Does Drake LeVeq figure into this, Val?"

Lenny said, "He looked like he wanted to toss us both into the nearest gutter."

Ducking the question, she replied, "He's descended from pirates. I'm hoping he can be cured."

Cole chuckled.

She then told them how she and Drake met. At the end of the tale both men were angry.

"And none of the men were brought up on charges?"

"Not as far as I know."

Cole said, "I'm glad he came to your rescue. But why would you want to stay here after that?"

Lenny expressed equal concern. "Even the Paris papers were filled with stories of the racial violence here, Val. This isn't a safe place."

"The country is full of racial violence. No matter where you go you can't escape it. Remember the Draft Riots at home?"

Their faces said they did.

She cared for Cole, and she cared for Lenny because of their affection for each other. But was she willing to pack up and move across the country now that she'd lived here on her own? Being in New Orleans with its long history of ambitious women of color like Julianna had shown her that she didn't need the societal stamp of a husband to achieve her goals. Having worked beside Sable, she knew how much work needed to be done and she wanted to do her part in hopes of making a difference. But could Cole and Lenny succeed without her being Cole's wife?

"How long are you planning on staying in New Orleans?"

"We'd hoped to scoop you up and be on a train heading west in the morning," Cole replied. "The two of us and the paper's owner sailed home on the same ship. We told him we'd meet him in San Francisco. Travel could take a month or more."

"Oh."

"We have time to wait if you need a few days to think about things. And maybe we'll learn what you see in this hot humid place."

"The weather is truly horrid. I'm told it'll be markedly worse as we get deeper into the summer months." She eyed them for a few thoughtful moments. "Let me think about what I want to do, and I'll let you know. I also promised Julianna I wouldn't leave while she was away, so if I do decide to go west, it won't be until after she and her husband return."

"Fair enough," Cole said. "If you decide not to join us, I'll be sad about not having you bossing me around, but I'll understand. Lenny and I will muddle through. Men like us have been doing so since the beginning of time."

Cole had shared his attraction to men with her when they were adolescents, and she'd guarded his confession like a dragon did its horde. He and Lenny met during the war. Val didn't claim to understand the hows and whys of their bond, but she cared for Cole enough that posing as his wife so the two men could be together while she sidestepped her father's choice of a husband had been an easy decision. Now, everything was up in the air, and, yes, Drake entered into the equation as well.

Archer stepped into the room. "Excuse me for interrupting. I'm returning to the Quarter. Would either of you like to go with me? If not, Drake's offered to drive you when you're ready."

Lenny stood. "I'll go back with you, Archer." He looked to Val and Cole. "You two talk. Me, I need more sleep. Cole, I'll see you later."

After Drake's earlier show of pique, Val wasn't sure how she felt about him being responsible for getting Cole back to the Christophe but decided to worry about it when the time came. "Thank you, Archer."

As he and Lenny exited, Val wondered where Drake might be, but turned her attention to Cole. "How's your leg?"

He looked down and rubbed the knee slowly. "Aches. Between the long ocean crossing, the train ride, and the humidity here, I probably should've gone with Archer, too. It needs rest."

He'd received the injury while fighting with the United States Colored Troops at the Battle of New Market Heights. Lenny had been a corpsman in the hospital where he was taken to recover. She was glad Cole hadn't been among the hundreds of men killed that day. However, he'd need the cane for the rest of his life.

He asked, "If you do decide not to accompany us to California, what will you do about your father?"

He brought up a question that was looming in the back of her mind like a threatening storm. "I don't know, but I won't be married off like Caroline. Seeing her so unhappy makes my heart ache."

"He's going to insist on you marrying though, and if you tell him no, as I know you will, he'll be on the first train heading south."

It was an apt prediction. Harrison Lacy was convinced his daughter's rebellious ways could only be cured by a husband's firm hand. He'd grudgingly consented to her marrying Cole because he worked for Cole's father and didn't want to jeopardize his employment. If Cole was no longer in the picture, he'd declare it within his rights to choose a replacement, and demand she meekly agree. The thought was infuriating, and admittedly, something she didn't want to think about.

They spent the next hour rehashing his trip to Paris, talking about his parents, and reminiscing on their shared past. Once they were done, he eyed her for a long moment before saying, "So you never did answer my question about LeVeq. Do you have feelings for him?"

She'd hoped he'd let the question lie, but he knew her better than anyone.

"You know you can be truthful with me, Val. We hatched this marriage scheme to cover for me and Lenny, but I won't have you sacrificing your chance to have what we have out of a sense of loyalty to us."

She thought for a long moment before asking, "What is love, Cole?"

He gave her a small smile. "Missing them when you're apart. The joy in waking up each morning and knowing that person is there, and how blessed you are to be given another day together. Wanting the best for them and them wanting the same for you. It's many things, Val, both large and small."

She let that fill her mind and heart.

"I want you to be happy, Val. You've always wanted to conquer the world. Love with the right person makes us stronger, not weaker. I hope what I've said helps?"

"It does. Thank you."

Although Cole had been doing his best to conceal the pain from his injured leg, she could see it in his furrowed brow and his tightly set jaw. "Let me find Drake so he can get you back to the Quarter. You need to rest."

He didn't argue. "I'd appreciate that."

She rose from her chair. "Be right back."

She found Drake seated in the gazebo with a cup of coffee. When he glanced up at her approach, she was flooded by memories of their passionate night.

"If you've come to scold me, you've every right," he said to her.

"You promised you'd be nice."

"I did, and I apologize. First, Archer woke us up, then you ran out to see to your guests. It wasn't how I'd envisioned our morning."

The gentleness in his tone touched her and she found his disappointment endearing, even if he had acted like an angry pirate. "Will you drive Cole back to the Christophe? His leg is paining him."

"Of course. Have you eaten?"

"No."

"I left you some food on the stove. We can go after you're done."

She wanted to protest taking the time to eat. The sooner Cole returned to his room, the sooner he could take the weight off his leg, but arguing would only delay the journey as well. "Okay. I won't be long."

He stood. "In the meantime, I'll go apologize."

As he loomed above her, she smiled. "Thank you." She knew from what she saw in his eyes that he was going to kiss her. When he did, it was soft, sweet, and satisfying. He drew back and ran a bent knuckle slowly down her cheek. "Come find us when you're done."

WHEN DRAKE ENTERED the parlor, he saw Cole tense. "I came to apologize for my rudeness earlier. My mother raised me better."

"Valinda said she's looking for a cure for your pirate blood."

Drake chuckled. "As far as the family knows, it's incurable. She and I will drive you back once she's finished breakfast. She'll be with us shortly."

"I don't mean to impose."

"You aren't imposing," Drake assured him.

Cole gestured. "Then sit, if you would. It'll give us a chance to talk. Unless you have something else to do."

"I don't." Drake sat. In a way, he envied the man for being her lifelong friend. He knew her in ways Drake might never know.

"So," Cole began. "How long have you been in love with her?"

Caught off guard, Drake studied Cole's lean face with its close-cropped beard and fearless brown eyes. "What makes you think I'm in love?"

"Just a guess. But what man wouldn't be? Val's smart, intelligent, beautiful. Has a pretty wide rebellious streak though. Never met a rule she didn't challenge."

"She told me her father calls her a hellion."

"Among other things. If she decides to stay, he'll be someone you'll have to contend with. He's been trying to put a bridle on her for as long as she and I have been friends. Don't let him."

Drake heard the undercurrent of steel in the last three words. "Did she tell you she's staying?"

"Not yet, but I think she's made up her mind. She's just trying to let me down gently. She likes New Orleans."

"We enjoy having her here. She and my mother get along well."

"You didn't answer my question about loving her, but that's okay. It's really none of my business after all. I just want her to be happy and cherished the way she deserves to be.

Lord knows her father isn't going to care about that."

Drake hadn't met her father, but judging by Cole's assessment, he was already not liking the man.

Cole continued, "When he learns she and I are no longer engaged he's going to come to New Orleans to take her home. Again, don't let him."

Drake nodded. "A stellar man in your eyes, sounds like."

Cole laughed. "Does it show?"

Drake had been prepared not to like Cole Bennett. Valinda had called him a good man, and Drake now understood why. "Know that I will do everything within my power to ensure she's safe and happy as long as she's here."

"I believe you. She told me about the attack and your role in her rescue. Anything happen to the men?"

"Other than my breaking one's face, no. They're soldiers. I know their commanding officer. Their behavior won't matter to him."

"Pity."

Val joined them. "Are we ready to depart?"

Drake said, "I'll get the buggy and meet you out front."

Outside, Drake sat behind the reins and

watched Cole lean heavily on his cane as he made his way. His wincing showed the pain he was in and Drake wondered if he'd been crippled all his life. It would be rude to ask, so he saved the question for when he and Valinda were alone.

Valinda said, "Cole, you take a seat up front. I'll sit in the back." The concern and worry on her face showed how close she held him in her heart. Drake tried to convince himself he wasn't bothered by it, but he again envied their bond.

Once everyone was inside, Cole, breathing heavily from the exertion, leaned back against the seat. "On days like this, I wish I had let the surgeon take my leg."

Drake looked over.

"I was at New Market Heights," Cole volunteered. "The bone in my leg was shattered in the shelling."

It was not the answer Drake had been expecting. He got the buggy moving and turned it towards the Quarter. "You men fought bravely that day," he told Cole.

"The generals weren't sure we'd fight, but we did and well."

"Fourteen Medals of Honor were awarded, if I remember correctly."

"Yes. Well-earned, but when the majors tried

to reward the honorees with raises in rank, the War Department refused."

Drake knew about the insulting episode.

"Did you fight?" Cole asked.

"I did. First Native Guard, then First Corps d'Afrique. In '64, the Army moved us into the USCT 73rd but by that time, maybe only 100 of the original thousand who'd volunteered were still in the ranks."

From behind him, Valinda leaned forward to ask, "Why so few?"

"They stripped our superior officers of their rank and replaced them with Whites who hated us. Throw in bad food, terrible conditions, and many men simply left their posts and returned home."

Cole added sagely, "But without the men of the race, the Union wouldn't have succeeded."

Drake agreed, and decided yes, he liked Cole Bennett, very much.

Their journey to the Quarter was slow. Last night's rain left the roads a muddy mess, and twice Drake had to get out and push the buggy's wheels out of the mire. As they entered the streets of the Quarter, Cole stared around at the thick traffic and the wealth of humanity on the walks. "I'm amazed at how busy it is here. I thought New York was crowded."

"Yes. Even after the sun goes down."

They came up on a man riding a cow, and the look on Cole's face made Valinda laugh. Cole asked, "People ride cows here?"

Drake smiled. "They ride whatever they can."

"Cows have been known to roam the streets back home, but no one rides them."

They eventually made it to the Christophe.

Cole slowly descended to the walk and as Valinda got out and joined him, Drake said, "I can bring Valinda in tomorrow if you want to visit with her again."

"I'd like that."

Valinda flashed him a smile, letting him know how pleasing she found his offer. "How about lunch?" she asked her friend.

The two decided on a time, and Drake said to Cole, "My mother is going to want to celebrate you and Leonard being in town, so plan on staying for at least the next two days. She'll be very disappointed if she doesn't get to meet you."

Valinda said, "The LeVeqs seem to celebrate everything under the sun."

Cole replied, "Val and I talked about my staying here for a few more days and I haven't been feted for anything lately, so I look forward to whatever your family has in store."

Valinda said, "Go on in and rest up." She hugged him and placed a parting kiss on his cheek. "I'll see you and Lenny tomorrow."

After they watched him make a slow walk to the door and disappear inside, Val rejoined Drake on the buggy seat. "I like your friend," he told her.

"I knew you would."

Drake turned the buggy towards home.

As they left the congestion on Canal Street, Valinda said, "Cole and Lenny are going to take over a newspaper in California."

He listened while she shared the details. He admittedly didn't care for the idea of her leaving. It wasn't his place to pressure her into doing what he wanted though, so he kept his opinion to himself. It was her life.

"Are you going to join them?" he asked, hoping his concern couldn't be heard.

"I don't know. The thought of moving west doesn't thrill me. Having to start over again. Finding a place to live and looking for a teaching position. Maybe I'm wrong, and everything will fall into place, but—"

"But?"

She shrugged. "I like it here."

"Did you and Cole discuss the possibility of you staying?"

"We did and he's leaving it up to me. He wants me to be happy."

"You could always go out and visit him in California."

"True."

He knew she was conflicted, but he wasn't. He wanted her to stay. With him. "If you do decide to stay, what will that mean for your engagement?"

"It would end. He and Lenny will go on with their lives and I'd go on with mine."

He turned to her. Drake hadn't answered Cole's question about whether he was in love with Valinda, but he was. The possibility of her ending her engagement and being free to court and, yes, marry made him want to yell with joy. But he kept that from his face. The decision still rested with her.

"I haven't decided yet though, so we'll see what happens."

LITTLE REBA WAS in the kitchen when they returned.

"How's your sister?" Drake asked.

"So-so. She fell stepping off the streetcar and twisted her ankle very badly. Doctor wants her to stay off it for a few more days. My cousin Renee is going to help out until she's up and around."

"Good to hear."

Reba said, "Your friend Hugh stopped by looking for you. Said to tell you the cars are at your place."

Drake's eyes sparkled with glee. "Thank you." He turned to Valinda. "I have a surprise for you."

"And it is?"

"A surprise."

Reba said, "Be careful of those LeVeq surprises, Valinda. Growing up, Beau brought me a surprise once. Turned out to be a two-headed frog."

Valinda laughed and asked Drake, "Is it a frog?"

"No." He gave Reba a look.

She laughed, and Drake turned back to Valinda. "Let's take a ride over to my place and I'll show you."

"I'd like to see a two-headed frog."

He grabbed her hand. "Come on."

They got back in the buggy. He wondered what she'd think of the cars.

"Is seeing the house you're building the surprise?"

"No, but the surprise is on my land."

"You built your tree house."

He scanned her curious face and he noted

how much joy it gave him. "No, and you aren't going to guess correctly, so just sit back. We'll be there shortly."

She offered a mock huff and sat back.

He smiled.

As they turned off the road onto his land, he wondered what her reaction to his house would be. When he initially gained his portion, the entire fifteen acres had been covered with trees as far as he could see: live oaks, pecans, hickory. And because of the nearby waterways, there were egrets and pelicans, turtles, frogs—none with two heads as far as he knew—a variety of fish, and, yes, alligators.

His workers were on the job. Some were putting the bricks on the kitchen, while others worked on planing and sanding the oak needed to complete the house's floors.

"This is a pretty piece of land, Drake."

"Thank you. I like it, too."

He saw her viewing the men and the activity. "Would you like a tour once the surprise is revealed?"

"Yes."

All day long he'd been wondering when he'd get to kiss her again. The quick one they'd shared earlier only whet his appetite for more. He was still grumpy about having their morning interrupted, but having gotten to spend this time with her was a boon he wasn't going to cry over. "Will you have dinner with me this evening?"

"Depends on whether I like the surprise."

He shot her a look.

She chuckled in response. "Yes. No matter the surprise. Dinner together would be fine."

Were it up to him, they'd have dinner together every night, and breakfast, too, but he reminded himself that she might not stay.

Seeing his foreman, Solomon Hawk, walking to meet them, he stopped the buggy and waited for him to approach.

"Valinda, this is my foreman, Solomon Hawk. Sol, Valinda Lacy."

"Pleased to meet you, ma'am."

"Pleased to meet you, too, Mr. Hawk."

Drake said, "I'm told Hugh's been here and brought something."

"Yes. Had him put them in the stand of pecans over there. Figured having them in the shade would be best."

Drake nodded. "Okay. We'll be back shortly. Thanks."

"Nice meeting you, Miss Lacy."

"Same here."

Drake drove the short distance across the

cleared land to the spot Solomon indicated and stopped. He came around to hand her down and said, "This way."

He escorted her to where the cars sat under the shade of the pecans and said, *"Voilà."*

"This is the surprise?" she asked skeptically, taking in the two listing, broken-down boxcars.

Drake wondered if she might think the idea insane. "I figured I'd fix them up and turn them into classrooms."

She stared at him for a long moment, turned her attention back on the cars, and walked over to take a closer look. "How long do you think it might take to get them ready?"

"A few weeks."

She peered inside, surveyed the interior a short while longer, and said, "This is really a good idea, Drake."

Relief filled him.

"I could put the children in one, and maybe adults in the other. What do you think?"

"I think whatever you do will be up to you. When Hugh told me about the cars, your request for a space to teach came to mind."

While she continued to scan them he said, "Hugh has access to more, so my plan is to use some of the salvageable wood from those to make the repairs on these. We can saw out a couple of windows in the walls, so it won't be so dark. Add some shelves, benches for the students to sit on. Make you a desk if you want one." He stopped. "Why are you crying?"

Her eyes were full of tears. "This is the nicest thing anyone has ever done for me."

He eased her into his side and draped an arm across her shoulders. "Does this make up for my rudeness to Cole?"

"Yes. It makes up for everything. All the disappointments and the setbacks. I can actually teach in these." She wrapped her arms around his waist and hugged him tight. "Thank you, so much," she whispered. "So much."

She drew back and looked up. "This is so much better than a two-headed frog. And you know what else?"

"What?"

"This seals my decision. I'm staying in New Orleans."

Drake wanted to howl his joy. "Then let's get these cars ready for your students."

He slid a finger over her cheek then over her mouth. He kissed her slowly, fully, letting the sweetness of her fill him. That she didn't believe in love made the prospect of courting her challenging, but he'd go slowly, even though patience was not one of his virtues. Reluctantly drawing away, he took her hand and they returned to the buggy.

Seated beside him as he drove back towards his partially finished house, Valinda couldn't believe he'd done this on her behalf. No one had ever gifted her with something so life-changing, and she was certain it would be, not only for her, but for her students, too. She imagined the subjects she'd teach, the good she'd do, and it was all because of him. Last night, he'd treated her to passion; today, he'd set her on the path to her future.

When he handed her down from the buggy, she got her first up-close look at the house he was building. It wasn't as grand as Julianna's or as large as Sable and Raimond's, but she thought it lovely. It was two stories and twin columns fronted the entrance. Large live oaks lined both sides. The roof was complete and there was glass in the windows.

"What do you think?" he asked.

"It's lovely, Drake. I really like it." She ran approving eyes over the structure.

"Let me show you the kitchen."

Like many kitchens in the South, it wasn't part of the main house. She supposed it had to do with the heat, but she'd never asked. His, like the one at Julianna's, was made of brick and connected to the house by an open-sided breezeway. The kitchen was still under construction, and when they approached, the men laying the bricks stopped work and Drake did the introductions.

From there, she followed him along a cleared path through the oaks to the shed where he did his blacksmith work. Val looked around the cavernous space, taking in the large forge, and the neatly stored assortment of hammers, files, and tongs. "I've never seen a blacksmith work. May I watch you in here sometime? I enjoy learning new things."

"Whenever you like."

She took a last look around, imagining the forge filled with white-hot coals, and him in his apron and mask. "Where to next?"

"I want to show you where I'm thinking of putting the gazebo and the tree house."

She smiled. "Lead the way."

The spot for the gazebo was close to the house, but the land hadn't been cleared yet. "How long will it take you to take down the trees?"

"Not too long, but I want to get the house done first. The gazebo can go in after I catch my breath."

She thought about Julianna's gazebo. "Are you going to put in flowers and shrubs like your mother has?"

"I suppose, but I'll leave that decision up to

whomever I marry. For now, I simply want a spot where I can enjoy a cigar and a glass of cognac after a long day."

Holding his eyes, she thought about him marrying a woman who'd get to share all that he was—his kisses, humor, surprises. She looked away. "Where are you putting the tree house?"

"Come. I'll show you."

They wove their way in and out of pecans, through a small stand of evergreens, and he stopped in front of two massive live oaks that were side by side. "I'm partial to these two."

She scanned the size and configuration of the branches. "They look a bit like the ones holding up the old one at your mother's house."

"You've a good eye. That's what drew me to them." He pointed out the branches he'd use to support the base and the ones needing to be removed.

"This is pretty ambitious, Drake."

"Big ambitions, big man. But it, too, will have to wait until I get the house done."

"How long before you're finished?"

"Barring any problems, another month at the most. Mama and Sable are going to help me pick out the furniture. They know that left up to me, I'd get a bed, a table to eat on, and be done. I'm not one for fancy lamps or settees."

"You'll need a place for guests to sit."

"Not one for guests, either."

She smiled softly. "Your wife will want to entertain."

"Will she?"

His tone and gaze froze her in mid-breath. She managed to whisper, "I'm sure she will."

"Good to know. I'll keep that in mind." After a few heart-pounding moments of silence, he asked, "Did you enjoy yourself last night?"

The memories of their time together rose and filled her with wanting. "I did."

"That's good to know, too."

Val's nipples tightened, and a familiar hum awakened between her thighs. Would he evoke the same reaction in his wife? she wondered. Her eyes strayed to his mouth and memories of its warmth added to her own.

"Do you think my wife would let me undress her in the gazebo under the stars, and enjoy being pleasured in the tree house?"

Her eyes closed, heat whispered through her, as she imagined being the recipient of that pleasuring.

"I'd undress her and tease her small, perfect treasures until they were hard as gems. Think she'd like that, too?"

She whispered, "Stop this, Drake."

He whispered in reply, "*Cheri*, I'm just getting started, but come. Let's drive back to Mama's where you can cool off. It's pretty warm out today."

That he could stand there and look so innocent after verbally reducing her to a bowl of pudding made her want to punch him in the nose even as her smile betrayed her.

"We really need to find you a cure."

"Pirates can't be cured. Many have tried."

"Just lead me back to the buggy."

He held out his hand.

"No. You might be contagious."

He laughed. "See, you are learning to banter."

She pointed firmly, eyes sparkling.

He laughed again and started walking.

She followed, wondering if Sable had any extra clotheslines.

ON THE DRIVE back, Drake looked her way. She'd been silent since getting back into the buggy, making him wonder what she might be thinking. Had he been too forward? Had he offended her? Annoyed her? Embarrassed her? He knew he could be overwhelming at times. "You've been quiet. Are you angry with me, *cheri*?"

"Why would I be?" she asked. There was mischief in her eyes.

Seeing that, he decided to proceed cautiously. "I thought maybe I'd been too forward back there?"

"Because you made me remember the way you undressed me and touched me last night? The licks? The kisses? The way you took me in your mouth?"

Drake hardened like steel.

"The way I sat on your lap with my legs opened so scandalously while you brought me to pleasure?"

He almost ran the buggy off the road.

She gave him a catlike smile. "Why would I be angry, Drake? I told you I enjoy learning new things."

Momentarily speechless, he stared.

She added, "It is warm out today, isn't it?"

Looking into those sultry eyes, it took all he had not to drive into the trees and show her explicitly how truly warm it was. "Are you poking the bear, Miss Lacy?" He was both impressed and amused.

"No, I'm simply answering the bear's question."

"He approves."

"Good."

"Will you still dine with me later?"

"I will."

Approving of that as well, he drove on.

He drew the buggy to a halt at the door. "I'll see you this evening."

"You aren't coming in?"

"I'm going to trade this buggy for Havana and ride home. I need to help with the house, but I'll be back for dinner."

"Thanks again for the boxcars."

"You're welcome, and thanks for the stimulating ride."

She smiled and walked to the door.

He drove away.

Chapter Twelve

$\mathcal{B}$y dusk, Drake was done with his work for the day. He was pleased at what he and the men had accomplished. The bricks on the kitchen were done and the flooring was being laid inside the house. Once that was finished, they'd cover the floors with tarps to protect them while the walls were painted.

He mounted Havana and rode towards his mother's place to have dinner with Valinda. All afternoon, while hammering more iron for the gazebo he kept thinking back to their surprising conversation. Who knew she could be so playfully seductive? She'd turned him to stone. He never imagined she'd repay him with such boldness and flair and he wondered what other surprises she might have in store. At dinner, he hoped to find out.

Hugh and five of his men were on their mounts in front of the house when he rode up. By their grimly set faces, Drake knew something was wrong. "What's happened?"

"Nothing yet," Hugh replied. "But you're going to have trouble tonight."

Drake looked from Hugh to his men. "Come inside."

The story he was told left him cold. Supremacists were coming to avenge the disappearance of Liam Atwater. Hugh had been tipped off by one of his infiltrators less than an hour ago. "You should probably get your brothers out here to help defend this place."

"Everyone's away. The only one in town is Archer."

Hugh blew out a breath. "Okay, then my men and I will stay. I sent a few others to round up as many veterans as they could. Hopefully enough will answer the call and arrive before anything starts. You and the family have stored up a lot of goodwill around here. Let's hope it pays off."

Drake concurred. "Which group?"

"Defenders of the Cause."

Drake was familiar with the name from his work with the Bureau. They were a small, loosely knit band known for terrorizing freedmen traveling on the roads. A few deaths had been attributed to them as well, but none of the men had ever been arrested or charged, as far as he knew. "Coming after me is a big step up for them."

Hugh nodded in agreement. "They took on a new leader a month or so ago. Wears a hood to the meetings according to my man inside."

"Hiding who he is."

"Yes."

"What does he ride?" Many men were known by their horses.

"Nothing distinctive. Different mount each time they meet."

"Smart then. Smarter than the illiterate cowards he's leading."

"Much smarter. Has his members convinced that targeting well-known people like you will scare the freedmen enough to make them think twice about registering to vote for the Constitutional election coming up this fall. It will also avenge Atwater."

Drake mulled over Hugh's words. "New members will flock to them in droves if they're successful. Not a bad strategy. I'd like to know who this new leader is."

"If he's riding with them tonight maybe we'll find out."

Drake had all the information he needed for

the moment. "Okay. There are two women here. Let me speak with them, and then you and I can talk about how best to meet this threat."

Hugh nodded.

"Thank you, Hugh."

"You're welcome. Can't have anything happen to you. Who'd I drink with?"

"Do me a favor. Send one of your men to the Christophe to let Archer know about this. It might make us one man short, but my brother will want to be here."

"Right away."

He went to speak with Reba and Valinda. He'd send them to Rai's house to wait things out with Sable and her children. His brother was still in Lafayette as far as Drake knew, so he prayed the supremacists didn't strike there as well. And then there was his own home. Drake knew it would be impossible to defend both his mother's home and his with the limited amount of men available, but the choice of where to make his stand was easy.

Drake viewed Val's and Reba's solemn faces. Reba had her rifle. She could shoot as well as any man and wasn't afraid to let it be known. "Stick to the woods," he told them.

He gave Reba a tight hug and did the same with Valinda. As he held her against his heart, he sent up another prayer that it wouldn't be the final time.

She whispered, "Keep yourself safe, Drake."

"I'll do my best." They kissed, parted, and the two women slipped out the kitchen's back door and into the night.

An hour later, the moon rose, and men began arriving to help Drake and Hugh defend the LeVeq home. A large contingent of Drake's fellow soldiers from the Louisiana Native Guard appeared first, followed by Hugh's man leading a mounted column of fifteen USCT veterans dressed in their uniforms. In twos and threes came armed freedmen, farmers, and men Drake had never met, one of whom explained his presence by telling Drake, "Miss Sable takes care of our kin. We came to take care of hers."

Emotion clogged Drake's throat.

By midnight, forty men, mounted and on foot, stood illuminated by torches in front of the house. Looking out at them, his heart swelled. They'd willingly put themselves in danger to aid his family and he'd be grateful for their presence for the rest of his life.

The men took up positions in front and back of the house, in the trees lining the road, and on the roof. Everyone was set when five more riders appeared. Leading them were Archer and

Raimond. Drake had never been so happy to see them.

Archer dismounted while Rai stayed in the saddle.

"I just got back and was at the Christophe when Hugh's man came," Rai said. "I need to see to Sable and my children. We'll talk after this is over." He rode off, trailed by the three men.

Archer said gravely, "Thanks for sending word."

Drake nodded. He and his defenders settled in to wait.

It didn't take long. Supremacists often began their nightly assaults by chaotically blowing horns to rouse the victim from sleep and into terror. Drake, hearing the horns, smiled coldly. He didn't know how many men were on the way, but they were more accustomed to riding down on defenseless families. They'd not be expecting forty-plus armed men, many of whom were battle-tested.

Moments later, ten men, faces hidden beneath old yam sacks, rode into view carrying torches and blowing their horns. Over the cacophony, a voice, amplified by a speaking trumpet, called out, "Drake LeVeq. Prepare to meet your maker."

Descendants of pirate Dominic LeVeq did

not give quarter when facing murderers. They didn't negotiate, attempt to placate, or turn the other cheek. When the Defenders of the Cause spurred their horses towards his mother's front porch, Drake yelled, "Fire!"

In the silent aftermath, the sacks were removed from the faces of the dead men lying in the muddy road so they could be identified. Torchlight revealed that nine of the ten were known locals, including Ennis Meachem, son of Liam Atwater's overseer, Boyd. The tenth man wasn't from Louisiana, but Drake recognized him instantly—First Lieutenant Josiah Merritt.

But it wasn't a total victory. The rising wind carried the acrid smell of smoke and kerosene. Drake stilled and looked west. The sky was dull red. Although he was too far away to see the flames, he knew what it meant. Tamping down his emotions, he turned his attention to thanking the men before they rode away. He'd grieve his loss later.

The bodies of the dead were placed in the back of a wagon. Hugh would drive them into town. Drake didn't know how the authorities would respond but there'd been soldiers of both races among his defenders. If he needed them to testify on his behalf, they would.

Before Hugh and his men took their leave,

he and Drake shared a strong brotherly hug. "Thank you again," Drake said sincerely. He'd be grieving more loss were it not for the big Tennessean's help.

"You're welcome. I'll ride over tomorrow and we can talk about rebuilding."

"Okay."

As Hugh and his Heroes of America drove away, Drake looked over at Archer, who said solemnly, "Sorry about your place."

"I knew it might happen. Better my place than here. Mama left the house in my care. Can you imagine how mad she'd be if I let it be burned down by a bunch of sack-wearing *cochons*?"

Archer snorted. "Let's see if she has any cognac."

Drake took one last somber look west and followed Archer inside.

At first light, he and Archer rode out to assess the damage. There wasn't much left of the house he'd built with such devotion and care. The outer walls were a scorched jagged shell and he could see clear through what used to be the front parlor to the trees behind the house. The porch columns, the newly laid floors, the windows, the roof. All gone. He was thankful none of his workers lived on site so there'd been no loss of life. They reined their mounts around to the back. The wood on the kitchen was gone, leaving the blackened bricks intact. His work shed was a total loss, however. He dismounted and toed at the piles of still smoldering ash, unearthing a few of his tools: a pair of tongs, the partially melted head of his hammer. He glanced up into Archer's grave face.

"You'll rebuild," his brother said.

And he would.

Hearing horses, he turned to see a mounted Raimond accompanied by a wagon driven by Sable. With her were Little Reba and Valinda. They got out and offered hugs and condolences.

Holding him tight, Val said, "So glad you're okay."

He looked down into her concerned face and admitted that having her near reduced some of his sadness.

Rai said, "Hugh's man told me a bit on the ride from Archer's. Fill me in on the rest."

Drake relayed the story beginning with Hugh meeting him when he arrived home and ended with finding Lt. Merritt among the dead supremacists.

"Do you think he was the mysterious new leader?" Rai asked when he finished.

"I don't know for sure, but my guess is, yes."

Rai's jaw tightened. "I'll do some asking around. General Pershing needs to be told and he's not going to be pleased hearing Merritt was involved. I'll also talk to Roudanez about putting the incident in his newspaper. People should know the truth."

Drake agreed. If anyone could get the proper people on his side, it was Raimond.

After a few more minutes of discussion, Rai left them to head to the Quarter.

"I need to get back to the Christophe," Archer said.

Drake understood. "I'm going to wait for Sol and the workers and start cleaning up."

Sable spoke next. "Val and Reba, I can drop you at Julianna's on my way home."

Drake wanted Val to stay with him, but knew she'd be having lunch with Cole. He assumed she'd get Archer to take her and bring her back. The way her eyes met his gave him the sense that she wanted to stay as well, but he knew she wouldn't stand up her friends. She said quietly, "Drake, I'll see you later?"

He nodded.

Ready to depart, Archer said, "Take care, brother. Let me know if you need anything."

"Same here," Sable said.

"I will."

Valinda held his eyes until Sable turned the wagon around and headed back to the road.

When his workers showed up to begin their day, they gaped at the destruction. He relayed last night's episode. After they recovered from the shock, they began helping him with the cleanup. What remained of the walls had to be torn down and the surviving planks of flooring pulled up. Once that was accomplished, he'd bring in draft horses and plow under the soot and ash, add topsoil, and level the site for the planned reconstruction. It was going to be back-breaking work, and it wouldn't be accomplished overnight.

True to his word, Hugh showed up as well. Upon seeing the damage, he said, "They did you pretty good."

"I know," Drake replied solemnly.

Seeing a rider approach, Drake went still. It was Boyd Meachem. When he neared, he glared down from the back of his horse. "You killed my boy!"

Drake was not in the mood. "Maybe he should've stayed home last night."

Boyd looked around at what was left of Drake's home. "Men who did this should get a parade."

"Go home, Boyd."

He chuckled. "Hope they get your mother's place, next time."

Furious, Drake dragged Boyd off his horse and held him up as he growled in his face. "Hope you aren't buried with Ennis next time!" He tossed him away and the wide-eyed Boyd landed on his butt in the ash and mud.

Shaken, he stumbled to his feet. "In the old days, you'da been hung for what you just did!"

"Get off my land."

With as much dignity as he could, Boyd climbed back into his saddle. "I won't forget this, LeVeq."

"Daniel Downs's wife and son won't forget, either," Drake countered.

Reining his horse around, he rode away.

As they watched him, Hugh asked, "When will this end?"

Drake replied angrily, "Probably never, because men like Boyd won't let go of the past."

AFTER RETURNING FROM lunch with Cole and Lenny, Val sat out in the gazebo, her mind filled with the happenings of the last day and a half. First there'd been their arrival, followed by the gift of the two boxcars from Drake, and her decision to remain in New Orleans, which meant telling Cole at lunch that he'd be traveling west without her. It saddened her knowing he'd be so far away, but as Drake reminded her, she could always train out and visit. She was certain he'd miss her presence in his life as well, but her decision had been met with his blessing because they'd always wanted only the best for each other.

Breaking their engagement would necessitate a letter home to her parents, and her father would not be pleased by the news. He'd not see her staying in New Orleans as an opportunity to make her own way in the world because he didn't believe her capable. She was a woman after all, and women needed husbands to guide not only their lives, but their thinking. Val didn't need anyone to guide her thinking, proven during her schooldays when she'd spent almost as much time in Mrs. Brown's office being scolded as she had in the classroom. Yet still, he'd want her to defer to his better judgement and do as she was told.

Her saving grace might be her age. She was past the age society considered marriageable and if he wanted to find someone to replace Cole, it might be so difficult he'd leave her be. She didn't mind being labeled a spinster if she had to walk through life alone. There were undoubtedly worse things than being an unmarried woman in charge of her own life, free to come and go as she pleased, free to explore pleasure.

She thought back on her most recent night with Drake and blushed. Well-raised women knew very little about their bodies, but well-raised pirates apparently knew quite a great deal. Which made her wonder if his blood was indeed contagious because bantering with him in the buggy the way she had wasn't anything she'd planned. The words seemed to spring from a place inside she never knew existed. After making her melt the way he had, he'd deserved a heat-inducing taste of his own medicine. In hindsight, she'd enjoyed her boldness and how powerful it made her feel. She guessed a woman wasn't supposed to acknowledge such things but being in New Orleans seemed to be remaking her in exciting new ways. It also seemed to encourage the suppressed parts of herself to rise and walk freely. She looked forward to the future, but not one chosen by her father. With that in mind she picked up her pen and began her letter.

But last night and Drake were on her mind, too. When he told her the supremacists were coming for him, she'd never been so afraid for another person in her life. The mad dash through the woods with Little Reba had been harrowing but paled in comparison to her fear for his safety. Waking up that morning, and not knowing whether her pirate was dead or alive had filled her with dread, but upon seeing him, the dread was replaced by a joy that radiated inside like the warmth of the sun.

Did it mean she was in love? How did a woman who'd had no experience with the word know? Admittedly, she enjoyed their passionate moments, but last night, the reality that she might never see him alive again, hear his voice or see his smile again, had left her heartsick. She thought back on Cole's description of love and decided she probably was.

After finishing her letter and preparing it for the post, she was just sitting down to dinner when Drake came in. He was covered with ash, dirt, and reeking of smoke. "How are you?" she asked softly.

"I've been better." He gave her plate a cursory glance. "I need to get cleaned up."

"I'll wait and eat with you if you'd like."

Some of the tension he'd entered with seemed to melt away. "I would."

"Reba said you'd be starving, so there's enough food in the kitchen to feed all the diners at the Christophe."

"Good. I'll be back shortly."

When he left, she went into the kitchen to alert Reba that he was home, then retook her spot at the dining-room table. Seeing his burned-out house this morning had filled her with such sorrow she'd wanted to weep. He'd taken such pride in showing off the place to her yesterday, letting her know the construction had been a labor of love. And now? The barely masked anguish she'd seen in his eyes after arriving with Sable and Reba had made her want to scrap lunch with Cole and stay with him, hoping her company would lift his spirits. But he'd wanted to begin clearing away the debris, and she didn't want to be in the way. At lunch with Cole and Lenny, she'd debated whether to tell them about last night's incident but decided to go ahead. Both men had been shocked by the story, and again voiced concerns over her decision to stay. She'd explained that turning tail and running away did nothing to help the situation. After all, the residents of New Orleans weren't going to just pack up and leave. They had lives, families, friends, jobs. They'd stay and do the best they could to help things change, and she would do the same.

A short while later, clean and wearing a simple white shirt and dark trousers, Drake entered

carrying a tray that had to be groaning under the weight of the mountain of food piled on the plates. Fried chicken, red beans and rice, yams, a plate of steamed shrimp, and a litany of other gastronomical delights, including a large piece of pie. Seeing her jaw drop, he smiled wryly and took a seat.

Digging in, he asked, "So, what did you do today?"

"Archer was nice enough to send Mr. Doolittle to drive me to the Quarter so I could have lunch with Cole and Lenny. I told them I'm going to stay in New Orleans."

He paused. "And their reaction?"

"They took it well. Since I'm not going with them they're going to leave on the morning train. Do you think we can take them to the train station?"

"Of course. Whatever you need."

"Thanks. I also told them about last night. They're worried about me staying, but I told them running away won't change anything."

"No, it won't."

"How's the cleanup going?"

He sighed. "As well as could be expected I suppose."

"Are you going to rebuild right away?"

"No, I'll wait until the fall when the weather

cools off. In the meantime, I'll take on some paying jobs so I can afford to rebuild. There is some good news though. Your boxcars are fine."

"That is good news."

"Fixing them up will help take my mind off last night."

She saw the shadows cross his face. "I'm sorry, Drake."

He shrugged. "It's the price you pay for demanding justice, I suppose. I'm just glad it was my place and not this one." He took a slow look around the dining room, and said wistfully, "This house holds so many memories: parties, christenings, arguments, laughter. The family would've been heartbroken had something happened to it, especially Mama. My place had none, other than the ones I had from building it. Hopefully the replacement will stand as long as this one and be filled with just as many good memories."

Moved by that, she wondered what it might be like to share a lifetime of memories with him. "That's a wonderful way of looking at it."

"It's all I have." Then, as if needing to change the subject, he said, "Tell me what you plan to teach once the boxcars are ready?"

She mulled the question over for a moment and replied with a request of her own. "When you begin rebuilding, do you think you'd have time to teach some of the students your skills?"

He forked up some gumbo. "Such as?"

"How to use hammers and saws. Lay bricks. Those sorts of thing?"

"I don't see why not. How often?"

"A day or two a week to start. Teaching them to be employable will be just as important as learning to read and write, don't you think?"

"I do."

"Do you think I can convince one of your brothers to teach navigation? Back home, it was one of the subjects the boys got to study along with astronomy."

"I can't speak for them, but you can certainly ask."

"I'd let the girls study the subjects, too, if they wanted. Unlike Mrs. Brown I don't think it would be a waste."

"Who's she?"

"The woman who headed up the school I attended."

"Is that what you were told? That studying such subjects was a waste?"

"Yes. In her words a woman's role was to maintain the household, raise children, and support her husband's endeavors," Val snarled and his smile made her show him hers. "When I refused to learn to knit, she made me sit outside in the snow as punishment."

"Sounds like you and Mrs. Brown crossed swords often."

"There were some days I wished for a sword. I'm not sure who was worse, her or my father."

"What did your mother have to say about all the ruckus you were causing?"

"To stop being such a troublemaker and do what I was told. My grandmother Rose was the only person who took my side. She said I needed to be more respectful though, and she was correct, because sometimes my sassiness was a bit much."

"An example?"

"Mrs. Brown once told us that we women should be content letting men make our decisions, and I told her that if my grandmother had believed that, she'd have spent her life as a slave instead of running away from her owner."

"You had a good point."

"She didn't appreciate it. Made me write 'I will not sass my betters' one hundred times."

"Did you learn your lesson?"

"Yes, I learned that Mrs. Brown was a horse's ass, but I kept it to myself."

"How old were you?"

"Nine? Maybe ten. In truth, my being such a troublemaker was my grandmother's fault. She and my grandfather were staunch abolitionists, and when I was a little girl, she would take me to rallies with her. When my father learned of it, he was furious and forbade it, so to get around him, she'd say she was taking me and my sister to the docks to pick up fabric shipments, or to the market. Because of her I heard speeches by Mrs. Frances Watkins Harper, Philadelphia's Mr. William Still, and the great Mr. Douglass himself. My grandparents also hid runaways in the cellar until they could be passed on to Canada now and then."

"So, you got your troublemaking ways honestly?"

"I suppose I did. When I crossed swords with Mrs. Brown, my grandmother would remind me that I didn't have to grow up and be who my teacher or my father wanted me to be. I could be who Valinda wanted to be."

"Sounds like a wise woman."

"She is."

She paused a moment and thought about how much she missed her grandmother Rose and made a pledge to write her in the next few days. "I wrote my parents about Cole and I breaking it off. They needed to know."

"Maybe your father will surprise you and accept your decision to stay."

She shook her head. "Only if someone has worked a spell and turned him into someone else, but we'll see."

Studying her face, Drake noted the sadness beneath the quip, and it made him want to fix this somehow. He didn't like knowing she had things weighing on her that caused her worry. He brought the subject back to one she could embrace. "What other things would you like to do for your students?"

"When Cole and I were children, a teacher at his school had a glass box in his classroom called the Mysterious Objects and Other Curiosities Case."

"And what was in it?"

"Seashells, rocks from faraway places, interesting, preserved things like lizards, insects, and birds' eggs."

"And you'd like to have one of these boxes."

"Yes. Your brothers sail all over the world. If I ask nicely, do you think they might start bringing me back those kinds of objects?"

"That's an interesting idea, *cheri*. I'm sure they'd be eager to help. In fact, Phillipe already has a collection of rocks from far-flung places. He'd probably lend you some."

Her eagerness was plain. "That would be lovely. I'll ask him."

Drake decided he wouldn't mind spending the rest of his life making her happy.

She said, "The children I'll be teaching will be very much like me as a child, in that they've never ventured beyond a few miles of home. I'd never been outside of New York before traveling here."

That surprised him. "Really?"

She nodded.

"Then traveling alone was very brave of you."

"It was either be brave or stay at home and endure my father chiseling away at my dreams." She went silent for a moment as if thinking that over. "You've probably seen the world, haven't you?"

"A good portion of it, yes. The next time I go, would you like to join me?"

"Where to?"

"Cuba? Spain? Mama has relatives there. We could see the Moorish castles. Or go to France where the LeVeqs are from. Or visit Brazil where Little Reba's people once lived. You pick a place and Rai's ships will take us."

"I'd like that."

He would, too. Were she his, he'd lay the world at her feet. "What else would you like to do that you've never done?"

He watched her think for a moment then responded wistfully, "Stick my bare toes in the ocean. See mountains up close instead of from a tiny window on a train."

Drake never knew listening to a woman's dreams could open his heart this way. "Anything else?"

"When I was young my mother would let me take a blanket outside at night so I could lie in the grass and look up at the stars. But only for a short while, and only while my father was off doing whatever he did away from home with his friends. I'd lie there and look up, and wonder why the stars and moon were there, and what they meant." She brought her eyes to him. "I'd like to do that but be able to lie there for as long as I want. You probably think that's childish and foolish."

"Never, *cheri*." He pictured his land in his mind and searched for the perfect spot for her and her stargazing blanket.

"I want to thank you again for the train cars. I meant it when I said no one had ever given me a more precious gift."

"You're welcome."

"I never knew a pirate could be so generous."

"And I never knew a schoolteacher could be so tempting."

"You're changing the subject."

"I know. Pirates can be single-minded some-times." In truth though, he didn't need her physically, at least not tonight. Their meal and conversation had helped drain some of his rage and anguish. She'd been the balm his spirit had been craving seeing that red sky.

They finished the meal and he asked, "Will you come sit in the gazebo with me?" He wasn't ready to end their time together. "Being with you has helped make a terrible day bearable."

She whispered, "Yes."

So, they sat side by side, and as the moon rose they talked about everything and nothing: favorite books, the dates of their birthdays, the dog the LeVeq boys once had that kept eating Julianna's shoes. They purposefully avoided talking about last night's violence and the fire, and that pleased them both. Val was tell-ing him the story of her sister's first attempt at making an apple pie, and how Caro used salt instead of sugar to sweeten the apples, when snoring sounded. Looking over she found him asleep. After the night he'd had coupled with moving debris most of the day, she was sur-prised he'd stayed awake as long as he had. It took her giving him a few spirited shakes to wake him up.

"I'm sorry, *cheri*. Didn't mean to fall asleep on you."

"It's okay. Come on. Let's go inside."

He ran his hands down his face, got to his feet, and walked with her back to the house. Reba had left a few lamps lit before retiring to her suite off the kitchen, so they doused them and climbed the stairs by the moonlight streaming through the windows. At the top of the staircase, he looked down at her and said softly, "Thank you for the company. I needed it and . . . you." In the silence he drew a slow finger down her cheek, then leaned down and kissed her gently for a long lingering moment. And what was intended to be a parting instead ignited the embers lingering from their last passionate encounter and the kiss deepened. Drake hadn't intended for this to happen but something about her nearness, her scent, the heat of her satin-like lips and skin, rose inside, bringing with it an unrelenting desire to do more than let her go to her room. She was like a balm to the hate that destroyed his dreams, and the lure in her seemed to banish it. He healed himself on her lush mouth then bent low to brush his lips over the sweet curve of her jawline while his hand began to explore her small frame. He mapped her spine, lean torso, and skirt-shrouded hips. He dropped his head to treat himself to an already berried nipple through the thin fabric of her blouse, and her soft gasps hardened him further. Buttons were undone, her shift lowered, and his hot mouth claimed her. He licked and dallied, making her arch for more, and he obliged soundlessly. He worshipped a finger over the skin above her breasts, then fed wickedly on first one and then the other, while boldly moving her skirt up her legs, exposing the plain, knee-length drawers.

Val had lost all sense of time and place. Her entire being was focused on his pleasuring. When he whispered boldly, "Hold your skirt for me, *cheri*," she grasped fabric rucked up around her hips, and wantonly widened her stance to allow him to sensually explore the warm damp vent hidden between her thighs through the slit in her drawers.

"So wet for me," he growled softly. When his finger slid inside her flesh, she welcomed it with a growl of her own and her hips responded to the languid enticing rhythm that began. They rose, sought, and a featherlight croon slipped from between her lips. A second finger joined the first, increasing the heat, and she rode both scandalously. Her orgasm gathered and spread, tempting her to succumb, but that would end the brilliant pleasure he was gifting her with, and she was too greedy for that. He withdrew, circled dewed, masterful fingers over the stiffened pulsing bud that made her woman, before reintroducing with a sweet force that made her shatter and cry out soundlessly against his hard chest to keep from being heard. He eased her back to herself with soft kisses against her lips and gentle strokes between her now-boneless thighs. In the quiet that followed, she opened her eyes. Filled with all he felt for her and still resonating with what he'd made her feel, she leaned up and cupped his bearded jaw. "Thank you for the pleasure."

He turned her hand and placed a kiss in the center of her palm. "Good night, *cheri*."

"Good night, Drake. Sleep well."

THE FOLLOWING MORNING, Val's mood was somber as she and Drake stood with Cole and Lenny at the bustling New Orleans train station. Their leaving felt like a chapter closing on her life. Although this next chapter brimmed with unlimited possibilities, she was going to miss Cole, very much.

"I'm only a train ride away," he reminded her. "Conductor said barring any issues, we should be there in a month or so."

She hugged him tightly. "Godspeed."

She repeated the hug with Lenny.

When she stepped back, Cole told her, "Try and stay out of trouble."

She smiled through her unshed tears. "I'll do my best."

Cole looked to Drake. "Counting on you to keep her safe, LeVeq."

"Don't worry. I'll protect her as much as she'll allow."

Cole laughed. "Spoken like someone who knows her well. Please give your mother our regrets for not staying long enough to meet her. No disrespect intended."

"I will."

The train whistle blew, signaling imminent departure. Val said to them, "Take care of each other."

They nodded. She knew she didn't need to worry but felt better having said it. Even though they were discreet, she was sure there'd been some distressing incidents they hadn't shared with her about navigating life together, so she hoped California would be all they hoped it would be. "Put me on your subscriber list and mail me your first issue."

"Will do."

She watched them walk to the waiting

train and her heart ached seeing the trouble Cole had ascending the stairs to the car. He looked back and waved a final goodbye and Val wanted to bawl. "I'm going to miss him," she said.

Drake gently eased her in against him. "You'll see them again."

She was sure she would. The knowing made her feel a bit better, but the sadness remained. As she and Drake made the walk back to the buggy, the voice of the old fortune-teller whispered inside. *You will lose a love, reject a love, find a love.*

Chapter Thirteen

The next day, when Mr. Doolittle brought Julianna and Henri home from the train station, Drake told them about his run-in with the supremacists and the fire. His mother's hands went to her cheeks and her widened eyes filled with tears. "Oh, Drake. I'm so sorry."

Crying, she opened her arms and he went to her, holding her tight. "It's okay, Mama, don't cry," he whispered emotionally. "That you had a house to come home to was my only concern."

Julianna wept softly.

Looking on, Val, Reba, and Henri wiped at their own tears.

After a few moments, she raised her eyes to his. "You'll rebuild, yes?"

"Yes."

"Good. I'll have to go to confession to seek forgiveness for my feelings about those men, but I'm glad they didn't harm you physically." Henri handed her his handkerchief. Pulling herself together, she asked Valinda, "And your intended. Is he here?"

"No." Valinda explained why and the decision she'd made.

"I'm sorry I didn't get to meet him and his associate, but I'm glad you're staying. I'm enjoying your company." She then greeted Reba and said after, "Henri and I are going upstairs to recover from the train. Can you bring us something to eat?"

"What would you like?"

"Pie. A large piece of pie and coffee."

"Coming right up."

Julianna gave her son a final hug then she and Henri retired to their suite upstairs.

IN THE TWO weeks that followed, the local authorities deemed the deaths of the Defenders of the Cause justifiable under the circumstances, so no charges were filed against Drake and the men who'd defended the LeVeq home. General Sheridan began an investigation to ferret out any Army officers who'd aligned themselves with hate groups and promised to keep Drake and Raimond informed. Determined to change the discriminatory practices of the city's transit system, William Nichols and two White friends boarded a Whites-only streetcar and refused to leave. The police were called, and he was arrested for disturbing the peace by entering a streetcar "set apart for the exclusive right of White persons." Citizens of all races eagerly awaited his trial to see how the court would rule.

While Sable handled the reins, Valinda sat beside her on their way back to Julianna's after yet another exhausting day of distributing food. Valinda had gotten much stronger from handling the heavy bags of produce, but it was still exhausting work. "Can I ask you a question? And if it's too personal, it's fine to say so."

Sable looked over. "Ask away."

"How did you know you were in love with Raimond?"

Sable chuckled softly. "I wasn't at first. He was far too arrogant for my liking. Made me so angry one time, I threw his wet laundry at him. Made me even angrier carrying me through the camp slung over his shoulder like a sack of yams, but that man had more charm than the good lord allowed. When I began missing him dearly when he was away, felt my heart light up when I saw him again, and looked forward to spending every waking moment in his presence, I knew I'd fallen and fallen hard."

Val stared. "And so you married him?"

"Months later and only because Julianna asked if I would."

Seeing Val's confusion, she continued. "After the war, the family needed funds to get back on their feet. There was money tied to a will from a relative but to gain access, Rai, as the oldest son, had to marry. Julianna chose me, unaware that he and I knew each other and hadn't exactly parted friends after I left the camp. In fact, he was furious with me. I never expected to see him again, but there I was walking down the aisle."

"Did he love you?"

"Julianna insisted he did. I was skeptical, but in the end she was correct. Wise woman, our Julianna."

"So you settled your differences?"

"After some disagreements, misunderstandings, and my making him miss his mistress's birthday celebration."

Val found the sparkle in Sable's green eyes intriguing.

"Let me simply say, he paid me a visit on his way to the party and ended up spending the night. With me, his wife." Sable eyed Val and asked, "Are you in love with someone?"

"I think I'm in love with Drake, but knowing nothing about it, I'm not sure what to do. Do I tell him? Keep silent?"

"I've seen the way he acts when he's with you. He's in love with you, too."

"Will he know that I'm in love with him?"

"For all their worldly ways, men can be uncertain about things like this, so at the outset, probably not."

"So, I should stay silent?"

"No two love matches are alike, Val. You'll know when it's the right time, and he will, too."

"That's not very helpful, Sable."

Sable laughed. "I'm sorry, but it's the best answer I can give you. On the other hand, I can't wait for you to be my sister-in-law."

Val was enjoying their growing friendship. Sable was honest, hardworking, and devoted to her causes, but to be sisters-in-law, she and Drake would have to marry and Val's reservations remained. "I'd enjoy being sisters, too, but I'm not so sure I want to marry him, or anyone else for that matter. In the marriages I've seen the women aren't very happy."

"Not all men rule their wives like angry kings."

Being around Sable and Rai, and Julianna and Henri, she was beginning to see the truth in that. "Thanks for answering my questions. I do appreciate it."

"Anytime you need me, I'm here. How are the classrooms coming?" Sable asked, changing the subject.

"They're almost ready." Val had been assisting Drake, Hugh, and the workers with the boxcars' transformation in the evenings. Having no carpentry skills, she made herself useful by hauling old wood, sweeping up, and doing whatever else she was asked. "I haven't been over there in a few days though. You and I have been so busy." And they had, crisscrossing the city, helping with food distribution, gathering donations of clothing and blankets from the churches, checking on the children at the orphanage. Val was also teaching Sable's orphans three mornings a week. Her days were exhausting, but she was proud of the work she was doing and knew her grandmother Rose would be as well.

Sable dropped her off at Julianna's and Val found Drake sitting in the parlor with his mother. They hadn't had much time alone since Julianna's return from Baton Rouge but seeing him always made her light up inside.

"Good evening, *cheri*. How are you?"

She nodded a greeting at Julianna and replied to him, "Tired." She collapsed wearily into a chair. "How was your day?"

"It went well. I've a surprise for you."

She thought back to the last time they'd discussed surprises and Reba's reply came to mind.

"Is it a frog?" she asked, smiling.

He laughed. "No."

Julianna looked confused.

Drake said, "Ignore her, Mama." Attention back on Val he replied, "I'd like you both to ride over to my place for a few minutes."

Julianna asked, "What is this about?"

"Come on. I'll drive."

In truth, all Val wanted to do was eat, take a long hot soak in the tub, and sleep, but she followed him and his mother out to the carriage.

The surprise was a glorious one.

The boxcars, sporting a fresh coat of red paint, stood glistening in the late evening sun. White ribbon ending in a large bow graced the doors of both.

"They're done?" Val asked excitedly, scrambling out of the carriage.

He nodded. "Finished them up late last night. Needed to let all the paint dry before I showed them to you."

"Thank you!" And she threw her arms around his waist in joy.

Julianna asked, "Can we see inside?"

He withdrew scissors from the pocket of his work trousers and handed them to Val. "You do the honors."

Val cut the ribbons. He slid the heavy doors open and gestured them inside. The interior smelled of freshly sanded wood and paint. Awed, she scanned the benches and the cupboards attached to the walls. She didn't know how many students she'd have but the three beautiful pine benches would hold at least five students each. At the front of the room was a lovely desk she didn't know he'd built. Seeing it brought tears. "Oh, Drake. It's lovely."

She ran a light hand over the surface, eyed the drawers on each side of the desk's compact top, and could already imagine herself standing behind it while looking out at her students' eager faces.

Julianna said, "You did a fine job, Drake. A fine job."

Brimming with emotion, Val asked, "How am I ever going to repay you?"

"Just give your students the finest education you can and that will be payment enough."

They inspected the second car. The benches

were a bit farther apart. "Adults will need more room for their knees," he said.

Julianna asked Val, "When will you open?"

"As soon as possible."

"This is very exciting," Julianna said. "Make a list of the supplies you'll need, and I'll help with the purchases."

Val was moved by her generosity. "Thank you." She looked to Drake and her feelings for him filled her so, she had no words. As if he could read her mind, he simply nodded and said, "You're welcome."

Val floated through the drive back to Julianna's house. She thought about lesson plans and compiling the list of supplies she'd need, and all the while her brain kept shouting, *I have a school!*

When they reached the house, Juliana asked Drake, "Are you having dinner with us?"

"No. Hugh's throwing a send-off for one of his men going back to Tennessee."

Val was disappointed that she wouldn't get to spend the evening with him but kept it to herself. They'd have time together eventually.

As she and Julianna entered the house, Reba appeared and said, "Valinda. Wire came for you while you were gone."

Puzzled, Val took the paper and opened it. The message it bore shattered the day's joy.

"Is everything okay?" Julianna asked.

"No. It's from my father. He's demanding I come home." Deflated, she refolded the paper and slipped it into the pocket of her skirt.

"What are you going to do?" Julianna asked.

"Send him a wire back that says no."

Julianna reached out and gave her hand a sympathetic squeeze. "We'll support you any way we can."

"Thank you."

Henri, back from a business appointment, joined them for dinner, but Val had no appetite.

After dinner, Julianna and Henri left for an evening at the Opera House while a gloomy Val sat outside in the gazebo. Once her father received her reply, she was certain he'd come to New Orleans hell-bent on dragging her home. She hated the thought of the shouting match that would follow, but she was not going back to New York. Her school would be opening soon and that needed to be her focus, not wondering how much time she had before he arrived. She blew out a breath and sighed. Maybe she could find a voodoo woman who could turn her into a bird so she could fly away and become herself again once he was gone. Or maybe she could run away and join the circus. That silly thought made her smile. She thought of appealing to her mother for support, but she'd never take Val's side in something so critical, so Val would find no help there. After much thought, she concluded that the only way to send her father back to New York was for her to already have a husband when he arrived. The chances of that were nil, so she'd have maybe two weeks to prepare herself for the shouting match. Hearing footsteps she turned to see Drake step into view. "Hello," she said quietly.

He sat beside her. "What's wrong?"

She took the wire out of her pocket and handed it to him.

He read it. "I see."

"I figure he'll be here in two weeks or less."

"You sure?"

"Once I send him my response tomorrow? Positive."

He gave her a comforting hug. "I'm sorry this ruined your day."

"I am, too."

"Maybe once you show him the school, he'll relent."

"I wish I could believe that." She doubted that would make a difference. He didn't want her to be on her own, especially so far away. That he didn't believe her capable of looking after herself was maddening. "I don't need his hand on my life."

"I know that, *cheri*."

She wished her father did.

"So, if he doesn't relent, then what?"

"Lots of angry shouting and tears, I suppose." She turned to him. "I have a beautiful new school thanks to you. I'm not walking away from that." Drake's generosity continued to fill her heart. He'd made her dream come true. To leave would say his gift meant nothing. "May I ask you something? And please know you can tell me no."

"Are two-headed frogs involved?"

She chuckled. "No. Will you marry me?"

He stilled.

She continued in a rush. "It won't be permanent. Just until my father leaves. If he believes I have a husband, he'll give up and go home. After, we can get an annulment, or whatever we need to undo it." When he didn't readily respond, she said, "Never mind. It's a harebrained idea."

"Maybe not so harebrained, but suppose, just suppose, I want to stay married?"

She froze and searched his face, trying to gauge his intent. "I haven't thought that far ahead. I—I just came up with this idea a moment ago."

"Would you want to stay Mrs. Drake LeVeq?"

"I—don't know. I never wanted a husband."

"I know."

"Well—" she said. "To get you to agree, I suppose I could."

"Your enthusiasm is very encouraging."

"Drake, I'm sorry. I'm trying to save my future and you're asking me trick questions."

"And yours wasn't?"

He had a point. "Never mind. Forget I even asked."

He stood. "I'll marry you if it helps you stay in New Orleans. We'll figure out how to undo it after your father leaves."

The ice in his voice filled her with sadness. "Drake—"

"Let Mama know she's getting a temporary daughter-in-law. I'll see you tomorrow."

Left alone she hung her head. Hurting his feelings hadn't been her intent, but she had, and she felt terrible.

DRAKE RODE OVER to Rai's. Sable answered the door, took one look at his face, and said, "He's in his office."

"Thanks."

Drake knocked on the closed door.

"Come," his brother called.

Drake entered. Rai, seated behind the desk, scanned his face and asked, "What's wrong?"

"Valinda asked me to marry her."

Looking confused, Rai asked, "And you're upset, why?"

"It's temporary."

His confusion deepened. "Okay, start from the beginning."

Drake wasn't sure why he'd come, but for all of Rai's bossy, sometimes insufferable, eldest-brother ways he was usually the one they all sought out when there was a problem, or they just needed to talk something over. When Drake finished the story, Rai asked, "So, are you upset because she didn't jump up and down and say yes, she wanted to be with you until death do you part?"

"Maybe."

"She's looking for a way out of her father's trap, Drake. I know you think the sun rises and sets because you walk the earth, all we LeVeq men do, but one thing Sable has taught me is that sometimes it isn't about us."

Drake's jaw tightened.

Rai said, "I know that's hard to hear but you're in love, brother. Your ego is going to be punctured on a regular basis, and after a while you're not going to mind, because you wake up every day beside the most beautiful thing in your life. A woman who could've chosen any other man in the world, chose you. Would you have been happier had she asked Archer, or god forbid, Beau?"

Drake's eyes shot to his.

"Exactly. Count your blessings. It will work out. Always does. Anything else?"

"No." Drake stood up and started to the door.

Rai said, "Drake."

He stopped.

"According to Sable, Val is in love with you, too. You're a LeVeq. If you can't figure out how to make it permanent, I'm disowning you, and putting your chair at Mama's table up for auction."

Amused in spite of his mood, Drake exited.

DESPONDENT OVER HER rift with Drake, Val was seated at the dining room table preparing lessons for her students when Julianna and Henri returned. "How was the opera?" she asked.

Julianna replied, "The soprano left a lot to be desired, but the Opera House only allows us to attend occasionally so we take advantage of their bigoted largesse when we can."

Val said, "May I speak with you for a moment before you go up?"

"Certainly."

Henri kissed his wife's cheek. "I'll see you upstairs. Good night, Valinda."

"Good night, sir."

Julianna took a seat. "Did something happen while I was away?"

"Yes, I'm going to be a temporary daughter-in-law."

She raised an eyebrow. "Temporary?"

Val explained, adding, "I hurt his feelings with my lack of enthusiasm." Guilt grabbed her, again. "I feel awful."

"Drake may be the biggest and strongest of my sons, but he's also the most tenderhearted. He keeps it hidden because his brothers often teased him about that when they were growing up." She paused for a moment as if thinking back. "When Drake was maybe five or six, he got very attached to the ducklings and piglets we had. He fed them. Played with them. I of course was raising them for Christmas dinner. Christmas Day comes. We're having dinner, and Archer, I believe, made a comment about how delicious Drake's duck friends were. Drake looked down at his plate, looked over at me, and his little face crumbled. He left the table crying. To this day, he won't eat duck."

"Aw."

"His brothers of course howled with laughter."

Val felt so sorry for him.

Julianna added, "He'd named the ducks Josephine and Napoleon." She went silent again before continuing quietly, "When I received word that my Francois's ship had gone down and all hands were lost, I had to tell the boys their Papa wasn't coming home. They took it hard, but Drake refused to believe it. Told me, he was going outside to wait because Papa always came home. He sat out by the road and refused to come in. Sat there for days. All day. All night. He didn't care that it was winter or that it was raining or cold. He knew his Papa was coming home.

"It snowed one of those days. I looked outside and saw him covered and shivering. I made Rai and Gerrold bring him inside. He fought them, kicking and screaming the entire way."

Val saw the sorrow in her eyes. "How old was he?"

"Eight."

Val now had more pieces of Drake to add to the ones that had already woven their way into her heart. "I wish I'd had time to think about his question before answering, but he caught me so off guard. I tried to make amends, but he walked away."

"When his feelings are hurt, he can close himself off, but that big heart of his always reopens. You two will work things out, and for what it's worth, I think your plan to sidestep your father is a good one. What happens after is up to you and my son."

"Would you want me for a daughter-in-law?"

Julianna smiled and stood. "Until death do us part." She gave Val's shoulder an affectionate squeeze. "Good night, Valinda."

"Good night."

Lying in bed, Valinda thought about his question again. Would she remain married to him if it were left up to her? Being around Sable and Julianna showed her that not all marriages had a detrimental effect on a woman's spirit. Julianna had her business interests. Sable did remarkable charity work. Both women seemed fulfilled in both life and love. Could she have that with Drake? Instinctively she knew she could. He was fun, caring, and passionate. He was a man of conviction and honor. He'd supported her aspirations and built her a school. She didn't see him suddenly forbidding her to use it once she took his name. Again, she wished she'd had time to think about his question, so she could've given him an honest, measured response. As it stood, things had gone off the rails and she didn't know if they'd be able to go back to the way they were. She wasn't sure if he'd gone to his room when he left her, but she was tempted to go see, so she could apologize again. However, she wasn't sure of her reception, so she turned over and hoped she could sleep.

Chapter Fourteen

$\mathcal{N}$ow that the boxcars were done, Drake spent the morning riding around the area letting contractors and builders know he was available for hire. They all knew him and his reputation for excellence, so he received a few solid offers. Pleased, he and Havana headed back to his mother's house. On the way, he saw a sign advertising a buggy for sale, so he stopped. The seller, an elderly White woman, answered his knock on the door with a smile. She was a widow and the buggy belonged to her. She'd only driven it to church, she said, and was selling it because she was moving to Biloxi to go live with her son and his wife. As Drake eyed it up close, he liked that it was compact, sported a cushioned leather seat, and that the four spoked wheels were in good condition. Although the leather awning was a bit worn, there were no holes or tears, and it could be lowered or raised depending on the weather. The price she quoted was reasonable. A sturdy even-tempered mare named Penelope came with the vehicle and that pleased him as well, so he paid her what she asked.

With Havana tied to the back on a lead, Drake climbed into the buggy, waved farewell to the widow, and continued the journey home. Between Valinda's teaching and charity work she needed a vehicle. He knew she'd be grateful even if she had frozen like a deer suddenly running up on a gator in response to his question last night. Admittedly, his pride still stung. The talk with Raimond, though pointed, had made him feel somewhat better, but Drake was a LeVeq and the men in his line had outsized personalities most women were dazzled by—except the women who captured their hearts. According to legend, their great-grandmother Clare had cursed Dominic in three languages when he kidnapped her from the British ship, and Sable had given Rai such a run for his money, Drake and the other Brats placed bets on how soon he would lose his mind. Rai claimed Val loved him. Drake wasn't sure whether to put any stock in that or not. If she did, she didn't love him enough to remain his wife and with that in mind, he'd guard his heart.

DRAKE HADN'T JOINED them for breakfast, and although Valinda had been disappointed, she had too much to do to get her school up and running to mope about it.

"Here's the list of items I'll need right away," she said, handing the paper over to Julianna seated behind the desk in her office. She hoped the older woman didn't find the final sum too costly.

Julianna said, "The ink pens and pencils we can get in the Quarter as well as the slates and chalk. The readers we may have to order."

"I know. I can handprint some of the exercises the students can share until the readers arrive."

"May I keep this?" Julianna asked.

"Yes."

Julianna set it aside. "Thanks so much for organizing my office. I can actually find things now."

"Just be sure to put everything back in the proper place so it doesn't get out of hand again."

"Easier said than done, but I'll try. In the next three or four days, we'll shop for your wedding dress."

Val stilled. "Wedding dress?"

"And shoes."

Val looked down at her mud-caked brogans. "I don't—"

"Yes, you do. There will be more than a few wealthy Creole women and their simpering daughters attending the reception and I want them to envy you not only for taking another LeVeq son off the market, but for being the most beautifully gowned woman there as well. I'll get a kick out of seeing their crestfallen faces, so indulge me."

"You're very bad, Julianna."

"I know. It's the pirate blood."

Val laughed. "Then who am I to deny you your fun?"

Her dark eyes glittered with amusement. "I have two of the best daughters-in-law in all of Louisiana."

"Temporary."

Julianna waved her off. "If you say so."

Before Val could respond to that, Drake appeared in the doorway. "Val. Mama," he said in greeting.

Val saw the distance in his face which let her know he was still wounded from last night. She inwardly sighed, wondering what it might take to salve his hurt.

"Valinda, I got you a buggy."

She eyed him, confused.

"Come look. It's outside." And he exited.

Julianna smiled and shooed her out, so Val followed him.

Sure enough, there was a small black buggy parked outside with a dun-brown horse attached.

"This is Penelope," he said, indicating the horse. "Her former owner says she enjoys apples and likes children."

Val walked over and stroked the mare's soft-skinned neck. "How are you, girl?"

"Catch," Drake called.

The tossed apple caught her by surprise, but she snagged it deftly, and shot him a look that earned her a ghost of a smile. Ignoring him for the moment, she fed the mare the fruit, while offering gentle words of welcome and praise. "How long may I use the buggy?"

"It's yours, so until the wheels fall off, I suppose."

She studied him. He was the most generous person she knew, but after last night, a gift like this was the last thing she'd expected. "Drake, I'm sorry about yesterday. I—"

"No apologies needed. It was a trick question. I was wrong to put pressure on you that way. We'll marry and when your father leaves, we'll dissolve it. Henri has a nephew who's a justice of the peace. I'll ask if he can handle the ceremony, unless you prefer a church?"

She shook her head. "A justice is fine."

"When would you like it done?"

"Sometime in the next week to ten days?"

"I suggest sooner as opposed to later. If your father has suspicions and asks around, you want him told that the marriage is real and that it's a love match. No one jumps willy-nilly into an arranged marriage."

Her eyes shot to his.

"Do you think you can pretend we have a love match?"

She cleared her throat. "Yes."

"The reception I'm sure Mama and Reba are already planning will help with the legitimacy, and we'll move all your belongings into my room, since I no longer have a house we can occupy."

She froze.

"LeVeq wives share bedrooms with their husbands."

She was a bit overwhelmed. On the one hand, she was glad he'd thought so far ahead, but on the other hand, she realized, she hadn't thought this through at all.

"I'll add your name to my accounts, so you can draw money when needed."

"That isn't necessary."

"Do you have funds of your own?"

She paused and admitted, "A small amount."

"Then it's necessary."

"Drake—"

"Valinda, if you need to purchase chalk or hairpins or a pair of shoes, you shouldn't have to ask for the money to do so. I trust you not to spend me into the poorhouse, so allow me to help you in this way."

Having no true counter, she let it go. "Okay." She wondered what her parents would think of him and his family. Would they be impressed? Would the ruse of a love match convince her father to return home and allow her to live her life in peace? And what about after? If she had to go to New York for some reason after she and Drake had dissolved the ruse, could she convince him to accompany her? Suppose he married someone else in the interim? How would that sit with whoever he married, and why did the idea of him marrying someone else not sit well, at all? Deciding to stop thinking about the clashing moving parts of her harebrained plan before she lost her mind, she glanced up at his distant bearded face. "Is there anything else?"

"Not that I can think of at the moment."

"I want to open the school the day after to-morrow. Will you help me spread the word?"

"I will. Do you need me for anything else right now?"

She thought to herself, yes, she needed him to accept her apology, so they could go forward, but she refused to beg. She had her pride as well. "No. I'm scheduled to teach Sable's orphans today. Now that I have a buggy, I'll go to the Quarter later and let Eb and Dina know about the school." She had no idea how many students she might eventually be teaching. It could be two—it could be fifty. The freedmen were hungry for education, especially for their children.

"Then be careful on the roads. I'll see you later."

"You, too, and thank you again for the buggy."

As he rode away, she wondered if chucking rocks at the maddening man she intended to marry could be considered an act of love. Blowing out a frustrated breath, she returned to the house for the items needed for her day. After giving Julianna her goodbye, she and Penelope set out for Sable's place.

The eager smiles and confident voices of the orphans as they read lifted her mood, and after sharing lunchtime with them and one of the staff members, her day with them ended.

Sable walked her out to the buggy. "How's Drake? Rai told me what happened between you two."

"Still stone-faced. I've apologized but it hasn't made much of a difference."

"Give him time. We all act like children sometimes when our feelings are hurt."

"I suppose."

"He loves you. You love him. Once this mess with your father is settled, you can work on the problem between you. Do you really believe he's going to come to New Orleans?"

"I do." And the thought continued to nag her like an oncoming headache. "Julianna wants to take me shopping for a wedding dress and is planning a big to-do reception."

"You'll need a dress, and Julianna isn't content if she's not celebrating something or other, and a wedding is special. It'll be fun."

"Not with a glaring groom."

Sable laughed softly. "He won't be glaring, trust me. Rai and I were ready to strangle each other the day before we said our vows, but by the end of the reception—let's just say, we had a very memorable wedding night. You will, too."

Embarrassment burned her cheeks. She'd never talked about the marriage bed with anyone but her mother. That discussion had been quick and apparently quite wrong, considering the way Drake laughed upon hearing about her mother and the recitation of the alphabet.

Sable said, "Didn't mean to embarrass you, sorry."

"No, you're fine. I need to go."

"Okay, but if you have questions, let me know."

Val gave her a tight nod, but then gathered her courage. "Will it hurt?"

Sable seemed to consider her words before replying, "I'm sure it's different with every woman, but I did have some discomfort. Rai took the time to prepare me though, so it wasn't awful or excruciating. He seemed to know more about my body than I and that helped a great deal."

Val thought back on her experiences with Drake. He, too, apparently knew more than she. "I think it's shameful the way society keeps us in the dark about things like this."

"I agree."

Val eyed the woman soon to be her sister-in-law. "Thank you for being so frank with me."

She smiled. "You're welcome. Everything will work out between you and Drake."

"I hope you're right."

That said, she climbed into her buggy and struck out for the Quarter.

Eb wasn't at work, but the woman who answered the back door said he was due in later that evening and promised to pass along Val's message about the school.

At the cigar shop, Mr. Bascom didn't appear pleased to see her. Val ignored his tight face and asked after Dina.

"She's not here."

"When will she be?"

His anger was reflected in the tone of his reply. "I don't know. She and my son are gone."

Val was confused by that. "Gone where?"

"North. The note Quentin left me yesterday said they were going to get married."

Surprise rendered her speechless. She'd been correct in thinking the two had feelings for each other, but to marry? As far as she knew, miscegenation was illegal most everywhere in the United States. Were they bound for Canada? she wondered.

Mr. Bascom continued, "I hired a Pinkerton to track them down and bring him back. I don't care what happens to her."

Val was saddened by that. Bascom, like her father, was determined to dictate the life choices of his adult offspring, but she kept that to herself and said instead, "Thank you for your time, Mr. Bascom," and left his shop.

DRAKE LOOKED UP when Val entered the parlor. He was pleased to see her but because he was guarding his heart, he kept his feelings hidden. Going back to the mechanical drawings he was working on, he asked, "Things go okay with the carriage?"

"Yes."

"Do you need me to unhitch the mare?"

"No. I took care of it. She's been watered and is in a stall."

He was surprised.

As if sensing that, she explained, "Cole showed me how when he taught me to drive because I asked him if he would."

"I can always do it for you."

"Thanks, but it isn't necessary. Is your mother here?"

Her steadfast determination to be self-sufficient was one of the many facets he found admirable about this woman so reluctant to link their lives. Her independent nature was one of the many aspects that endeared her to him. "Mama's gone to visit her friend, Aunt Vi. I believe that's her name. My brothers and I've never met her, but we assume she's one of Julianna's longtime friends. Did you talk with Eb?"

"No, but I left a message with one of the workers. She said he'd be at the hotel this evening. I also stopped in to see Dina. Apparently, she and Quentin have eloped."

Drake was floored. "How long have they been gone?"

"Bascom found a letter from Quentin last night, so less than a day, I'm guessing. He's hired Pinkertons to bring his son back to New Orleans. Said he didn't care what happened to Dina. Reminded me of my father."

The mention of her father brought Drake back to their disagreement.

"What are you working on?" she asked.

"A pump station for a large landowner. He and a group of men are looking to build one in an effort to drain a swamp so they can reclaim the land."

"Is that common here?"

"More and more. The city's expanding and dry land is needed to fuel that growth."

She walked over to view the drawings. "Can you explain what I'm seeing?"

So for the next few minutes he did—pointing out the pump house's structure, the boilers and engine it would need, and how the piping would be laid. He found the questions she asked a testament to her intelligence, another facet he admired. She was positioned by his side. Her nearness made him remember their last interlude, the softness of her skin, the feel of her nipples hardening under his tasting tongue, and how hard he'd been when he finally turned her loose. As if reading his mind, her gaze rose from the drawing to his. The contact lengthened, and it took all he had to not reach out and stroke a finger across the lush petal of her bottom lip. Reminding himself he needed to resist the lure she exuded, he said, "I promised to complete these drawings as soon as possible, so I need to finish them."

"Of course. My apologies for disturbing you."

Her icy exit from the room gave him pause. Since their falling-out, she'd been trying to apologize and his inflated ego had refused her olive branches like a petulant toddler eschewing a nap. Now? He felt a different type of sting. One that said, maybe he should've gotten off his high horse when he'd had the chance. If her steely departure was any indication, his lovely hellion was no longer offering peace. Playing the injured male had just widened the rift between them. If he didn't figure out a way to bridge the divide, she'd dissolve their marriage immediately after her father's departure, and Raimond would auction off his chair two seconds later. He forced himself to concentrate on the drawings, but Valinda remained on his mind.

Chapter Fifteen

Valinda drove onto Drake's land for the first day of school and past the plowed-over spot where the house once stood. Her disagreement with Drake aside, the sight always tugged at her heartstrings and she guessed it always would, at least until a new house filled the space. She was soon distracted by the throngs of people milling around the boxcars and stopped Penelope and stared agape. Small children and gangly limbed adolescents stood with their parents, along with adult men and women, young, middle-aged, and elderly. Some in the crowd were outfitted in their Sunday best, others in well-worn homespun. In talking with students at her old classroom, she remembered them saying they only wanted three things from Freedom: their families no longer forcibly separated, no more working under the lash, and being allowed to educate themselves and their children.

Drake rode up and she whispered emotionally, "Oh my goodness! Look at all the people!"

"They started arriving at first light," he said. "It's quite a gathering."

It was indeed. The newspapers had been reporting on freedmen flocking to schools all over the South, not only to the few still run by the Freedmen's Bureau but those being sponsored by churches, Black Civil War veterans, and even groups of former slaves.

As she urged Penelope forward, a voice called, "Are you the teacher?"

"Yes!" she called back.

As soon as she parked and stepped down, she was surrounded by people wanting to shake her hand and learn her name. She was peppered with questioning about where she was from, if she was born free, and if she could really teach them to read. One man even asked if she was married.

In the end, she gently asked for silence so she could be heard. She gave them her name and asked that everyone form two lines: one for children and their parents, the other for adults.

As they began sorting themselves, Drake

said, "Looks like you'll need help. What can I do?"

"Can you handle the adults? I'll take the parents and children. Write down their names, ages, where they live, if they can read, and what days and times they can attend classes." She quickly retrieved a writing tablet and pencils from her supplies in the wagon. "You can record everything in here."

He headed over to the classroom he'd built for the adults and she sat on the step that led into the one for the children.

At the end of two hours, they had the names of twenty-five children, fourteen parents, nine adult women, and twelve adult men, including two who offered Valinda marriage proposals. Of the sixty names on the list, three could read. Valinda made a note to get in touch with Eb. She hoped his daughter, Melinda, still needed a position because if everyone in the crowd attended classes with any regularity, the school would need another teacher. And there was no reason to think they wouldn't. Every person thanked her, some with tears in their eyes. In response, she fought back tears of her own.

She made a tentative decision to hold classes on Mondays, Wednesdays, and Fridays during the day for the children, and evening classes on Tuesdays and Thursdays for the adults. If any adults needed to bring their children with them, they'd be allowed.

Since today was Friday she announced that there'd be no teaching until Monday because she needed to look over the lists of names, ages, and preferred days of attendance to determine how large each class might be. Many people expressed their disappointment. But so as not to send them home with nothing, she and Drake took the time to write everyone's name on a piece of paper. She asked that when they came to class, they pin the names to the front of their clothing until she learned their faces. Most had never seen their names written down. She watched many of them study the words silently before reverently placing the paper in their pockets.

After everyone departed, Val and Drake took seats in the grass to catch their breath. "Thank you, Drake. I couldn't have done this without your help."

"You're welcome. It was exciting. You're going to be eternally blessed for taking this on, Valinda."

She noted that he no longer referred to her as *cheri*. It was a small thing but pierced her feelings like a thorn just the same. "I hope that blessing comes with a large helping of added strength because this is going to be hard work." She told him about Eb's daughter.

"I'll take care of her salary, if you need me to," he said.

"Some of the parents said they'll be able to pay. I know they can't afford much, but I'm hoping to use those funds to pay her. I've also been thinking about a fund-raiser?"

"Such as?"

"I haven't decided yet."

"Okay, but I can help if needed. I'd like to contribute in some way."

Val wondered if there was a more generous family than the LeVeqs. "Thank you. That means a lot."

"You're welcome. Where are you off to now?"

"Back to your mother's for lunch, then to the Quarter to talk with Eb about his daughter."

"Mind if I ride with you?"

She searched his features for evidence of his intent. His assistance had been a godsend, so to deny such a simple request would be mean-spirited and unworthy of her, so she said, "No, I don't mind."

"Thank you, *cheri*."

She froze. Searching his face again, she wondered what he was about. The eyes holding hers appeared innocent enough, but she sensed something had changed. She couldn't put her finger on it but decided to remain on her side of the fence they'd erected between each other, because her feelings stayed safer that way.

Julianna joined them in the dining room for lunch. After asking about Val's day and being amazed by Val's description, Julianna said, "Val, we don't have time to have a gown commissioned for your wedding, so I've a dressmaker coming tomorrow morning with a few ready-made samples for you to consider."

Val froze with her spoon between her bowl of gumbo and her mouth. The look on Julianna's face was pleasant but also firm, which meant the subject was not up for discussion. "Yes, ma'am."

"I also need you and Drake to be seen together in the Quarter. As we said, if your father decides to investigate the legitimacy of the marriage, we want people to relate the gossip they've heard about how much in love you two are."

The still-frozen Val glanced at Drake whose eyes told her nothing, but she still wondered if mother and son had formed a conspiracy pact. Seeing no way out, Val took the bait and asked, "And how do you propose to accomplish this?"

"I thought we'd start with a shopping trip to supplement your wardrobe."

"My clothes are fine, Julianna."

"No offense, dear, but you're wearing borrowed brogans that once belonged to Phillipe when he was small."

Val cringed at the tart yet gentle rejoinder. A few weeks ago, when her already well-worn slippers became candidates for the trash bin, Julianna offered to buy her a new pair but Val's pride wouldn't allow it. So, she was presented with a pair of barely worn, sturdy brogans Phillipe had outgrown. They fit well and she'd been wearing them since.

"I'll give you the names of a few of the shops Sable and I patronize."

"And what am I purchasing?"

"Blouses, skirts, stockings, shifts. Whatever catches your eye and enough to fill your armoire. Also, keep in mind that as a teacher you'll want to look the part. The students will be expecting it."

Val didn't know if she agreed with that. Her students were coming to soak up what she had to offer their minds. She doubted they'd care what she wore during the process, but arguing with Julianna was always an exercise in futility, so she replied, "Yes, ma'am. When do you want this shopping trip to take place?"

"Didn't you say you'd planned to drive to the Quarter this afternoon to ask about the young teacher you want to employ?"

"I did."

"Then unless Drake has something pressing?" She looked to him and Val prayed he did.

"I don't."

She sighed inwardly.

"Then that settles it," Julianna said happily.

But Val had one more very important question. "How am I to pay for the items?"

"They will be my gift to you," she replied.

Drake shook his head. "No, Mama. I'll take care of the bills. She'll be my wife after all."

Val would rather not be beholden to him for what sounded like an expensive undertaking, but before Valinda could argue the point, Julianna said, "Thank you, son."

With that, she pushed back from the table and stood. "Now, I'm going to have Mr. Doolittle run me and Henri to the docks for a meeting with some carpetbaggers who believe this poor, ignorant Colored female is going to say yes to their appallingly low bid for one of our warehouses. Have a good time in the shops."

After her exit, Val sighed loudly and looked to Drake who said, "I almost feel sorry for the carpetbaggers."

"Do you enjoy shopping?"

"No."

"Neither do I."

"Then this should be an interesting adventure."

Val had never owned anything store-bought before. "I know absolutely nothing about purchasing clothing. My seamstress grandmother Rose made every piece of clothing my sister and I wore until we were old enough to sew for ourselves."

"You sew?"

"I do. One of my few ladylike skills, but it was a necessity. There aren't many places to buy ready-made clothing and those that have them are very pricey."

"I at least know what goes into it, so we'll do fine. If Mr. Doolittle is ferrying Mama and Henri, we should take her carriage. Your buggy is a bit snug for me."

She nodded.

"Don't look so glum, *cheri*. It will be fun."

The last thing Val wanted was for people to say that the esteemed and wealthy Drake LeVeq was marrying a woman so ignorant she didn't even know how to purchase a blouse.

After she finished her meal, she changed clothes and joined him for the ride to the Quarter.

ON THE DRIVE, Drake glanced her way. He knew her to be a prideful woman and having someone else purchase even a hairpin for her wasn't something she'd want. Now, facing the idea of him spending money on her, and he planned to spend a costly sum, was undoubtedly distressing. He'd never met a woman who didn't enjoy shopping, but then again, outside of his sister-in-law, Sable, he'd also never met a woman so determined to make her own way. He ran his eyes over her tightly set face and wanted to soothe away the tension in her jaws and lips. He also knew it was time to make amends because he missed their banter and her sunny smile. "I want to apologize for being so unappreciative of your apology, *cheri*."

She turned.

"You've offered me peace more than once and I swatted it away. If you can't forgive me right at this moment, would you consider it sometime in the near future? If you give up on me, I'll have to live with it. But I miss you a great deal," he said sincerely.

She remained silent for what seemed to be so long, he didn't think she'd reply, but she did.

"That couldn't have been easy for you to say," she said softly.

He gave her a ghost of a smile. "Admitting wrong is always hard for a pirate, but for you? I'd do it a hundred times."

"That's a very sweet thing to say, Drake."

It was the truth. He wanted to ask her to stay with him until the end of time, but the decision was hers alone. Forcing her to answer before she was ready would only reopen the hole they'd fallen into and he didn't want that to happen again.

She said then, "Can I say that I'd like to pick up where we left off, and that I miss you, too?"

The bricks he'd built around his heart shattered into a thousand pieces and he felt alive once more.

"One last thing?"

He looked away from the road. "Yes?"

"I'd enjoy staying married to you after we send my father back to New York, if you still want me to."

He stared with wide questioning eyes.

"I would."

He stopped the buggy and studied her silently. He didn't know whether to jump up and down, or weep like a small child. "I'm honored, *cheri.*"

He reached over and gently lifted her clear of the seat and onto his lap. Holding her close against him, he whispered, "Very honored."

Raising her chin, he leaned down and the kiss that followed was sweet, tender, and brimming with what they both felt inside. When they finally and reluctantly parted, he paused and filled with wonder, viewed her small, perfect face like the pirate's gold he felt her to be. "Is it okay for me to tell you I love you?"

She cupped his jaw and kissed him softly. "Only if I'm allowed to tell you the same."

His joyful roar startled the birds in the trees into panicked flight.

She chuckled. "Whatever am I going to do with you?"

He ran a finger over her lush bottom lip. "Many scandalous things, I guarantee."

"Drive, pirate man. We have clothes to buy."

"Clothes you'll not be wearing for long or very often when I'm around, that's a guarantee, too."

"Good," she said, holding his eyes. She left his lap and they continued on their way.

Eb hadn't had time to find a new classroom, so he was excited to hear about Val's school. His daughter was still searching for a position, so to Val's delight, he promised to bring her with him on Monday so they could discuss her becoming the assistant teacher.

Next stop was the first shop on Julianna's list. The little bell above the door announced their arrival with a bright tinkle. The air inside was scented with a beautiful perfume. Mannequins dressed in the latest fashion were tastefully stationed in various spots to showcase the shop's offerings. On the counters and in glass display cases were stockings made of everything from silk and lisle to common black cotton. She viewed precisely folded stacks of expensive shifts sporting delicately embroidered necklines and hems, next to gossamer-thin nightgowns. One case was lined with lovely sensual corsets in a variety of style and colors. She gave them only a cursory glance because she'd never worn the uncomfortable, binding garments and had no intention of doing so. There was a small number of women dressed in well-made gowns, pert hats, and expensive-looking *tignons* perusing the merchandise. They discreetly eyed her in her serviceable skirt, blouse, and worn-thin black leather slippers—some disapprovingly, but their smiles showed unfettered approval of the well-attired Drake in his white shirt and pressed trousers.

A beautiful dark-skinned woman crowned

by an elegantly tied red *tignon* that matched her red, loose-fitting gown approached them with a smile. "Drake LeVeq. How are you? And this lovely lady is?"

"Hello, Oya. This is my intended, Valinda Lacy. Val, Oya Marie. She's the owner here."

Val saw more than one of the eavesdropping shoppers freeze and stare their way in response to the introduction. *Let the gossip begin*, Val sarcastically announced inwardly.

Oya showed a hint of surprise as well, but the smile remained warm. "Pleased to meet you, Miss Lacy."

"Pleased to meet you as well."

One of the women, whose light skin could've passed for White, walked up and interrupted the conversation, saying, "Drake, I thought that was you. How's your lovely mother?"

He eyed her coolly and in a matching tone, replied, "She's fine. How are you, Mrs. Renay?"

Val noted all the other women watching and listening. Oya shot Val a slightly raised eyebrow.

Mrs. Renay, hair hidden beneath a well-tied blue silk *tignon*, was Amazon-tall and big-boned. Her blue silk gown screamed wealth. She turned to Val. "I'm Blanche Renay, and you are?"

"Valinda Lacy."

"Pleasure to meet you, Valinda," she said in a voice that lacked pleasure but held lots of haughty disapproval. "So, you're marrying our Drake."

"I'm marrying my Drake, yes."

Blanche drew back. A small smile crossed Oya's lips before quickly disappearing.

Blanche looked Val up and down critically. "I must say, Julianna's sons seem determined to disappoint the well-raised marriageable young women of New Orleans. First Raimond graces us with a slave and now—"

Val asked quietly, "Are you always this rude?"

Oya coughed. Someone in the store cackled wildly.

Blanche Renay's blue eyes were saucer-wide.

Val's eyes grazed Drake's before she turned to Oya and said, politely, "Miss Marie, would you show me some blouses, please?"

Blanche Renay stood, beet red.

"It would be my pleasure, Miss Lacy," Oya replied. "This way, please."

Blanche stormed out.

In the end, Val's first foray into shopping was a good one. Oya had only a few ready-made selections in her size but invited Val into her back room, where she quickly took some measurements and promised to have the additional blouses and skirts made and ready in a week to ten days. Next came the choosing of fabrics and Val impressed the shop owner with her knowledge and sensible choices.

The purchases were summed up. Val tried not to show her embarrassment when Drake added a large assortment of stockings, shifts, and nightgowns he'd picked out to the list.

Oya said to him, "You've chosen well."

He smiled at Val.

An elderly woman leaning on a cane walked over and said, "Miss Lacy, I'm Millicent Candy."

"Pleased to meet you, Mrs. Candy."

Drake said, "Hello, Aunt Millie." He leaned down and placed a kiss on her pale papery cheek.

"Miss Lacy, I've known your intended since he built his first tree house. In fact, he's my godson."

Val eyed them both with surprise.

Millicent continued, "You may have heard me laughing when you gave Blanche that outstanding set-down a short while ago."

She remembered the cackling. "I did."

"I want to thank you for making my day. No one has ever dared challenge her. The way you turned her to stone you might be part Medusa."

Val snorted. "I don't think so, ma'am."

"Where's your home?"

"New York."

"Welcome to New Orleans. Drake, bring her by the house when you can so I can get to know her better."

"Yes, ma'am."

She smiled at Val. "Nice meeting you, young lady."

"Nice meeting you, too."

"Goodbye, Oya," Mrs. Candy said, raising her cane to wave.

"Bye, Mrs. Candy."

As Drake and Val prepared to leave, Val thanked Oya, who replied, "You made my day as well. Your garments will be delivered as soon as they are completed."

Thanking her again, they departed.

After stopping at another shop where she purchased more clothing along with bath salts and hair oils, they placed the wealth of items into the carriage's back seat and headed home.

That evening after dinner, they retired to the gazebo to celebrate their love with kisses and caresses that left Val pulsing and breathless and Drake certain he'd never walk again if the wedding night didn't arrive soon. He wanted her fully, nude and twisting on his bed while he worshipped her, devoured her, and made her climax screaming his name. Until then he was content to have her on his lap with her legs wide, her buttons undone, and her soft sighs rising against the night while he licked and sucked, teased and touched, and hardened further watching her wantonly ride his hand under the pale moonlight.

"I owe you an apology," he whispered after she'd come back to earth from the first orgasm of the night. He moved a finger over a bared nipple still hard and damp from his loving. "Sit on the table for me."

He saw her confusion. Instead of explaining, he lifted her easily and set her gently down on the tabletop in front of him. Leaning forward, he kissed her and slid his hands beneath her skirt to savor the satin length of her legs and the heated place so wet and warm hidden between them. He raised the skirt to her waist and said softly, "Lie back, *cheri.*"

Val had no idea what this was leading up to, but his talented fingers were reigniting her senses and she wanted to know, so she lowered herself to the surface of the table, her hips rising, legs parting in response to his circling invitation.

He reached up and spread the open halves of her blouse wider, moved a damp finger to a nipple until it pleaded and she uttered a choked groan.

"Do you like this?" He leaned up and took

the bud into his mouth and bit it gently. She replied with a whispered, shaky, "Yes."

"You'll like this even better."

He placed a worshipping kiss against the inside of each spread thigh and as the kisses fervently climbed, she shuddered with the heat that hit her like lightning.

"I should be on my knees for this but you're at a perfect height. . . ."

When he licked the bud at the entrance to her core, a strangled scream escaped, and she slapped a hand over her mouth and sat straight up. "What are you doing?"

He chuckled softly. "You were the one with all the questions about a man being on his knees to make his apology, weren't you?"

"Yes, but?" She viewed him in the moonlight with wide eyes.

"Do you want my apology or not? Lie back and let me pay my penance."

Still studying him wondrously, she thought about all the pleasure her lusty pirate had treated her to and that he knew more about her body than she, so she complied.

For the next few bliss-filled moments, he paid his penance so wickedly and languidly well, the powerful orgasm broke her quickly and she screamed his name loud and long into her hand.

Chapter Sixteen

$\mathcal{M}$onday morning, Val greeted Melinda, Eb, and five adults who couldn't make the classes set for Tuesdays and Thursday evenings, along with ten of the twenty-five children who'd registered initially, and ten parents. Melinda asked to take on the children, so that left Val to teach the adults. Inside the classroom she was telling the students about herself when a young man arrived carrying an elderly woman. Val guessed him to be in his mid-twenties. He set the thin gray-haired lady gently down on the end of the bench and said, "Sorry for being late. My name is Micah Green, and this is my granny, Miss Delia."

"No need to apologize," Val said kindly. "I'm glad you're here."

The old woman stared with wet unfocused

eyes and Val realized she was blind. Miss Delia said in a strong voice, "What's your name, young woman?"

The full voice was such a contrast to her frail body, Val was caught off guard for a moment. "Valinda Lacy."

"You don't mind me being here, do you?"

"No, but I'm not trained to teach someone with your condition."

"That's okay. Not here to learn. I'm just here because I can be. Spent all my life wanting to read. Figured it must hold power if the masters didn't want us to learn how. When my grandson told me there was a school being taught by a pretty little Colored lady, I told him I wanted to come. So, don't mind me, Miss Lacy. You teach. I'll sit here and listen to you, and enjoy the other folks getting to learn."

Wiping at the tears stinging her eyes, Val began the first day of class.

It was a long week filled with laughing children guided by Melinda and sometimes-frustrated adults in Val's class who found the introduction to the letters and the sounds difficult. Miss Delia came every day. According to her grandson, Micah, she was well into her eighties, had been enslaved since birth on a plantation west of the city, and had vowed to live long enough to walk free. Val found her to be the most inspiring individual she'd ever met. Drake was impressed by her as well. When Val learned that Micah was carrying his grandmother a mile and a half each day on his back, Drake immediately purchased the young man a wagon and a team to make it easier for them to get around.

By Friday evening, Val was exhausted but happy that her dream of teaching had finally taken root. She had a full roster of students, an assistant teacher, and, tomorrow afternoon, she'd be marrying the man she loved.

DRESSED IN A formal black suit, Drake waited at the bottom of the stairs for his bride. He'd never imagined his wedding day, and certainly never imagined playing groom in a situation that began as a ruse. The ceremony would be witnessed by the family only. Later, Julianna would throw open the doors to the people she'd invited. Never one for large social events, he prayed it didn't include everyone in the state.

And then, there she was, beautiful as a sunrise. Sable was behind her, but Drake barely registered her presence. Valinda's sweeping gold gown with its low-cut décolletage accented by a thin line of a paler silk tastefully showed off the sensual lines of her bodice and throat. Her hair was up, face accented by a touch of paint, and he had difficulty breathing.

Beside him, Rai said, "Breathe, brother. If I'm captivated by her, I know you must be inches from keeling over."

He was right. As she seemed to float down the stairs, eyes locked with his, he was glad they were no longer pretending to be love-matched. Their match was true, and all he wanted to do was sweep her up into his arms and retire to someplace private, to hell with the guests.

She stopped before him and she was all he could see. "You look very beautiful, *cheri*."

"Thank you," she replied with what sounded like a touch of nervousness.

"I have something for you." Unable to take his eyes from her, he reached into the pocket of his coat and removed the thin black box.

She gave him a curious look.

"Turn around, please."

She did, and he draped the ornate gold necklace around her neck and hooked the clasp. She fingered it and walked over to the large mirror above the mantel. Her eyes showed her shock. "Where did you get this?"

The necklace with its alternating stylized leaves and delicate posts that supported tiny beautifully formed rosettes had been in the family for some time. "Mama has a trove of family jewelry, and each son gets to pick a piece for our bride on our wedding day. I chose that."

"It's beautiful."

"It pales in comparison to the woman wearing it." He walked over and stood behind her. Her eyes held his in the mirror. He placed a soft kiss on the lovely curve of her bare shoulder and felt the delicate tremor that rippled over her in response. "The others are waiting for us at the gazebo. Shall we go get married?"

She nodded.

He gallantly offered his arm and escorted her out.

While Henri's nephew read the words of the ceremony Val stood beside Drake. She couldn't stop shaking. Still reeling from the ornate necklace, the expensive gown, and the gold-and-diamond-accented studs Julianna had given her earlier, it was as if she'd awakened this morning and stepped into some other woman's life. Surely this couldn't be her own. It was, however, and as she and Drake were pronounced man and wife, the kiss he placed on her lips left her reeling as well. He drew back but not before whispering, "There'll be more to come, later."

Her body caught fire.

And it stayed lit for the rest of the afternoon, and as the reception guests arrived, into the evening. Each time his eyes met hers, she felt stroked by his hand. Her nipples tightened, her thighs grew warm. It didn't matter if he was across the room or standing next to her while Julianna introduced them to people whose names she'd never remember, thoughts of the pleasure toyed with her lustfully. She longed for the festivities to end because she wanted Drake LeVeq—the sooner the better.

As the evening finally wound down, guests offered the newlyweds their congratulations and departed. Soon, only family remained. Drake, standing beside her, asked, "Are you ready to go up?"

She didn't lie. "I am."

He slid a knuckle over her cheek. "Anything in particular you'd like to do once we get there?"

"Bed games?" she asked.

He gave her his pirate grin.

After the reception, Julianna and Henri would be leaving for a ten-day trip to Cuba to visit relatives, so Drake and Val could have the house to themselves. Because Val's school had just begun, there'd be no honeymoon for the newlyweds but they planned to enjoy their time together as man and wife.

They shared hugs and goodbyes with their family members then climbed the stairs to Drake's suite of rooms. He wished he had a house to take his bride home to but knowing he would eventually left him content.

Upstairs, the quiet inside his room was a balm to the noise and commotion they'd dealt with all day and Val slumped tiredly into one of the chairs. Reba had left them a small buffet of food both savory and sweet, proving herself the blessing the House of LeVeq considered her to be. Drake removed his suit coat and tie and rolled up his sleeves. He walked to the terrace doors, opened them wide, and let in the cooling air of the evening. That done he settled himself on the arm of Val's chair, leaned down, and kissed her softly. "Thanks for agreeing to be my wife."

"Thank you for agreeing to be my husband."

That kiss led to another and another, and with each one that followed, passion burned bright. Soon, her dress was gone and gently set aside, and she was standing in the center of the room wearing only one of her new shifts, stockings, jewel-encrusted garters, and fancy heeled shoes. Drake asked in a voice tinged with confusion, "Where are your drawers?"

"In the armoire," she replied, showing him a sultry smile.

"You been walking around all day bare beneath your gown?"

"Pirate wives are allowed to do that."

"Get on the bed, Mrs. Pirate, so I can teach you a lesson about withholding secrets . . ."

She made an equally sultry stroll over to the bed, that hardened him instantly while he removed his shirt before joining her there.

And he taught her well, especially once she was slowly stripped nude. Dazzled by her beauty under the light of the lone lamp beside the bed, he took in the small high breasts with their gem-hard mahogany tips, the beckoning curve of her shoulders, the tempting flat plane of her torso, and the sweep of her lovely legs he could barely wait to feel wrapped around him for the first time. However, he had to make certain she was ready. He was a big man, she was a small chocolate drop of a woman. He needed to go about this final lesson with care because he didn't want her carnal introduction to be filled with pain.

So he began again, worshipping her tenderly. He loved the way her nipples responded to the flirting wickedness of his mouth and tongue, the way she crooned as he turned his attention to the scented skin below, and how seductively she arched when his fingers plied the responsive little bud at the apex of her thighs. Unable to resist, he lazily flicked his tongue against it, then gently sucked it in. Her cries of pleasure filled him like an expensive French aphrodisiac and he knew if he didn't have her soon, he'd explode. So, he left his harshly breathing, slowly twisting wife to rid himself of his trousers, short drawers, and socks.

Val never knew a nude man could be so beautiful, the ebony sculpted shoulders and arms, the muscled chest dusted with furred hair. She took in the button-flat nipples, his trim waist. Her eyes lowered, then fled to the more calming opened terrace doors. She moved them back but settled them high on the wry smile curving his lips.

"Men and women are just constructed differently, *cheri*."

He climbed back onto the bed and settled himself above her and looked down into her uncertain eyes. "We'll go slowly. Promise."

She gave him a quick tight nod, all the while wondering how in the world he'd fit, but she was soon distracted as he began making love to her and she had her first opportunity to relish how wonderfully warm his nude and powerful arms and chest felt under her exploring hands.

He entered her then, slowly, carefully, stopping along the way to let her body stretch and adjust. He coaxed and teased, kept her nipples hard with kisses and tugs, all the while advancing forward. "You can take all of me," he reassured her, gently. "There's no rush."

When he finally pushed past the barrier, the discomfort became acute, but he stilled as if to let her accustom herself to his size and girth. Only then did the lazy stroking begin. The pain soon dissipated and the bright pleasure that had flowed so lavishly before returned, but not from his hands and lips, but from the radiant bliss between her thighs. Catching fire from his rhythm her hips rose to greet him. Holding his considerable weight above her, he invited her to join him in love's version of call and response. The pace increased, she wrapped her legs around his body and heard his pleased growl.

Drake didn't know how much longer he could wait. She was so hot, so tight. He fought to remember her small stature, that this was her first time, but she was matching him stroke for stroke and his orgasm was rising. A few strokes later, she came, calling his name. He broke in her wake, giving her his heart and soul until he was spent. Not wanting to crush her, he gently turned her over and held her atop him until he could breathe and see normally again.

He ran a loving hand down the perspiration dewing her spine. "How was that?" he asked.

She raised up and smiled. "Can we do it again?"

He laughed, squeezed her hip lovingly, and said, "You really are a pirate's wife."

So, they made love a few more times and her body grew better at welcoming and sheltering him. When they were finally done, he carried her into the bathing room so they could wash and soak. The soiled sheets were stripped from the bed and replaced by fresh clean ones. Sated finally, they slept for the first time as man and wife.

AFTER LAST NIGHT's loving, Val was a bit sore but not enough to miss settling into the gazebo for a nice leisurely Sunday morning breakfast with Drake. While his plate held enough to feed everyone at her school, hers showed the small stack of flapjacks Reba had prepared. They were partially through the meal when she reappeared. Behind her was Val's father, and Val was so caught by surprise, she dropped her fork. Not surprising however was the anger clouding his face. "Hello, Father."

He took in Drake and asked sharply, "Who's this?"

"My husband, Drake LeVeq. Drake, my father, Harrison Lacy."

"Get your things, you're coming with me."

Val saw a coolness settle over Drake's demeanor.

Her father snapped. "Now, Valinda."

"Have you eaten?" she asked, hoping to deflate the situation.

"Don't be flippant with me. Get your belongings or you'll leave without them."

Determined to remain respectful, she held on to her temper. "As I explained in my letter, I'm a teacher here. I'm not leaving them, or my husband."

"You will do as I say." He was a big man, accustomed to using his size to get his way, but he was a good four inches shorter than the still-seated Drake, and his build was nowhere near as powerful.

"I'm sorry, Father, but I won't. I have a life here, now."

"I don't care about that. When we get home, I'll look into getting this so-called marriage dissolved. I didn't approve it, so it won't stand."

"It doesn't need your approval. It's all legal and aboveboard. I'm happy here. Doesn't that mean anything?"

"You'll be happier at home. Now, come."

"I'm sorry. I won't be returning with you."

"You will not defy me, Valinda."

"Father, I'm sorry."

"You ungrateful girl. Do you think I enjoyed knowing you engaged yourself to that nasty little nancy boy, Cole?"

She gasped at the vulgar slurring.

He gave her a brittle smile. "Did you think I didn't know about him and what he does? Everyone back home does. I've been shamed enough by you!"

She gritted out, "Go home, Father."

He shouted, "You will do as I say!" He raised his arm to strike her only to be stopped mid-swing by a furious Drake, who grabbed him, slammed him hard into the wrought-iron wall of the gazebo, and pinned him there with a muscled forearm against his throat. "Have you lost your mind?" he snarled.

Her father cried out with surprise and pain, clawing ineffectively at the iron arm cutting off his wind.

Valinda looked up to see her mother, her sister, and a man whose face made the hairs rise on the back of her neck. It was Reverend Comer, the man from her dream, the man who'd been seated on the wagon bench beside her father. He eyed her malevolently. She turned away. "Mother? Caroline?" Caroline was dressed in black.

Still holding her father in place, Drake turned and scanned the shocked faces.

Having no idea what this all meant and deciding to let her father live at least long enough to get an explanation, she said, "Drake, darling. Let him go."

"Are you sure?"

She nodded.

He grudgingly complied.

Ignoring her father's coughs and gasps as he fought to restore his breathing, she trained her attention on the others. "Let's go into the parlor. This way, please."

Inside, she shared a strong hug with her mother, and a teary one with her beloved sister. Val wondered if the black attire meant her husband had passed away, but kept her questions for later, and took her seat. Her angry Drake stood possessively by her chair. "Mother, Caroline, my husband, Drake LeVeq."

They nodded his way.

He nodded in response.

Her father joined them, glowering around a few last coughs.

Valinda glanced over at the reverend. Oscar Comer was short, paunchy, and a bit older than her father.

Viewing Drake disdainfully, he said, "I came to redeem your soul for aligning yourself with a perverse fornicator and was led to believe you'd be my wife." There was cold fury in the look he shot at Drake and then her father.

"And she will be," her father insisted.

Caro gave a tiny disbelieving shake of her head. "Father, do you not see that man standing beside Valinda?"

Her mother stared. She seemed as surprised as Val by Caroline's show of spine. Unlike the rebellious Val, Caro had always been meek and retiring. "I'm sorry you were misled, Reverend."

"So am I, but I can still save you from burning in the fires of hell."

"What happened to your wife?" When she left New York, he'd been married to a quiet woman named Bethany.

"She died a month ago."

"My condolences. But as you can see, I'm not available to replace her at your side."

"Renounce him, marry me, and you'll be saved from the pit."

"No, thank you."

Drake said, "I'm not sure what's going on here, but, Reverend, you should probably leave. Now."

The reverend bristled but he was in no shape to take on Drake and he knew it. He turned on her father. "The hack that brought us is still outside because your father assured me he'd have no trouble fetching you, and had the driver wait. Since that was misleading as well, I will leave you. Mr. and Mrs. LeVeq, may the lord have pity on your souls. Harrison, I expect my money the moment you return home. Good day."

Her father jumped to his feet. "Wait! Oscar, we can resolve this."

"Do you have the money you owe me?"

"No. Not at this moment, but I—"

For the first time, Drake entered the conversation. "How much does he owe you, Reverend?"

"Six hundred dollars."

The staggering amount stopped Val's heart. What was it tied to? How long had it been owed? She glanced Caroline's way and saw her staring off into the distance, her face sad. Her mother on the other hand wore no expression. Val had so many questions.

"I'll see myself out," Comer said, and left the parlor.

"Oscar, wait!" Her father scurried after him.

Val asked her mother, "What is this about?"

Before she could respond, Caroline replied bitterly, "Father thinks he's a slave owner. He planned to sell you to erase his debt, just as he did me. He gambles."

Val's mouth dropped.

Caroline turned on their mother and snarled, "How could you let him do that to me?"

Her mother replied softly, "I had no choice. You know how he is. I'm so sorry."

"It's not enough! My husband was an awful little man. God forgive me but I'm so glad he's dead."

Val looked up at Drake. He placed his hand on her shoulder and gave her an empathetic squeeze.

Caro added, "I told Father I wanted to help him convince you to come home. But truthfully, I came to say goodbye, Val."

"What do you mean?"

"I took every penny my husband had in the bank and I'm going to use it to start life somewhere else. Anywhere else."

Her mother gasped, "You can't."

"And I never want to see you or Father ever again."

Tears in her eyes, her mother looked away from Caro's quiet wrath. Her pain was plain.

Drake said, "You're welcome to stay here if you need time to think about what you want to do."

The generous offer filled Val's heart. She reached up and covered his hand resting on her shoulder.

Her sister looked between them. "I'd like that."

"Then consider it done," Val said.

Her father reentered the room and announced, "We're going back to the train station. Let's go. The hack driver's only going to wait a few minutes more." Apparently, his conversation with the reverend hadn't been resolved to his satisfaction.

Caro turned to him. "I'll be staying, so I'll get my trunk."

"No, you aren't."

Drake moved to Caroline's side. "I'll bring it in. Come and show me which one is yours."

Her father looked about to say something else, but a cool stare from Drake seemed to make him swallow his words. Drake escorted Caroline from the room.

"Mother, do you wish to stay, too? You'd be welcome."

Her father's eyes widened, and Val wondered if he'd ever considered what his life would be like without her, but her mother shook her head. "Your grandmother needs me."

Val understood. "Tell her I send my love, and that Drake and I will be up to visit her before the weather turns cold."

Her mother smiled. "She'll like that."

Her father declared, "Consider yourself dead to me, Valinda."

That saddened her, but it was to be expected. He'd come to New Orleans with fiery expectations that were now ash. He wasn't accustomed to losing and this was the response he felt would hold the most weight. "I'm sorry you feel that way. Have a safe journey home."

He gave her such an odd look, she asked, "Did you expect me to beg or cry? I have a husband who loves me with all his heart, and I love him even more. If you don't wish to be a part of our lives, so be it. We won't love each other any less."

She looked over and saw Drake standing in the doorway. It was the first time she'd publicly stated her feelings for him and she was glad he'd been there to hear them. He smiled. She smiled in reply.

Her parents left.

Chapter Seventeen

As spring merged into summer, Val melted in the heat. Her sister, Caro, had settled into a small town in California and opened up a small seamstress shop. From her letters, she seemed to be happy and Val was happy for her. Drake said they'd go and visit sometime next year.

Her school was thriving. They lost a few children due to their parents needing them in the fields, but she made sure they were sent home with the extra books from the third order of readers Julianna had delivered. Now each student, both child and adult, had a copy of their own. The parents of the children who had to work in the fields promised their children would return to school in the fall.

Having always been a baseball fan thanks to her late grandfather and his love of the game, she had Drake and Hugh field a nine-man team each. They used the open field by the school to stage the game. She sold tickets at a penny a piece to freedmen and a dime to everyone else. Many people showed up and the game went well until some carpetbaggers in the crowd began taunting some of the Republicans and a brawl ensued. Some people demanded a refund, but she refused. The money went to pay for school supplies for some of the freedmen.

Val didn't hear anything from her father after his departure and she and Drake had a talk about Cole and Lenny. He understood why she and Cole had wanted to marry. He praised her for her loyalty to her friend and revealed that he had a cousin in Cuba who took male lovers, but the family didn't care. The cousin was one of the best boat builders on the island and the only person Rai trusted to build his ships.

The supremacists continued their violence against the freedmen. There was talk of Congress working on deals that might pull the Army out of Louisiana altogether. Everyone was convinced people of color would truly suffer if that happened, so they prayed the politicians wouldn't leave the race adrift.

Val's favorite student, Miss Delia, died the day after the Fourth of July. As she'd requested the funeral was held on the school grounds. Her grandson, Micah, had no other family, so Drake hired him as a laborer, and until he got on his feet, Julianna let him live in the small apartment above her coach house.

Drake began work on their house. He hoped to have it finished and ready to move into by the New Year.

In late September, Valinda was floating on air as she left the apartment of the midwife. She couldn't wait to tell Drake her news. Thinking about how he might react, her musings gave way to surprise as she was suddenly grabbed by her arm and found herself face-to-face with her nemesis, Walter Creighton.

He smiled nastily. "Come on."

He propelled her forward and dragged her down the walk. She screamed, "Let me go! Someone help me!"

He gave her a strong shake and snapped, "Shut your mouth!"

She swung a fist that landed on his shoulder. He reacted with a raised fist of his own but was distracted when she pointed and said, "There's my husband! He's coming to send you to hell!"

Eyes round, he froze. As his head swiveled in the direction she pointed, his hold on her arm slackened, and Val broke free and ran.

"Stop her!" he cried. "She took my money!"

Val moved as swiftly as she could through the crowd filling the walk. Apologizing each time she slipped by people who greeted her sudden appearance with cries of surprise, she moved ahead. She knew if Creighton tried to forcibly do the same, a good citizen was going to protest being shoved aside by a man of color. And sure enough, when she took a quick look back, he was apologizing to a stout angry man in a suit while simultaneously attempting to keep her in sight. With him occupied, she thought it a good time to cross the street, so she stepped down, hiked up her skirt, and wove her way through the steadily moving traffic of horses, carts, buggies, and cows. Creighton took off after her. She ran over to an old farm wagon driven by an elderly Black man. "Sir! Can you give me a ride, please? Someone's after me."

He immediately slowed just enough for her to climb up to the seat. He then slapped the reins on the back of the mule to keep in pace with the rest of the traffic.

"Thank you!"

A glance back showed Creighton running to catch the wagon and due to the traffic's snail-like pace, he was gaining ground. "He's still coming. Do you have something I can defend myself with?"

The driver said, "There's a shovel and a pickax in the bed underneath those blankets, if that'll help."

Val crawled into the bed. The blankets were near the back gate. She chose the shovel. The wagon stopped. Her eyes jumped to the stalled traffic behind them and saw the sprinting Creighton's triumphant gap-toothed grin.

"Got a funeral up ahead, little lady. We may be here a spell."

The procession's mournful but celebratory music barely registered as she focused on Creighton's progress. He was almost upon them.

"You going to be okay back there? I'm too old to be fighting for your honor."

She replied through her anger, "I believe so, but in case something happens, the man after me is named Creighton. My husband's name is Drake LeVeq."

"Yes, ma'am."

Creighton was now only a few feet away. She picked up the shovel and rose to her feet with it hidden behind her skirt. He latched onto the back of the wagon, quickly clambered up the gate, and she swung the shovel with enough fury to make the crowd at a baseball game erupt with a mighty cheer. He fell back onto the street. Not caring whether he was dead or alive, she tossed the shovel aside and retook her seat.

The old man stuck out his hand. "Name's Abraham Lincoln."

Stunned, she chuckled. "Valinda LeVeq."

"Freedmen's Office said I could name myself anything I wanted after Freedom, so this is what I chose."

"Honored to meet you, Mr. Lincoln."

"Same here."

The traffic began moving again. She looked back to see Creighton being confronted by the man in the suit, but this time a policeman was there as well. Not caring about his fate, she turned to face the road. "Can I trouble you to take me to the Christophe? I'll pay you for your trouble."

"I don't need any money. The day my master went to war, I dug up all the gold he'd had us bury the day before. I'm set until the good lord calls me home."

She chuckled. "I appreciate your kindness."

"And I appreciate you making this a real exciting day. Can't wait to get home and tell my wife."

LATER, UPON HEARING Valinda tell the story, Drake laughed. "His name was Abraham Lincoln?"

Val was lying in bed in their room at Julianna's cuddled against the protective cocoon that was her husband. "The Bureau told him he could name himself whatever he wanted, so he did."

"And you know he's probably not the only one who took that name."

She did. "I don't think I want to name our child that though."

She felt him stiffen.

"Especially if it's a girl."

He turned so he could see her face. "You're carrying?"

"Yes."

He roared and grabbed her up and rolled her on the bed like an alligator. Laughing and screaming, she cried out, "Stop before we end up on the floor!"

He stopped, and stared down at her with wondrous eyes. "I'm going to be a father."

"Yes, and I hope it's a girl. I'm not sure the world can handle any more male LeVeqs."

He grinned.

She tenderly cupped his bearded cheek and kissed him softly. "Thank you for loving me. You proved love does exist and it changed my life."

He pulled her close. "You're welcome. Thanks for your love as well."

As they drifted off to sleep, Valinda Lacy LeVeq prayed for a strong, healthy baby girl who'd be as generous as her pirate father and as rebellious as her hellion mother.

She was proud of the life she'd carved out for herself. She'd dared to come to Louisiana alone. Then dared to help the freedmen and believe she could start a school. But the best one? Daring herself to accept Drake's love. The old fortune-teller's words rose in her mind: *You will lose a love, reject a love, find a love.*

Pleased that the prophecy had proven true, Val smiled and slept, dreaming of her daughter.

But she had a son. They christened him Raimond Drake LeVeq. He weighed eight pounds, nine ounces, and came into the world roaring like a bear.

Author's Note

I'm always excited to start a new series. Setting this first book in New Orleans, one of my favorite cities, made the writing even more of a joy. Since *Winds of the Storm,* my readers have begged for another visit to the House of LeVeq, so I'm hoping you enjoyed meeting Drake and Valinda, and looking in on Raimond and Sable and the rest of the family.

Reconstruction was a very volatile and bittersweet time. Dr. Eric Foner terms it "America's unfinished revolution," and I heartily agree. The years 1863–1877 held such promise, not only for the newly freed but for the nation as well, only to have the politicians set the race adrift during Redemption. However, Reconstruction gave rise to the historically Black colleges, public education in the South, and eventually the Great

Exodus of 1879. Fifteen Black men were elected to the U.S. House of Representatives from 1870 to 1887, and two men of the race served in the U.S. Senate: Hiram Revels and Blanche Bruce, both from the state of Mississippi. Such numbers wouldn't be matched again until the latter part of the twentieth century.

One of the civil rights battles highlighted in *Rebel* involved the New Orleans segregated streetcar system. Protests against it came to a head on April 28, 1867, the day William Nichols and two White supporters boarded a Whites-only car. When the driver tried to drag Nichols out, he went limp and was arrested. At his trial, the packed courthouse didn't get the definitive judgement they'd hoped for, but the judge did drop all charges against Nichols, who promptly sued the streetcar driver for assault. Hoping to avoid further lawsuits, the car company mandated drivers no longer forcibly evict Black riders, but to stop and not drive until Blacks left the car. Of course, that didn't work. Black people boarded the cars and sat and sat and sat. Eventually, the entire system ground to a halt, while other activists commandeered the cars and drove them themselves. Fights broke out between Black and White men. The police chief, in an effort to head off city-wide armed confron-

tations, personally ordered the cars be desegre-
gated, and the car company complied.

Similar protests took place across the nation,
not only in the South but Northern cities like
Philadelphia. Many of these campaigns proved
successful until nulled by the rise of Jim Crow.

Here are some of the sources I consulted to
bring *Rebel* to life.

Before the Mayflower: A History of Black America
by Lerone Bennett, Jr.

*Black Gotham: A Family History of African Ameri-
cans in Nineteenth-Century New York City* by
Carla L. Peterson.

*Reconstruction: America's Unfinished Revolution,
1863–1877* by Eric Foner.

The Original McGuffey's Eclectic Primer by William H. McGuffey.

*The Trouble They Seen: The Story of Reconstruction
in the Words of African Americans*, edited by
Dorothy Sterling.

So, there you have it. Stay tuned for book two
in the Women Who Dare series, and as always,
thank you for your support.

Happy Reading,
B

Some Like It Scandalous by Maya Rodale
Theodore Prescott the Third, one of Manhattan's
Rogues of Millionaire Row, has really done it this
time. The only way to survive his most recent,
unspeakably outrageous scandal is marry someone
respectable. Someone sensible. Someone like Daisy
Swann. Of all the girls in Gilded Age Manhattan,
it had to be her.

Life, Love, and the Pursuit of Happiness
by Sandra Hill
Merrill Good knows there are many different
kinds of exciting. There's the adrenaline rush he
experienced during his years in the military. There's
the thrill of starting up his own treasure hunting
company. But topping them all is the surge of
exhilaration he feels every time Delilah Jones
crosses his path. Smart, voluptuous, and outspoken,
Delilah is a bombshell with a secret that could
explode at any moment.

Her Other Secret by HelenKay Dimon
For Tessa Jenkins, Whitaker Island is a sanctuary.
Fleeing from a shattering scandal, she has a new
name, a chance at a new beginning, and a breathtaking new view: Hansen Rye. It's hard not to crush
on Whitaker's hottest handyman. At six-foot-three
and all kinds of fine, he's also intensely private—and
the attraction between them soon simmers dangerously
out of control.

REL 0619